SoWest:
Crime Time

SoWest: Crime Time

Twenty original southwestern tales from the
Sisters in Crime Desert Sleuths Chapter

DS Publishing
Scottsdale, Arizona

DEDICATION

To victims of crime everywhere, may justice neither be denied nor delayed.

ACKNOWLEDGMENTS

The Sisters in Crime Desert Sleuths Chapter membership wishes to recognize those individuals whose contributions made this volume possible. Huge thanks go out to: Deborah J Ledford, for her tireless efforts as lead editor. Co-editors Nancy McCurry, Susan Budavari and Merle McCann for their dedication and hard work.

Martin Roselius for yet another fantastic cover design.

Acclaimed, award-winning authors: Naomi Hirahara, Catriona McPherson, Hank Phillippi Ryan and Rochelle Staab, for taking time away from their writing to provide fantastic blurbs.

The worldwide network of our fellow Sisters in Crime for unfailing support.

The contributing authors, for their imagination and for the words that grace the pages of this anthology.

And our discerning readers for making all of our efforts worthwhile.

TABLE OF CONTENTS

TABLE OF CONTENTS

NEIGHBORHOOD WATCH
SHANNON BAKER

I've heard them say man's house is his castle, so a man's neighborhood would be his kingdom. Just how far should a king go to defend that kingdom?

I stood in the front yard cogitating on this while Beau watched me from the front porch of my cabin. He whined, as if apologizing for not dragging his old hide down the steps. He sank to the deck and closed his eyes.

An Abert's squirrel scooted across the pine needles and volcanic cinders that substituted for grass in this mountain community and lurched up a Ponderosa pine. Beau didn't even stir.

A flash of white zipped by me. My neighbor's bedroom slipper of a dog stopped at the base of the pine, jumping up and down, yipping while the squirrel chattered at him.

"Elmo!" Twyla's laughing admonishment wouldn't bring the dog back to her. But Twyla didn't let that, or anything else bother her much.

Nothing like my late wife, Nancy.

Twyla lived next door. She and Bud had been my neighbors for thirty years or more. I'd seen their four rug rats go from babies to grown-ups with all the bumps and scrapes along the way.

Twyla bustled into my yard. That woman was always in a rush. Usually chattery and cheerful. "How are you and Beau today, Jerry?"

You know how some people can start looking like their dogs? That was Twyla. She was about as round and short-legged as Elmo and had the same wispy white hair. With our saggy middles and more white than black hair, me and Beau might resemble each other, too. I probably had the same used-up look in my old eyes as Beau did.

"Finer' 'n frog's hair." I enjoyed Twyla's giggles.

Nancy wasn't prone to giggles. "Such a lovely morning," she

said.

I did love mornings here. Mountainaire, a few miles south of Flagstaff, was really just a hodge-podge of cabins, trailer houses and the occasional new-build. When me and Nancy moved in around the dawn of time, we'd been about the only year-round residents. Mostly it was summer folks from Phoenix who came up to the mountains to cool off.

With Nancy's job at Northern Arizona University, and my work on the railroad, we could have afforded a fancy house in Flagstaff. But we liked the quiet out here.

I nodded. "Everyone's at work or school. Just us rusty folks around to be the Neighborhood Watch."

Twyla slapped at my shoulder. "Oh, you! Speak for yourself. I've got a lot of life left in me."

I laughed. "I can see that."

Her eyes drifted to the front porch. "But Beau." She stopped and gave me that meaningful look women give you that says everything without words. Not my Nancy. Nancy would just out and say it.

Twyla couldn't look sadder. "He's in pain."

I had to swallow down her words before I could speak. It was time to let Beau go, but I loved that old dog. I'd miss him, maybe even more than I missed Nancy. "Nancy was good at this kind of thing. She'd make a decision and follow through. Me, I decide one minute and undecide the next."

Twyla nodded. "I'm like that, too. I always did things Bud's way. So when he passed and I had to start doing for myself, I came up with a little game."

"What kind of game?"

"Elmo! For heaven's sake stop that barking." Twyla tsked and hustled over to distract the dog.

While I waited for Twyla to return I surveyed the neighborhood, what I might call my kingdom. Our block ran north and south along the base of a mountain. Half a dozen roads wound up the side of the mountain creating a maze of houses and cabins. Maybe ten houses on each side of a narrow blacktop ran north of me and Twyla. Volcanoes created most of the landscapes around so crushed cinders and pine needles made up the yards. Not fancy, but mostly tidy.

The view south used to be the best. Now I avoided turning that way. The street petered out three houses down and the forest took over. At the right angle, from my front window I could see past the last house on the block to the edge of the forest. In years past, Beau and I spent a fair amount of time traipsing around the trails out there.

Elmo dashed around my ankles and I followed him to the edge of my yard. My back creaked when I bent to pick him up, a wasted effort since he sprinted away. I straightened slowly.

I tried to avoid seeing the last lot on the block but there it was. A faded plastic tricycle with shards sharp as knives tipped over next to abandoned toy trucks and decomposing plastic guns all of which had gone through dozens of snows and thaws. A mud-encrusted four-wheel drive pickup with no doors sat in the middle of the yard. Tires, tools, jackets, garbage, beer cans—too much trash to identify—piled in front of the house.

I despised the arrogant thirty-something living in the ramshackle ranch house with the splintered deck. Ron. Or as I called him, MoRon.

I could always count on two or three wrecked four-wheel drive mud-mobiles parked on the edge of the driveway and on the street, like war casualties on the battlefield. Come two or three o'clock, beer-swilling idiots would gather and laugh their stupid laughs, rev the worthless engines and carry on into the night. MoRon's bwha-ha-ha laugh carried farther than the elks' bellows in the fall.

Before I let myself get too irritated, I addressed Twyla. "You were going to tell me about getting a backbone." Something Nancy always said I could use.

"You're going to laugh because it's silly," Twyla said.

Twyla's brand of silly didn't bother me.

She grinned. "I always sing to myself." She belted out a tune.

I recognized that old "I Am Woman" song by Helen Reddy from way back. Nancy used to sing it at me, like some kind of challenge.

When Twyla sang, she paused between lines and added a "bum, bum, bum" for drums and falsetto for backup singers. Her version sounded like an anthem instead of an attack. I kind of liked it.

"I know it's silly. But when it says 'I can do anything,' it helps me."

An engine rumbled in the hushed mountain air. Wheels

screeched and even if I couldn't see it, I heard a car speed around the curve in front of the old grocery store and tavern two blocks away. A thrumping, booming base of something that passed for music accompanied the raging engine, as a souped-up rusted heap that was once a Honda Accord rolled through the stop sign at the corner a few houses up the street from Twyla's.

"Oh no," Twyla squeaked.

"Looks like the butt-head rodeo is starting early today." I scowled at the driver as he passed by way too fast.

Twyla clucked. "I'm going to make a chicken pot pie this afternoon. I'll bring it over for dinner." She was pretty good at throwing a blanket over everyone's anger. Her Bud had a temper and she'd learned to keep peace.

I didn't want her to think she had to manage me, too, so I grinned at her. "I do love your pot pie."

The Honda rumbled to a halt across the street from MoRon's house.

The front door of the house banged open. MoRon burst outside wearing baggy pajama bottoms. A wrinkled T-shirt and flip flops and black hair turned every which-way made it plain he'd just gotten up.

"Rodriguez! You're up early. Bwha-ha-ha."

Rodriguez stepped out of his car wearing baggy pants with the crotch to his knees, a hoodie big enough for a linebacker and scuffed white tennis shoes. He reached into the Honda and hauled out a 30-pack of Budweiser. They hollered back and forth, a guttural animal exchange.

Pine needles crunched underfoot as I headed to my porch. "See you later," I said to Twyla.

She gave me a sad smile and trotted off to retrieve Elmo, who sat staring at the squirrel in the pine tree.

I heard the bark of a big dog and just as I turned around, a brown streak hit the edge of my yard and raced toward Elmo.

MoRon's stupid pit bull. I lurched back to the yard.

Twyla screamed and lunged for Elmo. She pulled him close to her chest and turned her back to the attacking dog. I couldn't do anything but stand between the dog and Twyla, hold my hands up and yell my fool head off.

The dog stopped in front of me. His lips pulled back in a snarl, white teeth snapping. I gave him all the Alpha attitude my old bones could muster.

"Cujo, get your ass over here!" MoRon screamed from his front porch.

Of course, the half-wit would name his dog after a killer St. Bernard he saw in a movie because, sure as rain, he never read a book.

Cujo kept barking and snarling, strings of saliva swinging from his jowls.

"God-damn it!" MoRon clomped down his deck steps. He muttered as his flip flops carried him across his junkyard and into the street. MoRon stomped up and grabbed the beast's collar. He tilted his face up to me and in an Eddie-Haskell-your-dress-is-lovely-today-Mrs. Cleaver-voice, said, "Sorry about that, man."

Twyla's arms shook as she squeezed them around Elmo. "You need to keep that dog locked up."

MoRon's face darkened. "Maybe you and your rat ought to watch out. Me and Cujo might both like to chew on slow-moving white-hairs."

"Hey." I wanted to punch the punk. "Get off my property."

MoRon took a step forward. Cujo focused on Elmo and snarled again. "Mind your own damned business, old man."

I matched MoRon's step with one of my own and Cujo growled deep in his throat, straining against his collar. Darn that old-man quaver in my voice. "You're nothing but trouble."

MoRon loosened his grip on Cujo and he lurched toward Twyla and Elmo. Twyla screamed and jumped behind me.

MoRon jerked Cujo back.

"What's going on here?" A man's voice called from the street.

I hadn't heard Sheriff Turner's Bronco pull up. A mountain of a pale man climbed from the cruiser. He lumbered toward us.

MoRon gave him a face-splitting grin. "Nothing going on here, Bill. Cujo decided to take an unauthorized walk, is all."

You'd think I'd be happy to see the law but hearing MoRon on a first-name basis with the sheriff made me uneasy. I'd turned MoRon in a handful of times. For disturbing the peace, for operating a business out of his home. They didn't investigate as far as I knew and certainly never followed up with me.

"Actually, Sheriff," I said. "There is a problem. This dog is dangerous. You guys need to do something about Ron."

Sheriff Turner's eyebrows rose. "Is that so? You got a

problem with Ron?"

The way he belittled me reminded me of Nancy. I almost backed down, like I used to with Nancy. Instead, I glared at the sheriff. "That's right. I'm sure he's dealing drugs. Probably cooking them up, too."

Sheriff Turner and MoRon exchanged amused looks. When he shifted his gaze to me, the sheriff's expression hardened. "I know who you are, Jerry. You've called the station and badgered us with complaints. Don't get me wrong, we like you old guys keeping an eye on the neighborhood, but I suggest you find a hobby and leave Ronny alone before he files a harassment charge against you."

I hated my feeling of powerlessness. "He's a menace. Why aren't you guys doing anything about it?"

"Now, Jerry." Sheriff Turner's patronizing tone burned me. "Ronny is going through a tough time. His wife left and took their kids. Maybe you could be more compassionate like me. I lowered his rent by half until he gets back on his feet."

Now it made sense. MoRon rented the sheriff's dumpy house. He gave Turner a kickback from the drug business to pay for protection from the law. I clenched my hands in frustration.

Twyla pressed Elmo to her with one hand and grabbed my arm with the other. "Let's go."

I did what I usually did. Walked away from the fight.

With Beau settled onto his oversized cushion in the corner of the living room, I stared out the dining room window at Sheriff Turner and MoRon yucking it up in MoRon's yard.

I'd been happy here in this one-bedroom cabin. I'd fixed it up with big windows and skylights to make it feel like we were smack in the middle of the forest. And now MoRon ruined everything.

Living in Mountainaire, in this house, was the one of the few fights I'd ever won with Nancy. That was only because she spent more time on campus than at home and she didn't care where we lived.

MoRon's braying slipped through the walls. "Bwha-ha-ha!"

He needed to be stopped. I had to protect my kingdom, not just for me, but for Twyla, too. It was only a matter of time before Cujo took a chunk out of Elmo.

Then I had an idea.

I fired up my laptop and hummed "I Am Woman," feeling

better than I had in years.

Some time later, a knock on the front door startled me. I started to jump to my feet but I'd been humped over my computer and notes so long, my old bones protested. I leaned heavily on the table and rose slowly.

Twyla stood on the front porch, her arms filled with something that smelled delicious. Elmo slipped inside and trotted to Beau. Beau banged his tail once on the floor and they touched noses.

"As promised, chicken pot pie."

I hefted the fancy-schmancy basket she carried. "Hallelujah. I'll set the table."

"Just clear it off."

Before I could gather the pages filled with my old-man scrabbly handwriting and drawings, Twyla brought over plates. "What's all this?"

I shouldn't tell her. The less she knew, the better.

Then she gave me that look. The one Nancy didn't have. It said she thought I was funny and smart.

The look made me feel twenty—no, fifty years younger. I spread the papers across the table. "I'm going to fix MoRon's wagon."

"What do you mean?"

"I ordered a rocket engine. The rest of this stuff I found in a box in the garage from when I helped Stevie with his 4-H Rocket project." Bud had been as much a workaholic as Nancy. Since my shifts at the railroad often left me home several days at a time, I took up the slack with Twyla and Bud's kids.

She set the plates on the table and jogged to the kitchen, only three steps away. "That had to have been thirty years ago."

I plunged ahead. "I'm going to build a small bomb. Up goes one of those worthless junk heaps. No one gets hurt but MoRon gets the message he's not welcome here."

She clutched her chest in alarm. "This is crazy. You can't set off a bomb!"

I was John Wayne leading the cavalry. "Why not? The sheriff's not going to help us."

She plopped into a chair. "It's not like you to use violence to get your way. This is like Bud. He had to be in charge." Her voice dropped to a whisper. "If he couldn't finagle it any other way, he'd use force."

I froze and studied her. "Force?"

She held my gaze. "I never told anyone because I wanted to protect him."

"He hit you? And the kids?"

She swallowed hard. "You know, when he died from the Apnea and people wondered why I didn't hear him struggle, I told everyone we slept in separate rooms because of his snoring. But I slept in Stevie's old room with the door locked because I was afraid."

I had a hard time finding words. "We had no idea." It was a shock when Bud died twenty years ago. Overweight and a heavy drinker, he'd been sleeping with oxygen for years but I didn't realize his Apnea could kill him. They said he knocked the mask off in his sleep and something as light as a pillow over his face could have caused him to struggle for air that led to the heart attack. One of those fluke things.

Twyla jumped up and trotted to the kitchen, fussing with the basket of food. She started humming, "I Am Woman."

I pulled myself up and limped to her, then put a hand on her shoulder in support.

Twyla shrugged. "That's all over now." She stared hard at me. "But I hate that you're talking about violence. This could change you."

Maybe I needed change.

Twyla fluttered her hands. "You'll get caught."

The adrenaline rush of the charge surged through me. "That's the genius of this. I'll hook up a cord that connects the bomb to the controller in my garage. I'll attach the cord to my electric drill. After I detonate the bomb I'll turn on the drill and, ZURRRUP! It'll wind up the cord in a second."

Tears found a path through the riverbed of wrinkles on her face. "I like you the way you are."

† † †

The rocket motor arrived a few days later and I set to work in my garage. I filled the rocket base with Super Glue and when it dried, I buried it in a five-gallon bucket of fertilizer and diesel fuel. Before I finished, Elmo raced up to me. I quickly stepped out and closed the door so Twyla wouldn't see the preparations. I don't think I fooled her because she scooped Elmo up with hardly a hello for me.

As the sun set, second thoughts crowded in. Maybe Twyla was right. Violence would solve nothing.

Hell it wouldn't. It would get MoRon out of our lives.

Night came on and a sliver of moon rose. I sat at my kitchen table with the lights off and the curtain cracked open and watched MoRon's house. It was a slow night in Drugsville.

After midnight I rose from the table. I rubbed Beau's soft ears and he dropped his head.

The bucket of fertilizer and diesel smelled bad and it was darned heavy for an old duffer like me. I had to stop in the shadows of bushes and trees several times before I lugged the bucket across the junkyard to the truck. The wires from the rocket extended up from the lip like antennae with small alligator clips on the ends.

Sweating, my heart thumping, I lowered myself to my hands and knees. My joints creaked like a rusty gate. The ridiculously large tires made it possible for even a gimpy old man like me to maneuver underneath the truck, though I couldn't stop my grunts. The sharp mix of cinders and pine needles cut into my knees. I shoved the bucket as far beneath the truck as I could.

I pulled the cable from my back pocket, attached the split wire to each of the alligator clips and started to back out from under the truck.

An engine rumbled in the distance. Headlights jumped along the street. The boom of an obnoxious stereo invaded the neighborhood. Rodriguez's jacked-up piece of junk-mobile skidded to a stop in front of MoRon's house.

I shrank into the shadow under the truck.

MoRon's front door banged open. He stood outlined against the inside light. "You're late."

Cujo pushed from behind MoRon and raced down the porch steps, barking. He headed straight for the pickup where I lay like a juicy steak.

"Cujo, you idiot!" MoRon yelled.

Cujo paid no attention to MoRon. He was going to tear me apart, starting at the jugular. He sprinted toward me, eyes glowing with a fiendish red glint. At least, I imagined they glowed since I'd pulled my arms over my face and curled into a ball.

Suddenly Cujo yelped. I peeked from between my arms to see him crumple to the ground, whining.

MoRon let out that stupid bwha-ha-ha laugh. "Bought a shock collar." He clomped down the stairs and leaned over to grab Cujo's collar. He dragged him toward the house.

Rodriguez's chuckle sounded less than enthusiastic. "Got my stuff?"

MoRon disappeared into the house. In a few seconds he reappeared. Rodriguez crossed the yard, not four feet from my head. His dirty white tennis shoes draped with the overflow of his baggy black pants.

MoRon leaned over the wood rail of his porch. A small bag and a wad of cash passed between him and Rodriguez with practiced efficiency. MoRon watched Rodriguez and his thrumping-bumping music drive down the street, squeal around the corner and vroom away. He leaned on the rail and smoked a cigarette and I stiffened under the truck.

While I waited for MoRon to go back inside, I decided it was time to call retreat. I'd have to haul the bucket back to my garage and dismantle the bomb. Twyla was right. This was a stupid idea.

But by the time MoRon dropped his cigarette butt in the yard and went back inside, the best I could do was crawl out and stumble home. Even that nearly killed me. Each vertebrae in my spine ached. My knees groaned and I couldn't get my breath.

Beau opened his eyes when I staggered into the house, leaning on chairs and tables and finally dropping onto the couch. He pulled himself to his feet and slowly shuffled to lie next to me. I rested my hand on his back and let the pain throb across my body.

The vitality I'd felt while planning the caper drained from me. I wasn't born for action. I was like Beau, just an old man heading for the grave.

Before I dozed I remembered I'd left my garage door open. I thought about closing it but I'd never get my bones and muscles to work. I might just lie here until Beau and I both gave up the ghost.

† † †

The *ka-WOMP* brought me bolt upright and my feet swung around and hit the floor before my eyes focused. Beau jumped up and barked. The windows rattled and a faint glow pushed through the curtains.

Beau and I scrambled to the front door. I wrenched it open and stepped onto the porch.

My heart jumped to my throat and I fell against my house. My eyes popped wide with the scene. Flames leapt into the dark sky, the roar and crackle impossibly loud.

Neighbors in their robes and pajamas ran from their homes to the street. They shouted.

MoRon's house was a ball of flames. His house. Not the pickup in front. His whole dad-gummed house!

Sheriff Turner's Bronco squealed to a halt. He jumped out and stared open-mouthed at the flames.

Twyla stood in her driveway in a pink housecoat, her arms wrapped around Elmo.

I shambled toward her. My body recovered from the shock of the explosion and remembered that it hurt.

How did this happen? I'd left the cord on the ground next to the bucket.

The detonator sat in my garage. My garage. I spun—well, turned slowly—to my closed garage door, then stared at Twyla.

She shrugged and her robe slipped open. Black cinders and pine needles clung to the knees of her pajamas. "I've read that meth labs are very combustible. Accidents happen all the time."

Without a word I limped back to my now-closed garage door and peered into the window. My drill lay on the floor, black electrical cord wrapped around the drill bit.

Bedroom slippers scuffed the driveway behind me and I turned to see Twyla smiling at me. She sang softly, "I Am Woman."

† † †

SHANNON BAKER writes the Nora Abbott Mystery series, a fast-paced mix of murder, environmental issues and Hopi Indians. *Tainted Mountain*, first in the series, is set in Flagstaff, AZ. *Broken Trust*, due March 2014 from Midnight Ink, takes place in Boulder, CO. A lover of western landscapes, Baker can often be found backpacking, skiing, kayaking, cycling, or just playing lizard in the desert. She is a member of SinC, MWA, and Rocky Mountain Fiction Writers. To find out more about Shannon, visit: www.Shannon-Baker.com.

VANITY PAYS
SUSAN BUDAVARI

Minutes before the doors opened at Luxura, a high-end boutique in the Biltmore section of Phoenix, two saleswomen busied themselves at the cosmetics counter. Marianne, a slender redhead with a flawless complexion, knelt unpacking a carton of perfumed soaps. A cell phone chimed. Her co-worker, Eva, a curvaceous blonde in a snug pink smock, checked the phone screen then whispered to her, "I'm taking an early lunch today. Cover for me?"

Marianne looked up at the younger woman. "Max Lawson?"

"A-huh."

Frowning, Marianne reached over and touched Eva's hand. "Don't waste time on that loser."

With a toss of her head, Eva pulled away. "You'll change your tune when he gets his mother to put up money."

Marianne stood. "Look at you. Twenty-four and gorgeous. Max is in his thirties and has nothing going for him. So he dangles his mother's money. He'll say anything to hold on to you."

"I'll take that chance."

"Things are good the way they are without his money."

"Yeah, but you've always wanted to have a legit business. He can help make it happen."

Marianne only half-listened to her. Cunning as the girl was, she could be so naïve about men. "Then answer this, why doesn't he tell his mother you're dating?"

Eva picked up a perfume bottle and sprayed herself. "Honestly, it's my idea to keep it quiet."

"Why?"

"Better she doesn't know we're connected."

Marianne placed her hands on her hips. "Something's wrong with this picture."

Eva bit on her lip. "She's thinks she has to watch him and keep tight reins on the money."

Marianne's eyes widened.

"He screwed up a long time ago. Drugs."

"There you go," Marianne muttered. "It won't work. Stay away from him."

Eva rolled her eyes. "Anyway, his mother's coming in this morning. I'm gonna tell her about your face creams. I've been setting her up for weeks."

"Watch it, Eva. Rich people are different from us." *They'll walk all over you.*

"Oh, will you chill out already! The store's open. We have to get to work."

Marianne spotted a well-dressed woman in her sixties heading toward the counter and nudged Eva. "Be careful."

Eva gave her miniskirt a quick tug, plastered a big smile on her face and stepped out to the front of the counter. "Good morning, Mrs. Lawson. How may I help you?"

The silver-haired matron surveyed the counter and pointed to a brightly colored display. "Is this new, Eva?"

"Why, yes. It's the latest from La Nova. Totally awesome hand lotion. Wanta try some?"

Mrs. Lawson extended her left hand. A five-carat marquise diamond sparkled on her ring finger.

Eva swabbed the top of her customer's hand then applied the lotion. "How's that?"

Curling her nostrils as she ran her fingers over the treated area, Lawson said, "Unusual scent, but nice and smooth."

"Softer skin guaranteed in three to four weeks. Or your money back."

"Nothing seems to work at my age."

"Oh, go on," said Eva. You always look fabulous."

"Thank you, my dear." Mrs. Lawson glanced at herself in a hand mirror on the counter. "It's getting harder and harder." She picked up the display bottle and read the label. "I guess it's worth a try."

"There is something..." Eva mumbled as she went behind the counter to wrap the lotion.

"What's that?"

"Oh, nothing you'd be interested in. That'll be eighty-seven dollars and sixteen cents."

Mrs. Lawson handed over her charge card.

While swiping the card, Eva murmured, "What, I..." and

then hesitated.

"Out with it." Mrs. Lawson grimaced. "Oh. I bet it's that mystery product you've been hinting at."

Eva looked around then mouthed, "You're too sharp."

"Cut the flattery." There was a trace of annoyance in her voice.

Eva leaned closer. Nodding in her coworker's direction she whispered to Mrs. Lawson, "You know Marianne, over there."

"Of course."

"Her aunt in Romania is like the queen of cosmetics there. She gave Marianne a supply of the Roza face creams she makes—they're not for sale yet in this country. The only places you can get them are the salons in Paris." Eva paused, letting her remarks sink in. "They work miracles. Marianne swears by them. Look at her."

"Hmm. She has beautiful skin, but so do most women at her age."

"She's pushing fifty."

"Really? I don't believe it."

Eva nodded. "She gave me some creams for my birthday. I love them." She put her hand to her chest. "Believe me. I try everything in this job, so I know the primo goods."

Mrs. Lawson waved her hand in dismissal of Eva's remark. "You're young and beautiful. You'd look lovely no matter what."

Eva blushed. "Everyone in Marianne's family uses her aunt's products. I've seen pictures. They all look super. Like, even the really old ones."

"Enough. You've sold me. I'll try some."

Eva waited a moment then whispered. "They're expensive."

"I don't mind…as long as they work."

"Eva cupped her hand in front of her mouth. "You'll have to meet Marianne somewhere outside the store to get the creams. You understand."

Mrs. Lawson looked over at Marianne, who was busy with a customer. "Tell her to call me." She handed Eva a business card, took her purchase and left.

As Eva tidied up the counter, her cell phone vibrated with a text message. She texted back, then stashed her smock in a drawer and grabbed her purse.

When Marianne finished with her customer, Eva told her to

contact Mrs. Lawson and said with a wink, "I'm off to lunch." She headed to the store exit.

Eva stepped outside and inhaled the crisp March air. A moment later, a tall, thin man in jeans and a white tennis shirt appeared. She threw her arms around his neck and planted a lingering kiss on his mouth.

† † †

"Wow. Have you been away on vacation? You look so rested," Eva gushed when Mrs. Lawson stepped up to the cosmetics counter a couple of weeks later.

"It's Marianne's face cream." Mrs. Lawson moved her head from side to side to show off her skin. "It rejuvenated my skin." She put her finger to her lips. "My son Maxwell says I look younger than I have in years."

Eva smiled. "I guess you'll be stopping less at this counter from now on."

Mrs. Lawson chuckled. "I'd like a tube of my favorite lip gloss and some Le Mist perfume."

As Eva gathered the items, Mrs. Lawson added, "Marianne should start a business. There's a big demand for cosmetics that work this well for women my age."

"She'd love to have her own business." Eva rubbed her thumb and index finger together. "Money. It takes big bucks to get started, ya know." Eva shook her head. "Marianne's working really long hours to save up."

Mrs. Lawson thought for a few moments. "Have her call me. I may be able to help."

† † †

Shortly before noon, after a sleepless night, Marianne, dressed in her finest tailored spring suit, entered the coffee shop in Fashion Square Plaza for a meeting with Mrs. Lawson. She straightened up to her full height when she spotted Lawson waving from a table near the windows. Marianne had Googled the woman. Impressed by Lawson's estimated worth and business achievements, she thought Eva might be right. This could turn out to be her lucky break after all.

Mrs. Lawson glanced at her gold Tiffany watch. "I appreciate your accommodating my schedule."

"It's my pleasure. Wednesdays are good. It's quiet at the store until late in the day."

A server poured coffee for them and took their lunch orders.

Mrs. Lawson leaned forward. "I want to get more of your creams and discuss some ideas I have. And please, call me Adele."

Marianne nodded. She took a long sip of coffee, trying to steady her nerves.

"As I told you on the phone, I'm very impressed with your products." She stared at Marianne. "I pride myself on having a good eye for business opportunities. With my connections and expertise in marketing, we could form a company that would make a great deal of money for us both."

Marianne furrowed her brow and pulled back. "No disrespect meant but my aunt's getting old. She's entrusted me with her formulas to make sure her cosmetics continue after she's gone." She coughed to relieve tension. "It would be easy to just sell the creams on the Internet and make money. But that isn't what I want. I want to honor my aunt by establishing a high-level business. That takes lots of money to start."

Adele Lawson cleared her throat. In an authoritative tone, she said, "I've started several businesses—all extremely profitable. I know what is needed. I'm prepared to invest the effort and the necessary funds."

"A quarter-million dollars?" Seeing no reaction from Lawson, Marianne added, "To start."

"It'll take a lot more than that," Lawson asserted with a wave of her hand.

A thrill of excitement ran through Marianne. *This could work.* She allowed her eyes to water and kept her tone reverential when she spoke. "It's very important to me that the business bear my family name. I know in my heart, the Roza family products can compete with the best and most expensive ones on the market."

"My dear, I've done my research. I know a great deal about the Roza business and the product line. What I envision is something on a grand scale." She narrowed her eyes. "But, first, there is one thing that puzzles me."

"What?" Marianne reached for her coffee.

"Your last name is Stel. That name doesn't appear anywhere in connection with the Rozas."

Marianne's pulse quickened. She put her cup down. "My mother was born a Roza. Stel's my ex-husband's last name. He had no involvement in the business." Her hand jerked. She barely avoided spilling her coffee.

Mrs. Lawson stared first at Marianne's trembling hand, then directly into her eyes. "What really concerns you?"

Marianne felt challenged by Mrs. Lawson's tone. She wasn't going to talk about her old life back in Romania nor about anything in her past, for that matter. Her heart pounded as she groped for words. When the server appeared with their lunches, Mrs. Lawson signaled for Marianne to hold her response. Marianne took the moment to figure out how to shift the conversation.

When the server left, Marianne said, "I want to bring Eva in as my partner. From my share of the business, of course. She's done so much for me over the years." She hoped her voice didn't betray the uneasiness she felt.

"Really?" Mrs. Lawson's eyes narrowed. "And why is that?"

Before Marianne could offer further explanation, the older woman waved a hand. "It doesn't matter. I prefer to take a behind-the-scenes role, anyway, setting strategic directions for the company. You can handle the staff...and decide what role you want Eva or any other employee to play."

Marianne nodded slowly.

"Let's talk about important issues. Positioning, for example," Mrs. Lawson said. "What are your ideas?"

Marianne had rehearsed what to tell Lawson. "I want to target wealthy women forty-nine and over—boomers, who have a lot of discretionary money and want to look as good as they feel for as long as they can. I'd use beautiful mature women as models and sell only in the finest salons." Marianne's courage built when she saw Lawson nod in approval. She held up her hands with her thumbs and index fingers forming a frame and said in a strong voice, "'Fifty is fabulous, sixty is sexy.' We'll come up with something snappy for seventy. I have detailed plans. I've already shopped these ideas around to prospective investors and received some financial commitments."

"Forget about other investors. You provide the products and a small amount of money—say fifty thousand dollars. I'll put up the rest. Here in Scottsdale we have the perfect test market."

Marianne nodded, fretful, massaging her brow.

"Is there a problem?"

"I don't mean to offend, Mrs. Lawson…Adele, but without my products, there's no business, so why do I have to put up so much money?"

Mrs. Lawson gave Marianne a cold stare before her face eased into a condescending smile. "I'll be investing a great deal of money. Should we fail, I'll lose my money but you'll still have your aunt's creams. If you put in money too, then you're sharing the risk."

"I'll need time to think about it."

"Yes, of course. Meanwhile, I'll have my lawyers draft an operating agreement. I'll need your address and other information before we leave today."

Marianne wiped her sweaty palms on the napkin in her lap.

"I'm offering you a once-in-a-lifetime opportunity, my dear," Mrs. Lawson said firmly. "While I'm very interested in doing this, I won't wait indefinitely."

† † †

"So, how'd it go?" Eva asked Marianne the moment she returned to the store.

"Lawson surprised me. I thought we might get twenty to thirty grand out of her, but she wants in for much more. Not just to invest money, but actually, to finance the entire business."

"Way cool." Eva giggled. "See, I was right. I knew it." Her smile froze when Marianne frowned. "What's wrong now?"

"She's one pushy broad. Already trying to move in and take over before a dime has changed hands. I don't think I can tolerate that."

"What do ya mean?"

"I've gotten used to a certain way of doing things. Make some money in a place then move on. No commitments. No micromanaging bosses to put up with."

"But haven't you always dreamed about running a real business? Maybe even staying put here in Phoenix?"

Marianne nodded. "I've thought about it." Her voice trailed off.

"You always said you wanted that…one day. Here's your chance. Don't blow it. Don't settle."

"What about you? Is that what you want?"

"I'm in," Eva said. "Even if it includes playing up to Max."

Marianne arched her eyebrows. "You're not falling for him, are you?"

Eva blushed.

"Do I have to worry about your loyalty?"

Eva shook her head. "Never." She put two fingers over her heart.

"Good. I told Mrs. Lawson I'm bringing you in with me, partner. She agreed." Marianne gave Eva a warm hug.

"So where'd ya leave things?" Eva asked.

"I said I'd think about her offer. She said she'll have her attorney draw up the papers. But I'm not sure yet if I want to do business with her. I don't think I can trust her." *Or Max.*

† † †

That Saturday night, Eva and Max Lawson sat side-by-side in a small Mexican restaurant in Old Town Scottsdale. They had finished dinner and were lingering over drinks. Eva looked adoringly at him as she sipped her margarita. "You rock. You convinced your mother. It's so cool she's willing to put up all that money so Marianne can start a business."

"I told you I could do it, baby." He took a long pull on his third beer of the evening and leaned back in his chair. "I know how to use just the right words to make Mother think she's doing what she wants to do. She's vain. I tell her she looks terrific and that the creams are magic. The next thing you know she thinks they're the greatest and she's got to have them."

"In a way, it's a little weird. Why invest in a business? She could just buy all the creams she wants."

"Mother never lets a good opportunity get by her. She smells big money."

Eva studied her glass for a moment then looked into Max's eyes. "Good thing she's honest or I'd worry."

"Huh?"

"Seriously, I'd be afraid she might try to take advantage of Marianne."

He smirked and rolled his eyes.

Eva raised her brow. "Did I say something funny?"

"How do you think she became so rich? It wasn't by sharing the spoils."

"She's your mother. It sounds kinda spooky when you talk like that. Maybe it's not smart for Marianne to get involved with her."

He put his arm around her and drew her close, nuzzling her hair. "Baby, baby. No worries. Leave everything to me."

Eva gently pulled away and waved her hand playfully at him. "You're kidding around with me, right?"

Grinning, he signaled to the server to bring them another round of drinks then said to Eva, "We've got to plan for the future. Might as well start right now."

† † †

"I received the contract from Mrs. Lawson's lawyer," Marianne told Eva a few days later.

"You didn't tell me?"

"I'm sorry. I had a lot of thinking to do first."

"Where are the papers?"

"On my desk at home. I'm still going through them, then I'll hand them over to you."

"So, how do things look so far?" Eva's face beamed with anticipation.

"Pretty much as Lawson promised. I name the company and get the control I asked for. She handles finances. That may be okay initially, since it'll be mostly her money. It could be a problem later on."

"So you hire an independent accountant once the dough starts rolling in. But you can make changes in the agreement before you sign, right?" Marianne nodded. "Then somehow get her to give you access to the money."

"Believe me, I intend to. But there's still the matter of the fifty-grand she wants me to kick in."

Eva's jaw dropped. "What makes her think you have that kind of money?"

Marianne shrugged. "Probably hasn't given it much thought. To her, it's peanuts."

"Not to me," Eva said.

"I'll talk her into half now, half later, that is, if I decide to accept her offer."

"Why wouldn't ya? It's like a golden opportunity. What's to lose?"

Marianne stared back coldly. "The family jewels," she said. "But there's something else that bothers me."

"What?"

"She's pushing to set up the company in the Cayman Islands. Claims she has her business accounts there already. To avoid taxes."

"Makes sense to me. Lots of companies do that."

"Anyway, we'll need to talk to a lawyer. You know one?"

"I can get a name. I'm gonna talk to this banking guy I dated. He plays all the angles. He'll know a lawyer who'll take good care of us."

Marianne laughed. "I can always count on you to know a guy who knows a guy who…"

Eva locked eyes with a customer. "I'd better help that lady jingling her bracelets before she has a coronary. Hold that thought."

† † †

"Please take a seat, ladies," L. Martin Terrell, Esquire, said as he pulled out chairs for Marianne and Eva. Two weeks earlier Marianne had called his Camelback office at the recommendation of Eva's friend. Terrell handed them each a copy of the agreement.

"I got Mrs. Lawson's attorney to make the changes you asked for but he insisted on certain password protections. Take a few minutes to thumb through. The latest revisions are underlined. I think this version stipulates everything you wanted."

After they reviewed the agreements and signed them, Terrell said to Marianne, "I'll need the cashier's check for the twenty-five thousand."

Marianne reached into her purse, took out a check and handed it to him.

"I won't wire this money to Grand Cayman," Terrell said, "until after Mrs. Lawson has deposited her funds in the Roza account. At that point we'll have to supply the formulas for safe-keeping in the bank vault."

"That still bothers me," Marianne said.

"You have no choice," Terrell responded. "Lawson's showing good faith by letting you both draw funds from the company account, so she needs access to the formulas, to protect her interests. A bonded third party will control her access. That's spelled out in this agreement." He clipped the check to the signed documents and laid the papers down in front of him. He looked sternly at the two women. "Mrs. Lawson has an upstanding reputation in the business community. If you are to be partners, you need to demonstrate trust. Otherwise, ladies, you'd better reconsider this entire venture."

"It'll be okay," Eva asserted. "We understand Mrs. Lawson has a lot more money at stake than we do. She's entitled to some assurances and safeguards."

"But," Marianne added, "she also *has* much more money than we do. If I lose control of the formulas, I have nothing." Eva touched her arm. "But Mr. Terrell is right. Trust is essential to make this work."

Eva had just arrived home when her cell phone rang. She saw it was Max calling.

"My mother's made the deposit," he said. "Grab a pen. You have your codes for the Roza account. I'll give you my mother's passwords and tell you how to move all the money to our account."

She reached into her purse for a pen and paper. "Go ahead."

He gave her the information then said, "It'll all go just like I said. You're with me on this, aren't you babe?"

"Totally. I just want to be sure you don't have any second thoughts," Eva said. "Since it's your mother—"

"None, babe. She's got so much she'll hardly miss it. Now do it," he ordered.

"Okay. When did you say the money'll get there?"

"By tonight, tomorrow morning latest."

"Okay. I'm on it. I can't wait until we're together," she whispered. "I love you."

"Sure, babe. Me, too."

She heard his deep breathing and smiled as she hung up. She walked to her desk, opened her laptop and logged on."

After clearing airport security at Sky Harbor, Eva slipped on her shoes. Her cell phone rang. She let it ring three times before answering.

"I just checked our account," Max grumbled. "The funds haven't shown up," he shouted. "I've been calling you all morning. Where are you? What's going on? You made the transfers, didn't you?"

"Yeah," she said. "It's probably just some glitch. I'll check on it and call you right back." She hung up, took a deep breath and grinned. "I'd love to see his ugly face when it hits him he's not getting his greasy fingers on a dime."

As they rushed toward the Brazilian Airlines gate, Eva said, "Can you imagine? He actually thought I was dumb enough to let him grab the money out from under us."

She tossed her cell phone into a waste bin and shook her head. "He wanted to cheat his own mother out of the money, disappear, and was setting me up to take the fall."

With a grand gesture, Eva high-fived Marianne. "We did it. We fooled every last one of them. Can you believe it, Mom? We got it all."

† † †

SUSAN BUDAVARI has written over 30 mystery/suspense short stories and co-edited several award-winning anthologies. She has completed DEADLY LISTING and LEGACY OF LIES, the first two books in a psychological mystery series featuring a Scottsdale P.I. and his physician wife, and is at work on THE BARGAIN, the next book in the series. Prior to this, Susan was an award-winning scientific writer and encyclopedist. She is a Member-at-Large of Sisters in Crime Desert Sleuths Chapter.

THE LEGACY
YVONNE M. CORRIGAN-CARR

Melanie's hands shook as she wiped away rivers of mascara. She took in a deep breath, but it came out as a sob. She grabbed the edge of the bathroom sink to steady herself. Her daughter rushed into the room.

"Mom, are you okay?" Jennifer's face was a mask of worry.

Melanie straightened, put down the mascara and hugged her.

"I'm fine, honey. Give me ten minutes. Go down with your brothers. I'll be right there." Her arm around Jennifer's shoulders, she gently moved her daughter out of the master bathroom. "We have to leave soon."

Jennifer hesitated, then went downstairs.

Melanie reapplied her makeup and choked back tears. She buttoned her black suit and walked down the sweeping staircase. How many times had she and Jack walked these stairs arm-in-arm? Memories flickered...Jack hanging evergreen boughs on the banister at Christmas...Jim bounding down three steps at a time in his cap and gown...Jenny gingerly navigating the stairs in her first high heels...Jack Jr. racing to his father's study, waving his acceptance from Annapolis.

Designing every detail of their home had been a joy for Jack and Melanie. They planned to grow old here together, welcome grandchildren here. Melanie hoped for a wedding or two in the garden. Jack said they'd be here forever.

She steadied herself at the bottom step and looked out the wall of windows. The somber black limousine waiting on the circular drive stood in stark contrast to the bright spring day. Jack had been everything to her, devoted and loving to his family, brilliant and tough as the head of Arizona's premier law firm.

Jack Jr. stood as she entered the room. Tall and dark, he was the image of his father. Blue eyes searched his mother's face. The twins, Jim and Jennifer, hurried to her side immediately. She looked at her children and smiled.

"Your father would be so proud of you," she told them, brushing Jim's hair from his forehead. "Please stop worrying about me. Today is about your father…about celebrating his life and honoring his legacy. If he could, he'd have spent another fifty years with you. But, let's celebrate the time we had with him. Okay?" She hugged each of them.

"You're the most important part of our lives and you always will be," she said. "Nothing has ever mattered as much as the three of you. Nothing. I hope you always remember that."

"We know, Mom." Jennifer's green eyes pooled with tears. Melanie stroked her daughter's ash blonde hair.

For Melanie, walking to the funeral car felt surreal. Puffy clouds graced the azure sky. A breeze wafting through orange blossoms carried their scent across the lawn. It was a beautiful day, Jack's favorite time of year.

Melanie sank into the seat and closed her eyes. The car wound through Paradise Valley. Pain and despair engulfed her, as the previous three weeks whirled through her mind like an unrelenting movie reel. Their day-trip to Nogales, Mexico with Barb and Steve Ross had started in high spirits. Barb laden with designer handbag knock-offs. Melanie haggling with street vendors over everything she bought; Steve and Jack laughing, teasing their wives.

Their semi-annual jaunts across the border always included festive lunches and margaritas. Barb couldn't wait to try The Cavern, the newest restaurant in Nogales. Reviews were good and the others readily agreed to go.

"Oh, they have scallops *ceviche*!" Barb had almost squealed as she perused the menu. Tuxedoed servers moved effortlessly around the dining room. "Look at their sushi selection!"

"Ugh. Raw fish!" Melanie shuddered.

"Gross!" Steve concurred.

"I agree with Barb. It sounds great! Be a little adventurous you two. Take a chance once in a while," Jack had chided them.

Lunch was exceptional. Barb and Jack shared sushi, *ceviche* and imported truffles, while teasing her and Steve about their limited palates. Steve had Caesar salad and a filet. She chose pork tenderloin with apricots. Steve finished the meal with Kahlúa and coffee. The two seafood lovers opted for cinnamon sopapillas and wild honey.

"I'll pass on dessert," Melanie said. "I'm so full, I'm not

sure if I can get to the car."

"Have you decided to buy those gorgeous malachite earrings you saw?" Barb asked her.

"Yes. I'm going back to get them."

"The shop is across the street from José's Cantina. Why don't we stop there for margaritas and you can get the earrings at the same time?" Jack suggested.

"Absolutely!" Steve agreed. "We can't leave Nogales without one of José's margaritas."

"Okay, but if we're going to do that, Melanie should be the driver on the trip home," Barb said.

"Nothing new about that," Melanie laughed. Since she had never been much of a drinker, she didn't mind always being the designated driver.

She knew that Jack and Steve used these forays to blow off steam and ease the stress of their jobs.

Two hours later, the others had polished off three rounds of margaritas and Melanie was tired of drinking iced tea.

It was dusk when the four walked through U.S. Customs and across the border to their car. It was parked in one of the courtesy lots on the Arizona side. On the drive home, Barb dozed, Jack and Steve discussed a new IPO and Melanie listened to jazz.

An hour out of Tucson, Barb said, "I'm really thirsty. Did anybody bring anything to drink?"

"Of course." Melanie grinned. "I have cold water or raspberry iced tea. Jack, would you open the ice cooler?"

"Tea, please," Barb said. "You know it's my favorite."

"I'll have water," Steve said.

"Okay, we have one bottle of each left," Jack announced. "What will it be, Mel?"

"Well, since you like sweet tea and I don't, I think I'll take water."

"That's my Melanie, always plans ahead." He smiled at her. "Are you sure you weren't a Boy Scout?"

"You're lucky you have me," she quipped. "Empties go into the recycle bag under the seat, please."

It was after nine o'clock when Melanie pulled the Lexus into the Clearwater Hills subdivision and navigated the narrow road to the Rosses's Tuscan-style home.

"I think I'm having a delayed reaction to those margaritas,"

Barb complained. "I only had three, but I'm pretty tipsy. I feel very woozy."

"Uh, make that three margaritas, plus wine, plus half of my Kahlúa, dear. Of course, you could just be tired from lugging about fifty pounds of leather all over Nogales." Her husband laughed while hauling her newest acquisitions from the trunk. "Thanks for driving, Melanie."

"Talk to you tomorrow," Melanie called to Barb as they drove away.

At midnight, Melanie sat up in bed. The light was on in the master bathroom. She found Jack vomiting.

"Honey, what's wrong?"

"I don't know. Maybe I should have stopped at two margaritas, or maybe I should have listened to you about the sushi," he mumbled between heaves. "I don't think I'll ever eat fish again."

"Should I call a doctor? If it's the sushi, it could be food poisoning or something else serious," Melanie said.

"No. I could have picked up a bug this week at that conference. Once I get it out of my system, I'll be fine. Thank God tomorrow's Sunday. No court, no depositions." Jack heaved again. "Crap, this reminds me of my fraternity days. First you're afraid you'll die. Then, you're afraid you won't." His breathing was ragged.

"Jack, you sound really bad. Maybe I should just call Steve."

"Don't call Steve. He has real patients to worry about," Jack insisted. "Just help me back to bed."

By morning, Jack was too weak to get out of bed. He complained of blurry vision and his breath was labored. Still, he flatly refused to call a doctor.

"I obviously ate or drank the wrong thing. I'm not going to call a doctor over my own stupidity," he admonished his wife.

Melanie went downstairs and quietly called Steve. There was no answer, so she left a message. She then called Steve's cell phone, but the call went to his voice mail. Two hours later, she tried again with the same results. At noon, her phone rang.

"Melanie, it's Steve." His voice was strained. "Barb's in the hospital. It's serious. Her system is trying to shut down. It may be some kind of food poisoning, but we don't have the test results yet."

"Oh, no! Steve, Jack's sick, too." Racing back up the stairs, she explained his symptoms. When she reached the bedroom, she found Jack unconscious.

A nightmare followed. Neither Barb nor Jack regained consciousness. In the hospital, both were put on respiratory assistance. Melanie stayed at Jack's side, leaving him only to go to Barb's room, looking for any sign that she would recover.

Best friends for decades, godparents to each other's children, there wasn't a holiday, vacation, joy or success they hadn't shared. They had bolstered each other through troubles. Melanie took a leave of absence from Goldwater Medical Trauma Center and put her life on hold to care for Steve after his kidney transplant. She was there for Barb and the children as much as for the patient.

Barb had been Melanie's rock when Jack Jr. suffered a severe concussion and broken leg playing varsity football. Unconscious for forty-eight hours, he endured months of physical therapy. Melanie had been the stabilizing factor in Barb's life when Steve's affair with his physician's assistant came to light. Barb was devastated by his betrayal; but, with renewed commitment and professional counseling, they had put their marriage back together. Just when both couples had sent their last child off to college and a new phase started for them all, this had happened.

Protocol prevented Steve and Melanie from being assigned to their respective spouse's care, but, as a licensed nurse practitioner, Melanie could review their charts and ask questions. She realized how bad it was. By nightfall their conditions worsened again. Steve and Melanie called their children home from college. On Tuesday evening, Barb died. Thursday morning, Jack passed away.

Hospital tests were inconclusive, but indicated the patients had consumed whatever poisoned their systems. Various authorities interviewed Steve and Melanie. Both gave blood samples for testing. Both homes were examined. Nothing was found that could explain the deaths. By process of elimination, the conclusion was the toxin had most likely been in the meal eaten at The Cavern.

Nogales officials were notified of the deaths. Mexican authorities and the owners of The Cavern were outraged. Both refused to allow Arizona officials or any federal inspectors into the restaurant, insisting that their own inspections determined no contamination existed.

"Look at all the cars." Jennifer's voice startled Melanie out of her painful reverie. She shook her head hard as though that would clear away the anguish. She looked at her children. Three grief-stricken faces stared back at her.

The limousine slowed and turned into the church's driveway. The huge lot was jammed. Parking had overflowed onto surrounding streets. The limo glided past the front doors, to the side entrance, where the minister and the funeral director stood waiting.

"Mom, are you okay?" Melanie gazed at Jim's earnest face. He had been the closest to his father, determined from the age of ten to emulate him and eventually become a partner in Jack's firm. His red-rimmed eyes belied his resolute composure.

"I'm fine, Jimmy," she replied.

The service was a moving tribute to Jack and the legacy he left for his family, his community and the legal powerhouse he'd built. Steve gave the eulogy in his best friend's honor. His wife's funeral was tomorrow.

Tears streamed down Melanie's face as Jack Jr., stalwart and handsome in his Midshipman dress uniform, read the letter of love and farewell he and his siblings had written together. As instructed in his will, Jack had been cremated. His ashes would be interred later, with only the immediate family in attendance.

The partners in Jack's law firm hosted a luncheon following his funeral. The governor made it a point to speak to Melanie and to each of the children. Friends and strangers grasped Melanie's hand and told her what a fine man Jack had been.

Hours later, the family said good-bye and made their way home.

"Dad always said a man should lead his life as though one day it would be examined. I think he would have been proud today." Jack Jr. slipped his arm around his sister and hugged her.

"He told me my word was everything and my decisions would be my legacy," Jim murmured. "I wish I could tell him now I understand what he meant."

At home, the children wouldn't leave Melanie's side. Finally, she told them, "I appreciate your concern. But, don't worry about me. I'll be fine."

The phone rang and Jim answered it.

"It's Mac Drury for you, Mom." Five minutes later, Melanie ended the call with the probate attorney in Jack's firm and turned to her children.

"I have to find a file for Mac and it will take some time. You guys need to eat. The refrigerator is bulging with food from friends, so take your pick, but, please eat something."

She went upstairs to Jack's study, locked the door and went to Jack's desk. She had asked Mac to call tonight. There was so much to be done and timing was critical.

A stab of pain cut through her heart. Tears slid down her cheeks. *Things should have been so different.*

Melanie opened one of the drawers in Jack's desk. She pulled out several files and selected one. The first page was a typed list, with notations and numbers. She dialed Mac's number.

"Hello," Mac answered.

"Mac, it's Melanie, again. I'm so sorry to bother you. I was looking for a new book of checks in Jack's desk and found some files I don't recognize, possibly investments. Jack always handled this stuff, and now, I…I don't—" Her voice caught.

"Melanie, please don't worry. I'll take care of everything. Why don't I come over tomorrow afternoon? I'll sort it out for you." Melanie could imagine the silver-haired lawyer's face creased with concern. "I wish there was something more I could do for you. I can't even imagine what you are going through. To lose Jack and your best friend at the same time is inconceivable. Mary and I are so very sorry."

"Thank you, Mac. I appreciate your help. I just can't thank you enough." Melanie sat back and rubbed her temples. Jack had been the love of her life.

"If only…." She sighed. Then she straightened and scolded herself silently.

If only…what? If only she hadn't borrowed her husband's Jaguar last month? If only she hadn't found the disposable cell phone under the driver's seat and recognized her best friend's phone number? If only Jack had used something besides the initials and birthdates of his loved ones as passwords and user names on everything? If only she hadn't read the loving, blatantly sexual text messages and emails, between the two lovers dating back more than a year? If only they hadn't plotted to take every dime possible and leave their spouses and children behind, without regard to the lives they would ruin?

Stunned and heartsick at what she'd found, Melanie had returned the phone to its hiding place. She'd sat in his car shaking, feeling as though she were drowning …suffocating…fighting to breathe. She'd returned to their house, told Jack she had a sudden migraine and would sleep in the guest room. Embroiled in a major court case, he didn't notice the shift in her behavior. Steve and Barb were attending a medical conference in Hawaii, making it easy for Melanie to avoid Barb.

Days of private pain and anger had followed for Melanie until she'd found a strength she didn't know she had. She decided she would act normally, monitor their affair, and make plans of her own. The affair might burn itself out…or not. She had been a fool, blind and trusting; but, never again.

"Keep your friends close, and your enemies closer," she'd told herself.

She'd changed to night shifts at the hospital, giving herself time to search Jack's study while he was at work. Melanie had been torn between a career in nursing and one in computer science in college, so she'd graduated with degrees in both. She'd always kept her technology skills honed.

Slowly and carefully, she'd tracked his money and his plans. Though Jack had kept most information at his law offices, Melanie knew he could access all of his files remotely. She did the same while he slept.

Within days, Melanie had learned Jack had hidden millions of dollars from her and he was definitely leaving her and the children. He'd secretly bought a home in Costa Rica for himself and his mistress…her dearest friend.

The two couples often vacationed in Costa Rica together. Jack frequently told Melanie he wanted to retire there while still young enough to play away his days. He was going to do that, without her. After reading the messages sent between the lovers, Melanie realized she would never change Jack's mind if she confronted him. She knew him so well. He would pretend to repent, beg for forgiveness and swear the affair was over, all the time escalating his timetable and hiding money more effectively.

What happened to the man she fell in love with, the man who said your word was everything, and how you kept your word, regardless of the situation was your legacy? When she first realized he was willing to abandon his family for money and his mistress, the pain was crippling. But, it was nothing compared to how his betrayal would shatter their children.

Protecting them was her first priority. She had to stop her husband before he could leave them. Jack was destroying the very foundation they built their family on. She would not let that happen.

It hadn't been difficult to track Jack's money using the search history buried inside the computer's memory. Given his pattern with user names and passwords, Melanie had plugged in Barb's information; and, every account opened immediately. He really was predictable.

Ten days after she'd found the tell-tale cell phone, as Melanie watched the gardener working in the yard, realization struck her. She stared at the solution. With meticulous planning it would work.

She'd driven to FedEx/Kinko's in Tempe, close enough to get there and back quickly; and, far enough away that she wouldn't be recognized. Paying cash to use a computer, it took just minutes to research what she'd suspected about her lovely oleanders, so graceful and commonplace; but, so deadly when ingested. Another half hour reviewing reports of oleander poisoning gave her what she needed. She erased the computer's search history and left.

When Barb phoned about the new restaurant in Nogales and suggested they take their semi-annual trip the following week, Melanie recognized her opportunity.

She'd called the restaurant and asked about their menu. The seafood and sopapillas would bring her plan together. Neither Jack nor Barb ever passed up sushi, and the puffy pastry was his favorite dessert.

As soon as Jack drove out of the driveway the next morning, she shoved oleander leaves, blossoms and stems into a large saucepan with water. She kept the mixture at a low boil for hours. Removing the cooked foliage, she added honey and cooked it down to a concentrate, then poured it into a bottle and hid it.

The night before the trip, she used a syringe to inject the concentrate under the caps of the plastic bottles of flavored tea. The tiny needle prick wasn't visible. A diabetic, Steve couldn't drink the sweetened tea. But, Barb and Jack loved sweet tea, so odds were strong they'd drink her potion.

Once they were home from Nogales, Melanie told Jack she had an early morning meeting and wanted to fill her gas tank before turning in.

"Honey, it's late. You should have said something. We could have stopped on the way back."

"It slipped my mind," she'd explained. "I'll be back in a few minutes."

Melanie pulled into the Circle-K, gassed her car and dumped a sack with the saucepan into a trash can. At McDonald's she rinsed and tossed the empty bottles, wiping them to smear fingerprints. The cooler went into a dumpster blocks away. Returning home she wiped down the car's white interior with a mild bleach solution. She emptied new bottles of water and sweet tea, rinsed them and tossed them into the recycle bin scheduled to be emptied on Monday. She wiped out a duplicate cooler and put it away.

With Jack sound asleep, she'd removed Barb's information and inserted hers for the user names and passwords on the large bank accounts. She'd changed the log-ins on investment accounts to their children's data. She'd typed the list of Jack's secret account numbers and the new passwords and dropped it into the paper file she would give to Mac. Each user name and password on the list of accounts now reflected the devotion of a loving family man, not the name and birth date of his mistress. She'd deleted the password document and backup file. As always, she'd erased her search history, the cache and other electronic footprints. One could never be too careful. Though if anyone checked, it would appear as though Jack himself had used his computer that night.

A soft knock on the study door brought Melanie back to the present.

"Mom, dinner's ready," Jennifer said. "Please come down."

"Give me five minutes." Melanie replaced the files.

She thought of Mac's words to her just now. "Losing Jack and Barb...inconceivable," she mused.

Not really. It was quite conceivable if you arranged it carefully. Difficult, but, oh so possible when it was the only way to protect your children and safeguard their father's legacy.

If the hospital ran additional tests and detected oleander poisoning, Melanie knew from her research that myriad sources, ranging from the honey to the seafood, could account for it occurring at the restaurant. Previous deaths had been traced to bees extracting nectar from oleander blossoms which poisoned their honey; with more accidental poisonings triggered by equally bizarre circumstances. Without proof otherwise, Jack and Barb's death would always be considered a tragic accident.

She poured a glass of Jack's prized Chivas Regal Royal Salute and looked at the smiling faces of Steve, Barb, Jack and herself in the photo on Jack's desk.

"What was it you said, Jack? Take a chance once in a while?"

She drained the glass.

"How am I doing so far, dear?"

† † †

YVONNE M. CORRIGAN-CARR is a former reporter and feature writer for newspapers and magazines in Arizona and her home state of Michigan. She is an acclaimed national speaker and a full-time Realtor in Scottsdale, Arizona. An avid reader of many genres, Yvonne's first love is writing. Her first book, THE CARETAKER'S CALLER, is an inspirational novel. She is currently working on a new murder mystery series, which is based in Arizona. "The Legacy" is her first published short story.

DEATH BY DECEPTION
LAURIE FAGEN

I'm havin' a drink with the nice Mitchell employees out behind the hotel, under the stars, just mindin' my own business...when gunshots ring out. A tall cowboy in old leather chaps, black duster and a dark ten-gallon hat bursts in through the bushes, wavin' and firin' twin Colt Army revolvers, a wild look in his eyes.

"Listen up, you lily-livered city slickers! I'm L.W. Sweet, 'n don't any o' you move! I'm a bounty hunter 'n I wanna know which one o' you is *this* varmint?"

He pulls out a Wanted poster showing Charles Mitchell, owner of a local business in the small southwestern town of Deception, Arizona. The couple dozen good folks murmur amongst themselves as they recognize Mr. Mitchell, who buys and sells gold and other minerals at his local assay office.

As the law 'round these parts, I'd had enough of this pesky cowboy, so I step up behind him.

"Now, hold it right there, L.W."

L.W. froze.

"I already told ya once today ta git outta town. Now just what in tarnation d'ya think yer doin'?"

L.W. turns around real slow. Sweat is streamin' down his face and he looks near crazy.

"Well, Sheriff Richie, I'm just out for what's due me. I hear there's five hunnert dollars on this varmint's head, and that he's here somewhere. I'm gonna collect!"

He turns toward the people standing at small tables, staring at him, and looks for Mitchell in the courtyard.

I glance at the poster. "This guy? Only thing he's wanted fer is being a gol-durned good businessman. Runs a metal testin' outfit called Mitchell Assay, I b'lieve. And he loves to take his employees to fancy places out West and throw big parties."

L.W. perks up his ears at that. "Oh, yeah? What kinda metals is he into?"

"I hear tell it's gold, even diamonds, that kinda stuff."

"Well, I know a few things about jewels—"

"Hold it right there. I'm tired of repeatin' myself. I want you gone!" I realize all the nice people are watching us pretty close like, so I calm myself down. "L.W., I'm gonna be sociable 'n let ya have a drink down at the saloon before ya leave. But only *one*. Then I want ya ta make yerself as scarce as whiskers on a baby. I better not see ya again."

"Oh, yeah?"   He waves those danged guns around. "Or what?"

"This here badge means I can do anythin' I damn well please. 'Sides, I hear there might be a bounty on *yer* head. So don't cross me."

That ol' cowboy knows I'm right, 'cause he gets real nice.

"Anythin' you say, Sheriff, one drink 'n I'm gone."

L.W. scoots right out.

I give a squint at the hotel's roomers, whose eyes'r big as full harvest moons. "Sorry 'bout that folks, don't pay him no mind. Just be at the Silver Bullet Saloon right at seven, 'cause we got a big surprise for you!"

Them folks settle down 'n go back to drinkin'. I head to the office to see my deputy 'fore checkin' on the 'rangements fer this big whoop-ti-do at the saloon.

Bits of nervous laughter scattered across the outdoor patio, and soon all the employees of Mitchell Fine Jewelry were chatting about the scene that had unfolded in front of them over cocktails in the lush courtyard at the swanky Arizona Biltmore Hotel in Phoenix.

"Hey, Mr. Mitchell!" Tom, the head of marketing, yelled from across the open area. "That was a good photo of you on that Wanted poster!"

Charles Mitchell, a rotund man in his sixties, smiled and waved as if to say, "Oh, go on." Those around him laughed and helped themselves to appetizers offered by a waiter.

"Is this one of those interactive murder mystery plays?" asked Denise from accounting. "I've never seen one."

"That's what Stephanie in public relations must've meant when she said to pay attention to 'clues' tonight," replied Renee, a tall blonde standing next to her. "Don't know about you, but I'd like more 'clues' about that handsome Sheriff." Her friends laughed.

Denise said, "Hey, it's almost seven. Let's head to the saloon for that 'surprise.'" The group went inside the hotel, down a carpeted hallway, to the Frank Lloyd Wright ballroom.

A woman in a long, old-fashioned dress with a cinched waist and fancy hat passed out flyers at the door. "Welcome to the Silver Bullet Saloon. Have a lovely dinner!"

It was as if Denise, Renee and the others stepped back in time. Above a long wooden bar, right out of the movies, was an old sign that said SILVER BULLET. Behind the bar, a man dressed in a white shirt with black elbow garters served drinks. Off to one side at a round table, several men in garb from the 1800s played cards. A buxom woman wearing a satin, knee-length blue dress with lace around the edges and a plunging neckline flirted with the men. Large round dinner tables covered with white linens filled the ballroom.

A spotlight illuminated the character known as "L.W." at the end of the bar. He was slumped over, as if passed out.

When I get back to the Silver Bullet Saloon, all hell's broken loose.

"Sheriff, come quick!" The barkeep, Billy Bob, who is also the town's apothecary, catches me as I push through the double swinging doors, my spurs janglin'.

"What the...?"

There's that no-good L.W., half on a stool, half layin' flat across the bar. His hat is upside down on the scarred wood top, his hair slick with sweat. The fingers on his right hand clutch an empty shot glass. Cloth wraps his other hand, 'n blood is seepin' through the makeshift bandage. I walked over to 'im and inspect the dressing. When I unwrap it, there are small red puncture wounds on his swollen skin. A leather pouch hangs from his left pants pocket.

I give him a poke. Then another. But he is deader 'n a stone.

"Ah, hell, Billy, what happened?"

Billy Bob looks plenty nervous. "Well, he came in about an hour ago and ordered a drink, sayin' it was on you. He seemed to be dry as the gulch and awful hot. He just kept orderin' shot after shot. The more he drank, the meaner he got. Soon, he was lookin' sleepy, like he was gonna pass out. Kept sayin' he's seein' yeller.'"

"Then what?"

"Thought it might help if I offered him some of my special elixir. He gulped it down." Billy pointed to a row of apothecary jars on a shelf next to the whiskey bottles. "He kept demandin' more whiskey. Tried to bribe me with his so-called jewels, but I said no."

"Jewels?"

"I think it's what he mighta kept in that little leather bag."

I pull the pouch out of L.W.'s pocket, but it's empty as a hollow tree. "What happened next?"

"He had a to-do with Miss Sally. Afterwards he got in a fight with ol' Farmer Johnson over a card game. Later I went out back to stock up for the big party, and when I returned, he was out cold. I just thought he was sleepin' it off. I tried to wake him but I could tell he was dead."

"So what's in that elixir?"

"Nuthin' but tonic 'n quinine and castor oil. It's good for anythin' that ails ya."

"And that's all you gave him?"

"Of course!" he says indignantly.

Tom, from marketing, strode to Denise and Renee's table, carrying martinis to them. He looked serious. "I think the butler did it," he said in mock horror.

"Oh, come on, play along!" Renee grinned. "I think the bartender drugged him."

Denise laughed. "You can't know that yet. I'll bet there are other suspects."

"Including that good-looking cougar in the shiny dress?" Tom pointed. As a waiter served the main course, the co-workers shared a laugh, and watched the saloon girl saunter over to the sheriff.

I'm jus' tryin' to figure out what I should do first 'bout this dead cowboy, when next thing I know, someone's sweet-smellin' arms are sneakin' 'round my neck.

"Howdy, Sheriff. I love it when you come to see me." Long dark hair curls down to this gal's ample breasts, barely covered by a dangerously low-cut dress. Nestled in her hair is a long black feather that tickles my ear, and her lips are painted bright red.

"Now, Miss Sally, I'm here to investigate this death." I remove her hands. "You know anything about it?"

"Me?" Miss Sally says with fake surprise. "How would I?"

"I hear you had a little row with L.W."

"Is that his name? Well, I'd never seen him before he come in this afternoon, boastin' about bein' a bounty hunter, talkin' 'bout all the wanted men he's captured. Then he said somethin' about gettin' a job with that Mitchell company. He pulled out these big diamonds 'n rubies 'n emeralds."

Sally's eyes get big. "Why, I'd never seen nuthin' like them. We had a few drinks. He seemed nice at first, 'cept he was so drunk he could hardly walk. No wonder he was sick to his stomach."

"Then what'd you two do?"

"Well, Sheriff, he said he'd been on the road fer a long spell, so, you know, he 'n I went up to my room." She fluffs her hair. "But we didn't do nuthin'. No sirree, we weren't in the room a second when he's jumpin' on me. And *you* know, Sheriff, how I like to git to know a man first." She strokes the side of my face. "He wouldn't quit. So I kicked him out."

"Is that all?"

"I did use a little physical means of persuasion."

"Like what?"

"I smacked him upside the head with a spittoon that was inside my door!" She shows how she grabbed the metal bowl and whacked the air. "Hell, he'd had so much to drink, I doubt he felt it."

I wiggle the man's bag in front of her. "This leather pouch with the jewels you was talkin' about is empty. Do you know what happened to them?"

Miss Sally's hands flutter about her face. "How would I know? He probably…lost 'em in a card game to Farmer Johnson over there. He's been winnin' all night."

She points toward a round table covered with shot glasses, whiskey bottles and playin' cards. Five men are lookin' down at their hands, not movin' an inch.

"Farmer Johnson?" My eyes land on Jeremiah Joseph Johnson, a crusty old feller who owns a couple hundred acres and tries his best to grow crops, despite the drought we're in.

"Ah'm right here, Sheriff." He stands up slowly, wrapping his thumbs around the straps of his dirty blue coveralls. When he comes to town, he's a regular at the Silver Bullet, spending most his time in a poker game. He has no woman at home, and enjoys visitin' now and then with the folks at the saloon while puttin' back his share o' whiskey.

"Wouldja tell me what you saw this afternoon?"

Farmer Johnson gives a longing look towards Miss Sally then turns to me. He looks a little jealous.

"Well, that cowboy was carryin' on with Miss Sally, and pretty soon they went upstairs. But a few minutes later, there's a ruckus and he came down from her room."

"So then what happened?"

Johnson strokes his stubbly chin. "I'm jus' settin' here, playin' cards, when he comes stumblin' down the stairs. He was a mess after hittin' the whiskey hard at the bar. He come over and asked to play cards, so I said, 'Sure.' But pretty soon his cash is gettin' low." Farmer Johnson gets a downright smug look on his face, and runs his fingers over his four-day beard. "He wasn't a good player. Lost all his money. So he pulls out this ol' pouch and tried to ante with a buncha colored rocks. Hell, I didn't know if they was real, but I figured one hand wouldn't hurt. Next thing I know, he's pullin' an ace right outta his sleeve. Wasn't even slick about it. Hell, he was too drunk! Well, that got my goat, and…maybe I said some things I shouldn't of."

"Like what?"

Farmer Johnson removes his hat and rolls it around in his hands. "I guess I said something about if he cheated me again …I'd have to do something about it."

"Somethin' meanin…?"

"Well, dang, what anybody else woulda done if'n they'd been cheated! I told him…I'd kill him. But I didn't. I swear I didn't." He blinks a couple of times and looks at me real serious like.

"All right, then, Jeremiah. You might need to spend the night in town 'til we get this all sorted out."

"I will, Sheriff." He glances at Miss Sally. She smiles in return.

Mr. Mitchell and his wife, Eleanor, were finishing dessert at their dinner table with six other employees, each holding a pencil, studying their flyer with a crossword puzzle on it.

Sally, Mr. Mitchell's secretary, focused on her puzzle. "Oh, I know number two," she shouted. "'What is the nickname for the hotel where *Death by Deception*, the Mitchell event, is being held?' It's Jewel of the Desert!" They all wrote the answer on their papers.

Mike, an intern with the company, said, "I should know number four: 'The film *Blonde Bombshell* was shot in the Arizona Biltmore's stables in 1933. Who was the famous actress who starred in it?'"

"Jean Harlow," Mr. Mitchell said. "And she was quite a bombshell." He smiled shyly at his wife, who nudged him in jest.

"Anybody know the answer to thirteen?" Eleanor asked, reading out loud. "'The Arizona Biltmore was originally owned by the Wrigley family. What were they famous for?'"

"That's easy," Doris from H.R. said. "Chewing gum!" The group laughed in agreement.

"This is fun," piped up Sharon, the receptionist. "Whose idea was it?"

"Oh, you know those P.R. people. They always come up with something different for these weekend conferences."

A woman's heels tapped briskly on the floor, followed by a stern female voice calling out, "Oh, Sheriff!"

Mike whispered, "Listen up. I think something else is happening." The group looked up at the actors.

"Sheriff Richie."

I turn around to see one of the local townswomen bustling in, very prim and proper like. Theresa Robinson is wearin' her best go-to-meetin' dress and clutchin' a purse.

"I just heard the news," she says, looking over at the slumped over cowboy. "Oh my goodness, is he…?"

"Yes, ma'am, he's dead. Did you know 'im?"

"Not really. I was coming out of the mercantile when he rode into town. Later, I observed the run-in he had with you, when you told him to leave."

"Did he say anything to you?"

Theresa turns a bright shade of red and lowers her eyes. "He said some mighty unspeakable things," she whispers. "I wouldn't dare repeat them." She pulls out a handkerchief from her pocketbook and dabs at her brow. "After all, I am a proper church-going woman," she says louder than necessary.

"And did you do anything about it?"

"I was so mad, I gave him a good whack in the face with my handbag and walked away." She straightens her spine.

"And what does your husband, Hezekiah, do?"

"He catches rattlers and sells 'em for their venom and their skins."

"And I reckon you know how to handle snakes, too?"

"Me? Heavens no! Every once in a while I have to catch one that's gotten loose in the house, but otherwise, I don't have anything to do with them."

"So, you would know how to avoid being bit by one?"

"Well, now, doesn't everybody around these parts?"

I turn to the good folks from Mitchell. "Now listen up, ever'one," I holler, trying to get 'em to settle down. "We gotta figure out who killed this cowboy."

"Well, Sheriff," Miss Sally says smugly. "You heard Farmer Johnson admit he threatened to kill him for cheatin.'"

"But I did no such thing!" Farmer Johnson explodes from his chair. "I wouldn't be surprised if Billy Bob didn't slip him somethin' more powerful than that so-called elixir and poisoned 'im to shut 'im up."

The bartender is aghast. "No sir, I would never use my apothecary skills for evil purposes. However, I think Miss Sally stole those jewels when he was in her room, then hit him so hard it cracked his skull, doin' him in."

"Sheriff," says the townswoman, "you knew he had a bounty on his head. Would you murder him for that money, all in the name of the law?"

"The thought did cross my mind, Miz Robinson. I've had to kill a few men in my time, and I did want him outta town. But maybe you did, too." She blinks her eyes and gulps.

"Okay, folks, who knows how this cowboy died?"

An older man in a three-piece suit raises his hand. "I think I do."

"Then, tell us."

The man reads from his crossword puzzle. "While several people wanted to kill him, none of them did. Something else caused him to be extremely thirsty, to sweat profusely, suffer nausea and have a yellowish vision. He thought alcohol would be the cure for what produced the small red spots and bleeding on his hand. It was a rattlesnake bite, and he died from the venom."

There's a moment of silence, then the group erupts in cheers and applause, and a couple of people slap the man on the back in congratulations.

"Give that man a prize!" A sharp-lookin' woman in a fitted dress hands the winner a large basket filled with all kinds of wine and cheese. "That concludes our murder mystery play, *Death by Deception*. Please give a round of applause to our actors who played Billy Bob . . . Miss Sally . . . Farmer Johnson . . . and Townswoman Robinson."

The crowd claps enthusiastically.

"And give it up for L.W. Sweet!"

People jump to their feet in a standing ovation. But L.W. doesn't move.

"L.W. Sweet," I say again. But still the cowboy doesn't budge.

"He's just stayin' in character, folks." I hurry to the bar and give L.W.'s shoulder a shake. He feels rigid and cold to the touch. My hands shake as I ask, "Is there a doctor in the house?"

There's nervous laughter in the room until the audience realizes this is not part of the play.

"I'm a nurse practitioner," says a woman who runs toward the bar. She places her first two fingers on L.W.'s neck then looks up at me. "There's no pulse. He's dead."

There are murmurs in the audience. "Someone call the police," I say, trying not to sound too tore up.

It was midnight before Phoenix police officers let the Mitchell employees go back to their hotel rooms. Detectives kept the four other actors and me in the ballroom, and our shaken producer, Lisa, who had been in the audience, joined us.

"Maybe it was just natural causes," she whispered. "You suppose Lenny had a heart condition or something?"

The Maricopa County Medical Examiner wrapped up his inspection of the body, and conferred with a weary Detective Al Whitney, who jotted something on his notepad. He joined us where we sat, still in our costumes.

"The medical examiner estimated time of death of Lenny Olson between seven and nine this evening," Whitney said. "Who was the last one to see him alive?"

Bob Taylor, the actor who played Billy Bob, spoke first. "I saw him a few minutes before seven. He finished drinking a bottle of water and got into place. But he did mention being extra tired and having a stomachache. I figured he'd picked up a flu bug."

The detective took notes. "Anybody know what might've made him sick?"

"Probably too many doughnuts while we were rehearsing," Theresa, who played the townswoman, grumbled.

"Who brought the food for the actors?" Whitney asked.

"I did," Lisa squeaked. "But they're all commercially prepared items."

"Someone could've slipped something into that water, I suppose," the detective said. He paused and referred to his notes. "The M.E. says the purported snakebite was just make-up, and he won't be able to check Mr. Olson's stomach contents until he gets him back to the lab. But he noted a rather large contusion on the victim's head." He turned toward Sally. "Sally Rogers? Did you actually hit the victim with that spittoon?"

"Of course not," Sally huffed.

An officer approached, carrying a large brass vessel. "Detective, this might be the weapon in question." His fingers pointed out a deep depression in the metal. "M.E. says the indentation right here was similar to that of the vic's head wound." The officer also handed him a small, clear plastic sack that the detective examined.

"No, that's an old prop. Of course it has lots of dents in it," Sally exclaimed.

"I understand you didn't like the guy who played L.W. very much. Another actor said Lenny was always coming on to you and other women in the production. Is that right?"

Sally turned a deep shade of red. "He wouldn't keep his hands to himself," she said through clenched teeth. "I had to pull him off a young production assistant he was groping during rehearsal last week."

Another police officer brought a nearly empty water bottle to Detective Whitney, whispering something in his ear and pointing to the bottle. He also had a paper test strip he showed the detective.

"Good work, Edwards." The detective flipped pages in his pad. "Theresa Thomas, you say you work in a doctor's office?"

"Part-time," Theresa answered.

"So, you would have access to syringes."

"Well, I'm just a receptionist. I don't give shots or anything."

"That's not what I asked," Whitney said. "Did this actor, Lenny, also make unwelcome advances toward you?"

"He does that to every female he meets."

"Are you the same Theresa Thomas who filed sexual assault charges against Mr. Olson three months ago?"

"I didn't want him preying on other women."

The detective nodded. "All right, gentlemen, you are free to go. You, too, Ms. Powers. But don't leave town, you understand?"

Tom, Joe and Lisa hurried out, but I turned back when I heard, "Ladies, you are coming downtown with me."

Sally shot a glance at Theresa. "What? Why?" Sally sputtered.

"Ms. Thomas, we found a tiny hole in this water bottle. I believe you injected a poisonous solution into Olson's water." He waved the small plastic bag. "And Ms. Rogers, we also found a couple of hairs most likely from the vic's head on that spittoon."

Detective Whitney pulled a pair of handcuffs from his waistband and nodded to an officer to do the same. "Hey, sexual harassment is serious," Whitney said. "But you should've just got him prosecuted, not killed him."

"Sally Rogers and Theresa Thomas, you are under arrest for the murder of Lenny Olson. You have the right to remain silent. Anything you say may be used in a court of law…"

† † †

LAURIE FAGEN is a long-time "writer by habit" who has written for radio and television news; corporate video, films and documentaries; and magazines and newspapers. Formerly publisher of a Chandler, AZ community newspaper, she is also a jazz singer and artist. An honorable mention in *Alfred Hitchcock Mystery Magazine*'s Mysterious Photograph short story contest and a life-long love of reading whodunits led to her mystery writing debut in Desert Sleuths' 2012 anthology. This is her second published short story.

GUY WALKS INTO A BAR
KATHERINE ATWELL HERBERT

No one knew where Maggie was.

I walked out of the heat and into the cool twilight of Pete's Hangar, a watering hole whose better days ended when I was still racing my Big Wheel down sidewalks. I inhaled the past when I saw the patina of the well-worn bar and the frayed padded booths where trysts or illicit schemes were plotted. I heard it in the drone of an aging air conditioner that counterpointed Davis or Coltrane and smelled it in the stale beer odor that hung in the air. Built before Phoenix sprawled every which way, Pete's was probably the only bar of its kind left in the city. Crammed between two towering office buildings and opening to the sidewalk, it was my post-work Thursday escape.

I always expected to see cops fly in the door and hustle out the unsavory looking characters who often huddled in the back booths. Maybe that's why I kept coming back. Or maybe I was waiting for them to come for me. It would happen one day.

Right away I saw that the barstool Maggie kept warm was empty. For the past month, as sure as heat in July, she was on that perch with her cigarettes and the *New York Times* crossword. She was becoming a fixture, like the neglected collection of model airplanes hanging from the ceiling above the bar. Since Maggie started coming in, Pete established two smoking zones: one at the end of the bar for Maggie, the other at a corner booth. He was skirting the law. No one gave a damn.

But where was Maggie tonight?

I glanced into the perpetual dusk, but all I saw were the regulars in their cheap suits. The only other drinker was Efrin Cruz, a solidly built guy who had the bar to himself until I sat down. Pete drew a Bud, poured a shot of Maker's Mark and walked them over to me. "Is it going to rain, Mitch?" he asked. Pete, craggy looks and shock of disobedient hair, was the living picture of a tough guy. He'd had lots of careers. His last was crop-dusting, that is before the Hangar.

"I think it's trying," I said. "I got a few drops on the way in." He nodded then looked at me like he wanted to say something. I waited, but he was silent. I tilted my head toward the end of the bar.

"Where's your girl?"

"Mags?" Pete asked. "Dunno. This is a first for her."

"Maybe she found somewhere better to hang than this dump," Efrin said in a tone that had a smile in it.

"That would be *any* place," I added as I loosened my tie.

Pete coughed a laugh. "Bull!" Pete didn't smoke anymore, but his voice didn't know that. It was an angry rasp.

Not for the first time, I asked myself why a woman like Maggie came to the Hangar. With her looks, her clothes and a shape that could seduce any guy who wasn't six-feet under, Maggie could class up the Ritz. I never came up with an answer.

"She's too stuck-up," Efrin said. "Doesn't talk, doesn't smile, just does her puzzle, drinks and leaves.

"She doesn't want to be hit on by the likes of you," Pete said.

Efrin raised his arms in surrender. "I'm not in that race."

"That's what they all say," the bartender mumbled.

Pete didn't know that Efrin had tried to tap that keg. I was coming back from the head one night when I spotted him hitting on Maggie. I didn't hear what she said but her look had a finality to it. He went back to his stool like a chastised schoolboy and never looked her way again.

I didn't know then if I wanted to chance the humiliation or not. I don't break cameras when my picture's taken but I won't be voted sexiest man by *People Magazine* either. It may not be an advantage, but I was born and raised in Phoenix and recently returned to take a civil engineering job at McKendall Construction Group. If you're into demographics, I'm a reasonable catch. College degree, not too old, around two-hundred pounds, and I'm not burdened with ex-wives or spare children. But, I wouldn't wish myself on any hopeful bride-to-be.

The phone behind the bar rang. Pete answered and handed it to Efrin with an unspoken apology. Efrin sighed and grabbed it.

"Yeah," he said into the receiver then lowered his voice.

Efrin was a nice enough guy. We jawed now and again,

mostly about baseball. We both played in college. Phoenix was due for an expansion team soon and we wondered about the chances of actually getting one. Pete put his hands on the bar and looked at me like a father about to give a lecture. "Have you gotten to know Maggie?" he asked quietly. "I mean outside of this place."

I didn't want to answer him. "Why? What's up?"

Before Pete could respond, Efrin slammed down the receiver and charged to the exit, nodding us a furious good-bye on the way. When he blew through the door, the airplane-shaped sign, PETE'S HANGAR, ESTAB. 1976, rattled against it. "Glad I'm not facing what he is," I said and looked back at Pete. "You were about to say…"

"Odd thing," he began. "When Maggie was leaving last Friday there was someone just outside waiting for her. She said to the guy, 'Now I'm sure it's him. We got him.' Then she mentioned McKendall.'" He watched for my reaction. I kept buttoned up. "You work there right?"

I nodded. My mind raced. Who was she talking to about me? Why? Or *was* she talking about me? What the hell did, "We got him" mean? I tried to stay cool but prickles of unease ran through me. Could it have something to do with the trouble I had in Kansas? Is this it? I wondered.

"I was going to the back room when she left," he continued, "but I forgot the key and came back. That's when I heard her."

"You sure that's what she said? 'McKendall'?"

"Sounded like it. I knew you worked there. That made it stand out, ya know?"

"Hmm," I said, trying to keep the growing panic down. "Strange."

Yes, I knew Maggie outside the bar. One night when I left Pete's, heading for my car, I saw her coming down the sidewalk, her skirt fighting a stiff breeze. Sexy as hell. She had left earlier and I assumed she was half way home to some remote gated enclave. As soon as she saw me she smiled. She never did that inside.

"Hey," I said.

She looked at me as if I were an old friend. "Hey back."

"I thought you were long gone."

She hesitated a beat or two before she said, "I live in The Lofts, next door."

"Metropolitan Lofts? Whoa. I figured you for Scottsdale."

"Oh no. I'm urban. I like a little grit."

"That accounts for Pete's."

She nodded. "What's your excuse? You don't look like a guy who would hang out at Pete's."

"You noticed, huh? I'm hiding from my fans." I couldn't help but smile. This was getting more interesting.

She laughed. It was melodious and made me feel like I was seventeen and wooing a high school junior. It had been a long time since I flirted and meant it.

"Hiding, huh?" She looked at me slyly.

"Sorta." It was a lame comeback. We were silent. "Want to get something to eat?" I couldn't exhale. I felt foolish. "I know a place close…" I sounded desperate and I figured my chances were slim. The wind pressed her skirt against her thighs again. Damn.

She looked like she was deciding if I deserved to be seen with her. Finally, after what seemed like hours, she said, "Take me somewhere. Get me out of this awful heat and wind." I breathed again.

During dinner we did the getting-acquainted conversation. When we walked back to her place, she didn't ask me up and I didn't push it. I asked her to have dinner with me that Saturday and held my breath. She gave me a quick peck on the cheek and said, "I was hoping you'd ask." All I could do was smile like an idiot.

We went to Vincent's and afterwards to some forgettable movie. When she stroked my inner thigh, my restraint gave way. I grabbed her arm and whispered, "Let's get out of here."

At her place we shucked off our clothes but as I tried to pull her to the bed she stopped. I hit the sheets by myself. She stood cooler than an ice sculpture and said, "Before we go any further, we have to agree on something." In my state I would have agreed to send my mother to prison. But the chill radiating from her deflated the urgent mood. "Sure," I stammered, "anything."

"Let's keep this quiet."

"Agreed." I reached for her. She pulled back a step.

"And…" she continued.

I started to get up but she pushed me back down. She may have been clear-headed, but I was incapable of spelling the word "a" while she was naked.

"Let's keep our lives up to this moment off limits."

"Sounds good." And it did. I've tried to strip a couple of chapters from my life's memory book.

"And let's rule out—"

"We don't have to talk at all if you don't want to."

She laughed.

I reached for her again. "Now will you come down here?" Again she pulled away.

"Promise you agree."

"Sure. What, are you married or something? Hiding from the mob?"

"Shh. I'll tell you when I'm ready to share." She smiled and fell on me.

After that we met as often as possible, either at my place or at hers. We still showed up at Pete's and acted as if we didn't know each other but sometimes we would catch each other's look and struggle to keep a straight face. I knew we were acting like a couple of kids getting away with something, but I didn't care. The pay-off was a blur of pleasure. Until now.

I drained my glass. Pete poured another. What could it possibly mean, I wondered, "I've got him"?

Then I remembered a night last week when Efrin and I left at the same time. As we got to the sidewalk he said, "Does Maggie live in The Lofts?"

"I don't know," I lied. "Why?"

"I saw her going in there last week with some big dude, real linebacker type. They were pretty friendly." A little charge of negative electricity ran through me.

"You think she's sellin' it?" he asked.

"Not at Pete's."

"Yeah, she's stone cold in there," he said.

Later that night when I saw her, I asked Maggie about the guy Efrin had seen her with. She said she couldn't imagine what he had been talking about. She didn't know anyone like that. I let it go.

I took another hit of the Maker's Mark and calmed down. I told myself to let the evening play out. Wait for her to show. After an eternity of thirty seconds, I lost it. I had a bad feeling about this.

I called Pete over, smacked some cash on the bar and said goodnight. I hoped I sounded unconcerned.

"Stay out of the storm," he called after me.

A tune from "Bitches Brew" followed me to the door. Not a good omen.

Out on the sidewalk I saw a guy with a linebacker's build entering The Lofts. Was this the man Efrin had seen? I expected someone classy. This guy wore shapeless jeans, a faded polo shirt and dirty running shoes. I followed him. The lobby was a mausoleum: marble walls, tiled floor and silent as a church on Saturday night.

I hit the buzzer for Maggie's apartment. No answer. An elevator was coming down. I flattened myself against the wall next to the doors. When they opened, the night security man gimped out. I held the door and slipped in. The guard wouldn't notice me—he'd probably been collecting Social Security since Ike was in office.

I went to Maggie's door and knocked. Silence. I wondered if I should be here. I might not like what I'd see. I knocked again. I stood for another long minute. "What the hell," I thought and tried the door. It was unlocked. That prickly negative charge ran up my back again. I sucked in a breath, quietly turned the knob and stepped inside. Except for the sofa, the place was as bare as a dumb blonde's brain. All that fancy furniture was gone. I went into the bedroom. Only the bed remained.

I remembered another incident. One night after Maggie left my place, I noticed the desk drawers were slightly ajar. I thought I had locked them all. I always did. When I opened them, it looked like someone had stirred up the papers there. I reached for the phone to call her but stopped. Maybe in my hurry to get her in bed, I had done it myself. Besides, everything in the drawer always slid around. I was probably just being paranoid. I skipped the call.

I slumped to the bed in the bare room. Elbows to knees, hands on forehead, I thought I was going to heave. Maggie had been playing me all along. The toe of a dirty running shoe appeared on the carpet below me. I looked up. The Linebacker stood over me. He looked even bigger up close. I got up.

He rolled his neck before he said, "Maggie wants to see you."

I didn't move.

"Come on," he said flatly.

"You her errand boy?"

He reached behind his back and brought out a small gun from his waistband. I stared at him. This didn't feel real. He waved the barrel in the direction of the door like a TV goon.

"Oh, hell no. I'm not following you. Just tell me where she is."

He came toward me, serious now. I turned my palms to the ceiling. "Whatever, Mr. Universe," I said, "just relax. I'm not going to argue with a thirty-eight."

Downstairs he shoved me into the car then got behind the wheel and turned to me. "One more thing," he said.

I faced him. His fist hit my jaw like a guided missile and a growing blackness drew me in.

The world was shaking and something was pressing against me. From a distance a harsh, "Come on," rang through the fog. I forced my eyes open. The Linebacker's hand was squeezing my shoulder. "Get out of the car," he said.

I didn't want to get up. I wanted to go back to sleep. He pulled me out.

I lurched forward. The blackness evaporated as I took a couple of steps and I shook off his arm. He took out the gun again.

"This way." He shoved me forward. I looked up. We were at the six-level airport parking garage McKendall was working on. It was just a skeleton. Behind me he said, "Over there." I turned to him. He waved his gun toward the construction elevator. I stumbled across the rubble.

"This your idea of a good time?"

He looked at me like I was a virus then rolled his neck again as if his overdeveloped muscles had to be stretched regularly to keep them from freezing up. We passed a sign that read: MCKENDALL CONSTRUCTION, ESTIMATED DATE OF COMPLETION: AUG. '92.

"There's been a mistake. Maggie couldn't be here."

"Shut the hell up," he said.

We got to the elevator cage and stepped on. The bruiser pushed the button for the fifth level. When we reached it, he shoved me out and led me to a large metal box near the edge of the rough cement floor. "Sit," he commanded. The wind from the coming storm blew through the open building and whipped against me.

"Now what?" I asked. But when I turned there was no one there. I stood and looked into the dark.

"Sit back down," The Linebacker demanded from somewhere in the half-light. That's when I saw him and Maggie coming toward me.

"Maggie? What's going on?"

"Sit down, Mitch," she said harshly. "And listen."

Her sidekick pointed the gun at me again. I sat down.

"Your new life? Say goodbye to all of it. It's over Mitch. You're going to get what you deserve."

"What?"

"You know what I'm talking about. You shouldn't keep mementos of your past." She tossed my old Kansas driver's license at me but it caught the wind and swept across the floor.

"My old license? Really? This has something to do with why we're here?"

"You're the man I've been looking for."

She opened the tote-bag she was carrying and pulled out a news clipping. She read out loud. "Three Kansas City men fell to their deaths today when portions of a new hotel under construction collapsed. Buddy Samuelson, Angel Guzman, and Robert Hardcastle were working on the eighth floor when it gave way."

She looked at me with pure white anger. "Robert Hardcastle was my brother." She pulled out another article. "A panel of state experts has concluded that the concrete was watered. The investigation is continuing. Chasson Construction is also conducting an internal investigation."

"You bastard." She began putting the papers back in the tote. The wind ripped them out of her hand and blew them into a swirl. They both grabbed for them.

It was the only chance I was going to get. I ran to the elevator.

Maggie screamed, "Get him."

The Linebacker sped after me. I opened the door, flew into the cage and hit the ground floor button. I tried to pull the door closed but Mr. Universe ripped it open. I threw myself at him with all my weight. He stumbled backwards and fell.

I took off to the stacks of building supplies and equipment shadowed in the darkness at the far end of the floor. Their pounding steps echoed, getting closer. Where could I go? Every nerve jangled. I saw a pile of air conditioning ducts and I dove behind them, paralyzed. I didn't move as they came even with me on the other side of the equipment.

When I heard them continue on, I braved a glance over the metal forms. I caught sight of their backs moving in the opposite direction, searching among the materials for me. I inched along, approaching the elevator. I stood up and spotted them and dashed to the lift.

They barreled after me. Muscles caught me with a flying tackle. We both went down hard on the cement. I struggled under him. He clutched his gun but when he swung it around at me I knocked it out of his hand. It skittered across the floor and flew off the edge. Rising above me, he struck my right jaw again. I stayed awake but couldn't tell you what day it was or how to stand up.

The bruiser scrambled off and towed me like a sack of cement to the edge. I thought for a second I was going off, but he held me steady.

"Your expiration date's arrived, Mitch," Maggie began. "You're going to die like my brother."

The wind was meaner now. I knew I'd get blown off.

"Maggie," I pleaded. "Don't do this. You're not a killer."

"Quiet," she said.

"I didn't do it."

Disgust filled her face.

"I discovered that the cement had been watered." I looked at her. I had to say this out loud to her and to myself. "But I didn't do anything about it."

She looked at me, then at the Linebacker. "Push him off, Jason."

"What?" he said.

"Push him off!"

"Wait a minute, Maggie." Jason demanded.

A gust of wind caught me. I hung on desperately. "When I came to work the next morning," I continued while they stared at each other. "I confronted Chasson's son. Told him I knew he had watered the mix. He didn't deny it. He laughed and told me to prove it. Tell his dad, see what he would say."

"Shut up Mitch! Jason! Do it."

"I can't, Maggie. I'm sorry. I thought we were going scare the hell out of him then take him back to Kansas to turn him in.

But if it was a Chasson…you won't be able to touch that family."

Maggie paced. "Don't you care that he helped kill my brother? And the other two?"

Maggie balled her fists and let out a long frustrated moan.

Jason looked dumbfounded. I inched away from the edge.

She stared into the middle distance looking like she was about to shatter. The wind howled. The rain started, coming in powerful gusts. I had to get to a safer spot.

Maggie paced. "I've been looking for you since that day you disappeared, and now I've got you," she said.

"You've got the wrong guy," I said without conviction. "Or maybe I'm not the wrong guy."

She looked at me, confused and full of pain.

Jason rushed at me, and grabbed me from behind in a bear hug. I threw my head back and caught his nose. It sounded like it broke. He fell back shrieking. I turned and swung at him. He feinted to the left and grabbed my wrist mid-air, twisted my arm behind me, grabbed my other wrist and forced me to the edge again. Raising my arms overhead, he swung me out where there was nothing below me but air. I dangled there in the rain and wind with no way to get any leverage to crawl back to the floor. He couldn't hold me for long.

"Okay, Maggie? This what you want? I'll do it," Jason yelled. "But what if he's telling the truth about Chasson's kid?"

She froze.

I was slipping from Jason's grasp. I looked up at Maggie.

Jason waited. Maggie blew.

It started with tears and turned into screams. She fell to the floor. Jason pulled me back up and dropped me on the cement.

I scrambled to my feet. Maggie's sobs continued. I started brushing myself off when suddenly Maggie, like a maddened animal, rushed at me in a crouch. I stepped out of her path and she hurled toward the edge. I reached out and grabbed her arm.

She fell forward but I caught her and swung her back onto the floor. She crumpled into a ball. Jason and I stared at each other in silence.

Finally I scooped her up and held her next to me. "Maggie." I brushed her hair off her face. "I am guilty. I didn't *do* it. But…" I wished I could hug the pain out of her somehow. "But I didn't stop it. I didn't stop him." She stared at me, hollowed out, absent. "I just quit. That day. And left."

I thought I saw a flash of sympathy cross her face but it was probably my imagination.

We all boarded the elevator. At the bottom she held my gaze for a long time before Jason led her to his car. He glanced back at me once, nodded, then got in and took off.

I raised my face to the sky and let the rain pour over me.

It wasn't cleansing.

†   †   †

A Hollywood veteran, **KATHERINE ATWELL HERBERT** is the author of three books on screenwriting as well as television and film scripts. The variety of material she has written includes newspaper articles and film, theater, and book criticism, magazine articles, and poetry. She was also a publicist and chairman of the film program at Scottsdale Community College. She recently completed her first mystery novel.

CROSSWIND
MACHELLE LANGSETH

The man and woman stood out of sight, in a narrow alleyway between the empty hangar and a chain-link fence imbedded with tumbleweed carcasses. Since it was April, the temperature was only ninety degrees and the sun, growing in strength, hadn't yet turned brutal. The heat, however, diminished small plane traffic and once again Chandler airport sank into its afternoon torpor.

"You know I'm right." The statement, delivered in his flat nasal twang sent a charge down her spine.

"But killing him?"

"Brit, it'll look like an accident. How many times..." He exhaled through his nose, did a quarter-turn of impatience and began again. "Think about this. He made promises, right? Did he come through for you?"

She shrugged off Willie's words, moved deliberately down the steel wall, then through the hangar door. Cal and his plane, both absent, left the building hollowed out like her stomach. The gray epoxy floor reflected the light, sans oil stains and dust. She told Cal she'd clean up, kept her end of the deal, as usual, and was about to leave when Willie appeared like a demented Genie popping from a bottle.

Weeks ago they'd shared a six pack, spinning out daydreams and 'what if's; things that *could* be done, if only they had money. In conventional parlance Willie was an 'airport bum', a ramp-rat, a nobody. He hung about, like a vulture, waiting for scraps of flying time others might pass on to him. For many, his presence was like a splinter, persistent and irritating.

Since that night, spent at her apartment, he managed to sidle or squirm into some portion of her day, every day. A few times she dodged him but today, when the rattle of his dilapidated Vespa scooter echoed between the hangars, the big door stood open. There was no place for Brit to hide.

The whole thing was a mistake. She never should have started with him. He hovered behind her and watched as she dumped rags into a trash bag for the wash, and spilled dirty water onto to the tarmac.

A waft of putrefying manure danced in on a hot breath of air, the only thing that stirred. Few traces of rural life still clung around the airport, but subdivisions elbowed toward the runways. Like other desert towns, this sprawling suburb of Phoenix, boasted endless miles of stucco walls, oceans of red tile roofs, and possessed the charm of a desert gulag. The San Tan Mountains lay to the south, a smallish crumpled ridge, a throw away. The Superstitions and their lesser brothers and sisters lay to the east. Those, jagged, blackened heaps were to be the exclamation point at the end of Cal Morrison's life.

Brit pictured it, saw it sharp and clear. The white and blue plane streaming black smoke from the engine fire, Cal would nurse it down, prop feathered, looking for someplace level to slide it back onto terra firma. He'd show more skill than hanging it on a cliff.

From eight feet away she smelled Willie, a mix of tobacco and sour sweat and she had to power down her gag reflex. The first night, had it been that bad? Had she been that drunk or that pissed at Cal that she let him touch her? Brit spun, squaring her shoulders, "There's no way I'm doing this."

"Really?" His hand snapped out, fingers dug down to her humerus. He jerked her close, spray of spittle hitting her face. "Miss Priss, do I have to remind you what's at stake here? What happens if we don't get that money."

"Then," he sneered, "there's that other matter. The little problem that you wouldn't want to turn into a big one. Right?"

"Now, once more, just because I *know* you aren't stupid. The plan is foolproof. A small chunk nicked out of the gas line. I tape it well enough it doesn't leak. Well enough for takeoff and climb. It starts to loosen. By the time he's over the mountains, the line is spraying gas. Engine fire. No place to land. Tragic accident. Catastrophic mechanical failure."

He raises an eyebrow, and a smirk that passes for his smile slides across his face. Willie leans closer, softens his voice and continues, "It's an older plane. He's an older pilot. Could happen to anybody."

With a blistering twist she pulls free. "He's A and P certified.

If they found the—"

"That's the beauty of it. Everything will burn, don't you see? No hoses, no tape, nothing left but twisted metal pasted to the side of a mountain."

Then a quiet whisper echoes from her dark place.

Maybe.

Cal promised her the money. He did promise, and on that promise hung the rest of her life.

Her voice comes out thick, strange in her own ears. "I can't be the one to call him."

"You have to be. Don't you see? You're in Globe, truck broke down, out past the Indian casino. You got a ride back to the casino. It's right across the road from the airstrip, and you have to get back to the Valley for work. Your truck's being towed in, you'll get it later. Can he come pick you up?"

She hugs herself and stares sightless at the hangar walls papered with the flotsam of Cal Morrison's flying life. Over eight of his sixty-five years have been spent aloft. Airplanes are his true love, the passion that lasted above all others. His wife, cut loose early on, didn't last five years. There were no photos of her, though Cal said she came from money, and never let him forget she'd married beneath her. Their child, a son, absorbed his mother's arrogance, and improved on it.

A consummate gentleman, Cal Morrison never mentioned romantic conquests but Brit was sure he'd had lovers in all four corners of the planet. Wherever wheels squeaked down onto a runway, if he was lonely there would have been someone to fill his bed. The man did not lack charm; to that she could attest.

Early pictures of him came to mind; impossibly good looking with a smile to tear your heart out. Later pictures showed a man comfortable in his own skin, taking life on its terms, a bit world-weary around the eyes. Thoughtful frown lines were around his mouth, a mouth that still twisted readily into a lopsided grin.

"You know where the money is, right?" Willie's voice brought her back.

She closed her eyes. "Yes, I know."

"And you can get to it easily, right?"

Silence.

He continues, undaunted, "So what are we waiting for? A little drive up to Globe. You call. Cal takes off. You wait. You wait some more. He never shows. Pretty soon you call me. I come pick you up and we drive to the Chandler airport. Report him missing." He dusts the palms of his hands together and blinks his deep-set black eyes for emphasis. "When it's dark we make a small detour with a duffle bag to pick up that stack of Franklins."

He rocks forward slightly onto the toes of his oil-stained sneakers. "Any luck, it won't take long. They'll find his plane right away. Someone might even spot the fire. You'll be devastated. Your best friend gone, all because you were stranded and asked a favor of him."

Brit can smell it: the sour, acrid smoke that would drift from his wreck; oil, rubber, plastic with just a hint of burning meat. She dips to clear her brain and focuses on the vanishing wet spot in front of the hangar door, in a few more minutes it would be gone, vaporized, like Cal if she makes the phone call.

Willie slides a hand to her hip. With its pressure come his words. "I know...I know this is hard. You really care about him. But it's the only way. You know that."

She moves deliberately, jams the mop into the bottom of the empty yellow bucket. *Th-thump, th-thump, th-thump*, the bad wheel clatters back at her. Cal kept saying he'd fix it. He'd fix all of it. But he hadn't, had he? Endless days of work and empty nights. The plans she'd so carefully stitched together because of that promise. Gone in a blink.

Willie shadows her to the corner, determined to seal the deal. "It's not like it was hard-earned money. He got it in the eighties bringin' in coke for the cartel. Cal *told* you. *Showed* you the cash just sitting there in a dresser drawer, for Pete's sake."

She spins. "He was drunk, you bastard. He trusts me."

"You trusted him too, what did that get you?"

A turn back toward the big door gives her a particular slant of sun. It reveals the invisible airborne world: dust motes, a wavering silver spider thread, and the ghosts of the life she might have had.

"I won't go to Globe. I can call from here. On my cell."

"No. I heard they can check the location. Find out where you are, like with GPS. Besides, we need to have the timing down right. If someone sees you here we're toast." He comes around in front of her, squats slightly and catches her chin in his fingers to lift her face. "You'll never see him. Okay? A phone call, that's all. Then, he'll leave here and just…"

He makes the poof sound to punctuate. "Besides, I'm sure he'd rather end his days in a flaming crash than sitting in his own piss, gumming JELL-O in a nursing home."

She nods. Then pushes her fingers into her eye sockets so hard stars burst.

Cal asked her twice what else was wrong. It couldn't just be that her truck had broken down. What else? Whatever it was he'd give her a hand. He had a bit of paper work to do, then, he'd head to the airport. He'd see her in a little over an hour.

After the call she paced the dingy aisles of slot machines paired with leaning geriatrics. The stale reek of vanished smoke and rotting carpet suffocated her. Outside, in the sunlight she strode across the empty parking lot. A quarter mile she reckoned from light post A to light post L. She lost count after fifteen roundtrips.

Back inside.

Two shots of tequila. The scorch of booze and bitter lime. Then, a slight ease, she can breathe again.

Wait. Just wait. It's done. Out of my hands. That's it. By now he's on his way.

Her mind tripped over itself and fell back in time. It still stung. The humiliation burned invisible, like a boil gone septic.

She and Cal had known one another over a year before he leaned over one day and kissed her long and deep. They sat side by side in the cockpit of his Mooney, the intimacy of flight just ended. A flight where he'd handed her the key and told her to fly left seat, something he'd never done before.

The kiss was exceptional. Soft and persuasive and when she pulled back, startled, his eyes teased her.

"Like kissin' your dad?" he queried.

She'd shot back something like, "Not hardly." And leaned forward to wipe away his smile with a kiss of her own, hungrier than his.

As affairs went, it was comfortable—what you'd expect from people who shared other passions and interests. He owned a modest bungalow in an older neighborhood and after the first few weeks, gave her a key.

Sometimes she spent an entire week in his bed, other times,

when he worked charters, or ferried planes for people, nine or ten days would drift by before she'd get his call and an invitation to meet him at Guedo's for tacos and beer.

Three months to the day after that kiss she helped him paint his kitchen and late that night sitting in the debris of drop cloths and empty beer bottles, under the glare of bare light bulbs, she'd mentioned how much money they'd saved him doing the job themselves. He shrugged and said money was never a problem. He had enough tucked away to be comfortable.

She must have flashed an 'Oh really?' look because he pulled himself out of his chair, crooked a finger at her and led her back to an unused bedroom, crowded with extra furniture and waist deep in boxes. He shifted a stack of old *Trade-a-Plane* magazines and tugged open a dresser drawer. Nonplussed, she glanced down at three neatly folded polo shirts, each sporting a different resort logo. She knew Cal well enough to wait for the other shoe, and a moment later it dropped. He snagged a shirt, snapped it out of the drawer and gave her a wink and a smile.

It took a moment to register what she was looking at through the blur of a thick plastic bag.

Money.

Stacks of banded hundred dollar bills.

He regaled her that night with tales of the secret life he'd lived. August of 1982 he began flying for one of the larger drug organizations. After three years he'd wanted out, and was lucky enough to manage that as well. That night her whole view of Cal shifted. Somehow the hidden man became more intensely interesting, someone to care about, someone *she* might trust.

It took several weeks to work up the courage to pop the question. Not marriage, something that mattered much more to her, something she fell asleep holding close and woke up to embrace the next day.

Her Air Transport Rating.

It was the Holy Grail she'd pursued for ten years. It would buy her a job doing something in the sky for the rest of her life. She'd worked three jobs to get the money for her instrument rating, then her commercial ticket. But, building hours and snatching that final gold ring was still as distant a dream as becoming an astronaut. It all came down to money, something that always seemed to dance beyond her fingertips.

She'd made him a favorite dinner: stuffed pasta shells,

homemade cheesecake and a couple bottles of killer Pinot Noir to finish the feast. Finally, she laid it out, how much she needed, and for how long. What kind of return she'd be able to manage on the loan. When she finished, she sat back, dry mouthed, ready to throw up. He hunched over his dessert plate, silent, then, with a slight uptick of his chin she knew to be confirmation, he said: "I don't see why that wouldn't work. Sure, you can count on it."

She flung herself at him, nearly knocking him unconscious in her excitement.

"Let's wait until I get back from Portland, okay? You know I promised a buddy I'd go help him out. I'll be gone a week, ten days tops."

The first week evaporated, as she made arrangements for instruction and modifying her work schedule. After that, time inched along at a glacial pace, taunting her racing mind. Two weeks later she paced her apartment.

It had been days since they'd spoken, not unusual when he traveled, but now she had a stake in his return. She'd know quickly enough if there'd been an accident. There was a possibility he was visiting friends on the way back. Or, maybe he was taking a couple days off for fishing. But why didn't he call? Her patience, finally exhausted, she decided to visit her old friend, Bumpy Harrison.

An airport, like any small town, has its share of intrigue, scandal and backstabbing. For Chandler Municipal, Bumpy, junior mechanic at Sierra Aviation, was the guy who knew everything. It was an accepted fact that any dirt you might want to dig up would be instantly available from him, along with editorial comments.

On her way to ferret out what he might know, she practiced questions about Cal in her head. She hoped they'd come off casual, and planned to mix them with queries about other pilots. Brit claimed the only shady parking spot near the Sierra hangar, slid out of her truck, and stopped dead.

Cal and a stunning brunette strolled out of the administration building twenty yards away. As they walked he slid an arm around her shoulders and gave her a momentary squeeze. Almost as tall as Cal, with legs Tina Turner would envy, she wore a brightly colored sun dress that accentuated her curves. He opened the door of a convertible for her then stopped long enough to give her a hungry kiss.

Within four days, half a dozen people asked if she'd met Cal's fiancée.

At first Brit tried to squelch the rage with reason, *He'd keep his word. Cal of all people would understand. The Air Transport Rating would change her life, forever.*

Another week of silence from Cal painted it out in giant capital letters.

Their relationship was DONE; dead as the petrified moths on her window ledge. She threw up at least once a day, her stomach felt like she'd swallowed a cup of ground glass. Sleep came only with an empty bottle of wine and three magic pills.

Finally she got the call.

His voice, breezy, unchanged: Where'd she been keepin' herself? Could she stop by? He needed a hand with some things if she was interested in earning a little cash...

She walked into his office, dropped the house key on his desk, gave him a kiss on the cheek, told him: *So happy for you. A real surprise. Love to meet her.*

Not a word about her plans or his promise. Not a word about the woman, or the For Sale sign taped to the hangar door. The only glimmer of hope came when he handed her back the key with a wink.

"Keep it. You never know how things will turn out."

Now she stood outside the Apache Casino, the sun bearing down on her shoulders and watched a mini-bus unload yet another batch of pensioners waiting to be scalped.

It was an hour since she'd placed the call, time to walk across the road to the Globe Municipal Airport. One runway, six tie-downs, two gas pumps and a rotting Beechcraft trapped in knee high weeds.

Willie told her to sit on the tarmac and watch the sky so that someone would see her. They'd notice and later confirm she was waiting for Cal to fly her back to the Valley.

Twice, she tried to force her feet toward the highway and the airport. Twice, they took her in a large meandering circle. The wind freshened behind her, tugging strands of hair around her face, snaking it into her eyes. Brit looked across the road toward the windsock pivoting at the far end of the field. A crosswind made the landing trickier but Cal would notice.

He noticed everything, everything that related to flying, that is.

Her knees began to wobble and she found her way to the concrete base of a light standard. She wondered idly which outcropping would end it, would snag the white fuselage and roll it up into a blackened wad. Which of the nameless mountains they'd flown over so many times, dismissed as terrain.

The shaking started first, then the tears. She didn't bother wiping them, didn't try to stop, just closed her eyes and rocked gently. Later, she dug her elbows into her sides and glued her lids together until she heard a hint of the sound. Finally, that sound pried her eyes open. Dark tear splotches decorated her shorts and she squinted through the salt blur.

She closed her eyes again and saw him in her mind. He'd fly south of the strip, turn ninety degrees and cross midway. Then he'd lay-up, slide the plane to earth and grease the landing out smooth as butter. The sound, it had to be, had to be.

Brit broke into a trot, scanning the sky, letting her feet find their way without her help. Centerline of the highway the sound was off to the east, and her head followed, pivoting to the left. She squinted against the curdled milk sky. The engine was running rough, wavering but drawing near. Then, a pinprick of light flashed bright as the pilot banked.

Half a breath later the grill of the red pickup lifted her off her feet and flipped her effortlessly end over end.

After the hollow-melon thunk of Brit's head impacting the top of the windshield there was nothing but silence, and she flew, unencumbered, for the first time in her life. Later, when she lay in the dried weeds of the barrow ditch, the squeak of tires on a runway filled her unhearing ears.

A life-long scribbler and storyteller, **MACHELLE LANGSETH**, has resided in the Phoenix metro area since 1980. During this time she's worked primarily in the travel industry segueing into owner/operator of a commercial cleaning enterprise in 2001. Husband, Allan is first reader and chief editor of many words. Any remaining time in her life is devoted to grandchildren Luke and Micaela and age appropriate outdoor pursuits for an older, not *old* gal.

CLEAÑORITAS, INC.
Isabella Maldonado

The two cleaning ladies glared at each other in the dining room of the sprawling estate. "Oh, no you don't, *chica*," Rosa said as she tried to snatch the revolver out of Consuela's pink-gloved hand. "You got to do the last guy. It's my turn."

Consuela's grip tightened as she pulled the gun away and tucked it into a pouch hidden under her starched white apron. "No, the last one didn't count, I just ran him over with a truck. I didn't get to shoot him."

Rosa stooped to pick up a large pink feather duster and brandished it at Consuela. "Yeah, and if your shooting is as bad as your driving, we might need to get some extra bullets."

"Hey, I couldn't help it, that dude was fast. He kept darting back and forth all over the street like a monkey on crack. Do you have any idea how hard it is to aim an old piece of *caca* Chevy pickup?"

Rosa tugged down the hem of her black maid's dress and rolled her eyes. "And you call yourself a pro? *Caray.* You gotta' work around that stuff. You're just lucky he ran into that dead-end alley or you never would have nailed him."

Consuela raised her chin and crossed her arms over her chest. "Are you dusting with the Pledge, or sniffing it, *mamacita*? I get this one and you can have the next one."

"No way, I get this one!" Rosa's voice echoed through the quiet house. "Don't make me call Sofia."

Consuela unfolded her arms and flapped them up and down. "*Cállate*, Rosa, you are making too much noise. We will settle this now. Let's do rock, paper, scissors."

They each held out a fist and swung it up and down three times. Rosa poked out two fingers. Consuela's hand shot out in front of her and flattened. Rosa clapped her calloused hands, "Ha! Scissors cuts paper, I win."

† † †

Arthur Bastion sat in his study, his fingers drumming on the large mahogany desk. He looked up at Sofia and realized he was holding his breath. He exhaled loudly and ran a hand through his hair. "Is it done?"

Sofia smiled coyly. "Oh, yes, about two hours ago." She glided to one of the two overstuffed leather chairs in front of the desk and perched lightly on the edge of the cushion. "One of my cleaning ladies, Consuela, screamed when she discovered your brother's body. She ran to the other end of the house to get Rosa, who had just started cleaning the kitchen. They were both hysterical when they called the police. I imagine the authorities will be calling you soon."

Arthur grinned and shifted in his seat. "Okay, remind me what's supposed to happen next. I don't want to get anything wrong."

"You remember that you ordered the Tamale Package. That means it will look like your brother got shot by a robber before my cleaning ladies arrived. You made sure you had an alibi during the time frame like I told you?"

"Sure," Arthur nodded. "I was playing eighteen holes at the Phoenix Country Club with my attorney and his paralegal. We were going over some matters concerning an upcoming corporate merger I have in the works. I just got back here five minutes before you arrived."

"Good," Sofia said. "Lots of witnesses, and not too close to this part of Scottsdale."

"I made sure I never left the course and that my attorney was by my side the entire time." Arthur grinned and blew out a sigh. "Whew, I didn't even realize how nervous I was. Now that it's done, I feel so much better."

Sofia tilted her head slightly and peered at Arthur. "I don't normally ask for a lot of details, but I am curious to know why you wanted to…um…get rid of your brother in such a brutal way."

His eyes scanning the ceiling, Arthur paused before speaking. "My hideous mother, may she rot in peace, finally went to that great full service spa in the sky." He lowered his head and leveled his gaze on Sofia. "The nasty cow put a no contest clause in her Will. If my brother or I file any sort of appeal or contradict the Will in any way, the entire amount will go to her cats. Can you imagine? Over fifty million dollars for a bunch of mangy cats!"

"Didn't she just split it between the two of you?"

"Oh, no. That would actually be fair." Arthur's face darkened and his fists clenched on the desktop. "She used that inheritance to control every aspect of our lives. She would change the Will every few months. She used to tell us that one of us would inherit everything and the other would get one dollar. She would decide which one she thought was treating her better and change it. Then the other son would fawn all over her and she would switch it back. For decades we tripped over ourselves groveling to her constantly. It was sick."

"So when she died, who was in favor?"

"I was. I made sure of that before the old bat—" Arthur's fingers sketched quotation marks in the air, *"accidentally* fell down the stairs at her mansion." Arthur's jaw tightened and a little vein on his temple pulsed. "Then my worthless brother told me he was going to file a contest in court. He laughed in my face and said he would rather see the cats get the whole thing than for me to get his share. I tried offering him ten percent, but he turned it down. He told me to give him half, or see the cats poop in solid gold litter boxes."

Sofia pursed her lips. "Seems like the two of you could've worked something out."

Arthur glared at her. "No way. I earned that money kissing up to the old battle axe all those years. Even though she had enough domestic staff to run a small country, she made me massage her bunions, clip her toenails and clean out her cats' litter boxes. Do you have any idea how disgusting that is?" He shivered.

"Mr. Bastion," Sofia said in a low tone, "I have scrubbed people's toilets, pulled slimy mats of hair out of their drains and picked up maggoty dead mice from behind their refrigerators. I wasn't doing it for the hope of fifty million dollars either."

Arthur sniffed and steepled his fingers. He leaned back in his chair and looked down his long nose at her. "My situation is different. There are other considerations. What you don't know is that I am also blessed with a harpy of a wife who spends money faster than I can make it. Always the most expensive cars, jewelry and fashion. She idolized my mother. She's even started collecting cats!"

"Well, you certainly seem to have solved your problem with your brother."

"Since we're speaking frankly, Sofia, I wonder if I might ask you something."

Sofia inclined her head.

"How did you ever get started in this business?"

Sofia smiled. "Normally I don't talk about it, but I have a feeling I can trust you to keep your silence. I was raised by my *abuelita*, my grandmother, in Mexico. She was the local problem solver in our village. If your neighbor stole your stuff or your drunken stepfather beat you, or a *pinche* woman tried to take your husband, you called my *abuelita* and she took care of things. Sometimes permanently."

Arthur's jaw dropped. "You learned the trade from your grandmother?"

"She was much respected. I used to help her sometimes. Then I decided to move to the United States, the land of opportunity, to make my fortune." A wistful smile spread across her face as Sofia gazed out the window. "I crossed the border at Lukeville and made my way to Phoenix. I was very young, had no money and hardly spoke any English. I began cleaning the houses of rich *gringos* in Scottsdale. When I came to clean one day, the lady of the house told me that her *cabrón* husband was beating her."

Sofia's eyes refocused and shifted back to Arthur. "She could not leave him. I offered to solve her problem, for a price. It was perfect. She made sure she was out with her friend shopping on the other side of town all day. I took care of the husband and then pretended to discover his body when I came to clean the house. No one suspected me. I had been working there for months, so what did it matter if my fingerprints were everywhere? What motive would I possibly have for killing my boss? Besides, people don't take cleaning ladies seriously. We are like the landscapers and busboys. Invisible."

Arthur leaned forward, listening earnestly. "How did you come up with your business model? I mean, that 'menu' you provided for me—pure genius. What were the options again?"

"The cheapest is the Tamale Package, the one you ordered. Unknown suspect kills the person you want dead. The next level up is the Enchilada, we just make the victim disappear. Then there is the Burrito, we make it look like the person died in an accident. Finally, there is the Chimichanga—the most expensive because it takes out two people. That's the one where we kill a person you choose and frame somebody else. A lot of work goes into that, let me tell you."

"Incredible!" Arthur said as he leaned back. "Would you be interested in a business partner?"

Sofia shook her head. "Mr. Bastion, do you remember how we first met?"

"Of course, my cleaning lady told me about you after my mother's tragic fall." He winked. "She overheard me arguing with my brother on the phone and approached me afterward. She advised me that something could be done about my brother. When I pointed out that one too many accidents might be suspicious even to the most dunderheaded police detective, she told me about her employer, a woman named Sofia, who could help me out—for a price."

"Exactly. You did not find me in the phonebook or on a website. After we spoke, I was able to persuade your brother to try my housekeeping service by offering him one month free. We cleaned his house many times and he was very happy. My ladies are the best at what they do, whatever kind of cleanup is necessary."

"What does this have to do with a partnership?"

"Mr. Bastion, I run Cleañoritas Incorporated the way I want. I personally recruit my workers and screen my clients. I only agree to a cleanup service when I feel that the victim is someone who has it coming—"

"That was my brother all right. The selfish bastard!"

Sofia continued as if Arthur had not interrupted, "Everything about the menu options from my company is word of mouth and nothing is written down. I even have a favorite spot far out in the desert for the 'disappearances.' I've been in business for many years and no one has caught on. There is no reason to take on an outside partner when I can train my own people how to do things the right way." She folded her hands in her lap and winked. "I will let you in on a little secret, Mr. Bastion. I plan to choose one of my cleaning ladies to set up a business in another city. Soon there will be Cleañoritas franchises everywhere. I love this country."

"Ah, well. I'll just have to remain a fan of your work. Who

knows, I may need to order an Enchilada Package for my wife someday."

"*Que será será.*" Sofia shrugged and turned her palms up to the ceiling as she smiled.

Arthur tensed when a young woman wearing a black house dress, white apron and bright pink rubber gloves opened the office door. Sofia looked up at her, "Ah, Consuela, I see you have returned from your questioning with the police."

Consuela nodded, "*Sí,* Sofia, it went good. Rosa and me had to promise to stay in town for more questions. The police drove us back to our van at the brother's house and we came here. Rosa is waiting outside."

Sofia angled her body toward Consuela and spoke in rapid Spanish. "Did you bring the gun?"

"Of course," Consuela answered, pointing at her stomach. "It's behind my apron."

Arthur snapped, "I don't like the two of you speaking Mexican to each other. What are you talking about?" His eyes drifted down to settle on Consuela's slightly bulging midriff. "What's going on?"

Sofia turned her gaze to Arthur as she switched back to English. "Mr. Bastion, there might be a problem."

Arthur tore his eyes away from Consuela to glare at Sofia. "What problem? I paid you good money so there would be no problems!"

Slipping her right hand under her apron, Consuela stepped backward until her back pressed against the office wall. She kept her gaze on Arthur as she slowly edged sideways. She bumped into a small ornamental table and cursed. Two pairs of eyes turned to Consuela as she righted a wobbling Tiffany lamp with her left hand. "Sorry," she mumbled.

"What in the hell is going on here?" Arthur demanded. "What are you hiding under your apron?"

Sofia cleared her throat and raised her voice. "Speaking of money," she watched as Arthur's head swiveled back to her. "There is always a final payment when we finish our job. An additional fifty percent."

Arthur's face turned an unhealthy shade of puce. "How dare you? You never said anything about a final payment. Is this some sort of shakedown?"

Consuela sidled against the wall until she was past Arthur's peripheral vision. She hesitated, then began to creep forward.

Sofia bristled and stiffened her spine. "I do not, as you say, shake down my clients. This final payment is for expenses."

Arthur's fist pounded the desk. "Expenses! What kind of—" His words were cut off by the loud report of a revolver being fired. Consuela stood motionless for a moment holding the gun in her pink-gloved hand precisely where Arthur's temple had just been.

Sofia stood, smoothed her skirt and spoke after waiting long enough for their ears to stop ringing. "Works every time. When I raised the price, he went *loco*. He forgot all about you. And that's saying something because, Consuela, you crashed around like a drunken burro. You've got to work on that."

Consuela started to speak, but snapped her mouth shut.

Sofia's eyes twinkled as she beamed at her young protégé. "Anyway, we need to act quickly, *m'ija*. The police will come soon to notify him of his brother's death."

Consuela lifted Arthur's right hand and wrapped it around the gun's grip. She pushed his index finger onto the trigger. "Where do you want me to fire the shot?"

Sofia pointed to the fireplace directly facing the desk and plugged her ears with her fingers. "It's a good thing this house is on five acres. Shoot it in there." After the second shot rang out, Sofia withdrew a pair of pink rubber cleaning gloves from her pocket and pulled them on. "Get the cleaning supplies and the vial of blood from Rosa in the van. Tell me in detail everything that happened at the brother's house. Did you kill him early this morning?"

"Yes, I made sure it was done a half hour before the time frame you told this one." She jerked her chin toward Arthur. "So his alibi is useless. After we took care of the brother, Rosa and me snuck out the back and returned around two hours later in our Cleañoritas van to pretend to discover the body."

"Excellent," Sofia nodded. "Tell me how you arranged the scene."

Consuela gently placed Arthur's hand, still holding the gun, down on the desktop. His torso was slumped in the leather chair. "Everything went perfectly. Rosa shot the brother, and then took off her rubber cleaning gloves. She put the gloves, gun and a little tube of his blood in our special kit bag. I went out through the back door and walked about a mile away. I hid the bag in a hole in a wash area behind a cactus. When we were done with the questioning, the police took me and Rosa back to our van at the house. We let them see us drive out of the neighborhood, then circled back through another street and got the bag."

"Good work. Now go out and get me the vial of the brother's blood and I will finish up here and bring you and Rosa your payments tomorrow. Remember not to flash the money around for a while and to spend it slowly."

After Consuela left, Sofia padded softly over to Arthur's crumpled form. She uncapped the glass tube and carefully smeared a drop on the side of his shoe. Finally, she looked down at him and murmured, "You shouldn't have been so cheap, Mr. Bastion. Your wife...she ordered the Chimichanga Package— with the works."

† † †

ISABELLA MALDONADO, PhD, is a retired police captain. Her previous short story, "Diablo Ranch," was published in the 2011 Sisters in Crime, Desert Sleuths anthology, *SoWest So Wild*. She is currently working on a novel featuring a Phoenix Police Detective in pursuit of a serial killer. She lives in the Greater Phoenix area with her husband and son.

MURDER AT WICKERSHAM FARMS
MERLE MCCANN

Strains of "Mack the Knife" pierced the air.

Scottsdale Homicide Detective Molly Raines dashed from the bathroom to answer her phone. "This better be good, Lar," she growled. "You got me out of the shower."

"Sorry, kiddo. We have a homicide not far from your place. Wickersham Farms."

Molly gasped. "Wickersham? That's a major equine breeding farm. Is Patrol there?"

"Securing the scene now. Body's in the mud between barns. You take the lead on this, given your background in ranching. I'm also assigning Wilson and Schmidt."

"I'm on it." Molly glanced at the droplets on her skylight. "Did it rain again last night?"

"Yep. Wear boots. Lieutenant Simmons of Patrol will meet you at the first gate."

Wickersham Farms, owned by a retired industrialist, was located near Tonto National Forest. Their lead stallion was world famous for producing champion Arabian halter and performance horses.

Minutes after receiving Lar's call, Molly turned off the main road and followed the white four-rail fence that surrounded emerald pastures. She drove through the gate and spotted the lieutenant standing near a smallish barn with a wide porch. Across the roadway, three black and whites were lined along the low wall of a training arena. She parked next to the building under a giant mesquite, pulled on her gloves and got out.

"Morning, Detective." Simmons motioned to her to follow him. "The body's this way. It's badly beaten."

"What's the victim's name?"

"Todd Lampell."

Molly recorded the name on her smart phone. "Everything handled so far?"

"EMTs just left. They confirmed death. CSS has been

dispatched and the scene's secured. We talked to the night watchman who found the body. He's pretty shaken. Says he didn't hear or see the fight."

An engine purred in the distance, a voice shouted in Spanish, and a chorus of whinnying horses grew louder. The ranch's day had begun.

Ahead, three large metal barns sat side by side. Behind them a second row of identical barns had been built. All were painted white and well-kept.

Simmons pointed ahead. "Let's cut through this barn."

Inside, the air was pungent with the combined scent of hay, grain, liniment and fresh manure, provoking pleasant reminders of growing up on her parents' ranch near Kingman. This was life as Molly wished it could be, calm and tranquil. She recognized the irony of the situation. A murder investigation had brought her to this serene setting, and she was about to view a corpse. Her hands curled into fists. Would she ever get used to it?

They walked through the barn and out into the wind, then turned right. The twenty-foot roadways separating the stables were muddy bogs from the recent rains. Molly picked her steps between water-filled ruts. In a small paddock at the corner of the last barn, a gray mare, heavy in foal, paced.

Yellow crime scene tape, strung from building to building and tied off at either end of the corral, approximated a circle. In the center the body lay half submerged in mire, arms askew, one leg bent at the knee. By the look of it, he lay where he and his attacker had thrashed it out.

Simmons pointed to two men speaking with his officers, their breath rising in the air. "C'mon, I'll introduce you to Mr. Wick and his business manager, Dan Halyard."

Wick wore a Burberry scarf tucked into his khaki down jacket. Molly shook his hand and noticed the sadness in his eyes.

She was curious about Halyard. She hadn't expected a business manager to be in a denim jacket, baseball cap and running shoes. The briefcase he gripped in his gloved hand gave him some credibility, at least. Tall with dark eyes and a square jaw, his body language was tense and all business. He stood with his back to the victim and it appeared he intended to keep it that way. It wasn't unusual. Most people are uncomfortable around a dead body.

Molly addressed Wick. "We need to keep everyone away

from here."

"Of course. I'll tell our people." Wick checked his watch. "Visitors will arrive soon. This time of year folks come from around the world. Can we make arrangements with that in mind?" He looked at Dan. "You work with Detective Raines, and I'll deal with visitors." He smiled at Molly. "Danny can show you around and answer questions." Wick glanced back at the body. When he turned, there were tears in his eyes. "I'll have to call Todd's parents. They'll be devastated." He headed toward the house.

Dan rubbed his jaw. "Detective, can we place vehicles at the end of these roads to block the view of our clients and visitors? I'll lock the barn doors that open on to it, also."

"As soon as we transport the body," Molly said.

"Thanks," Dan said. "This is an important time of year for us and this…" His voice caught. "This death will go hard against our reputation."

"We'll do our best to keep a low profile. Tell me, how many people work here?"

Dan didn't hesitate. "Six trainers, nine grooms, twelve barn-cleaners and four grounds keepers, plus two veterinarians. Mrs. Wick works in the home office." He checked his watch. "I've some calls to return. If you don't need me for now, I'll be in my office in the stallion barn, the building with the porch."

"That's fine. Once I'm done here, I'll catch up with you." She watched him turn away, then grabbed her cell and punched in Wilson's number. He picked up promptly, and she explained she needed his and Schmidt's help with interviews. "Lot of employees. Come as quick as you can."

Molly turned to examine the victim. The muck made it hard to assess the damage. She began at his battered head. He had bled from his mouth and nose. She hesitated, not wanting to soil her slacks, but then knelt for a closer look at a mark on his jaw. *Birthmark?* She sketched it. Working her way down, one arm and several fingers were undoubtedly broken. *Poor guy took a real ass-whooping.*

Next, she walked the roads between the barns, sketching the tire tracks. She made notes regarding the shoe prints she found. Before leaving, she took a last look. Something in the grass surrounding a fence post caught her eye. She picked up a scrap of cloth containing a pearl snap.

Minutes later, Molly walked into Dan's office. He closed the file on his desk and smiled. The office resembled an elegant reception area with overstuffed chairs and sleek tables. Dan's desk filled one corner. A window behind him looked into the stallion barn.

"Would you like a tour of the ranch?" he asked.

Molly checked her watch. "Let's talk here." She reached for her phone, prepared to take notes. "Any idea who'd want to kill Todd?"

"No. Everybody liked him."

"Tell me about him."

"Typical young guy. Loved horses, girls and the computer. Sort of a nerd. Liked to flirt but in a nice way, never aggressive, more on the mysterious side. The ladies loved him."

"What was his job?"

"Junior trainer. He worked with Chad, one of three senior trainers. They work with the juniors, teaching them our methods."

"Any idea why he'd be around the barns in the middle of the night?"

"A long-hauler dropped off a horse. The gray mare you saw in the receiving paddock."

"Is that usual?"

He nodded. "Haulers come at all hours, all year 'round. The trainers load and unload, never the drivers. The job's assigned by the month. It was Todd's month. The hauler rings the trainer from the back gate. The phone there is programmed each month with a trainer's number. I've already reprogrammed it to Alejandro, another trainer."

"So, Todd would've gotten the call and met the hauler?" Dan nodded. "What time was that?"

Dan opened a manila folder. "The mare came in at two-ten a.m. She'll foal out and be rebred. Then she'll go home."

"Would you make me a copy of that report?"

"No problem."

"Did the hauler know Todd?"

Dan picked up a form. "John Everly's Equine Hauling. Local company. Making a return trip. I've known him a while. He's married with two girls. Oldest is about seventeen. He and Todd might have had a run-in."

"Over his daughter, you mean?" Dan nodded. "He must

drive a heavy rig. There're deep tracks in the mud."

"Yeah. John pulls a nine-horse trailer. Eighteen wheels."

She looked up from her notes and spotted a young woman in a pink cap leading a handsome horse from the barn. "Who's that?"

Dan looked over his shoulder. "That's Big Bonny and Rothman, our lead stallion."

"She doesn't look so big." Molly said.

Dan chuckled. "We have Little Bonny, a new groom, and Big Bonny, a junior trainer. It's how we distinguish them."

"Tell me about the grooms."

"Same as the trainers. The junior grooms are here to learn from the seniors.

"How about barn cleaners?" Molly asked. "I noticed they're almost all Hispanic. Are they legal? Did they get along with Todd?"

Danny pursed his lips. "Yes, they're legal. We check each applicant thoroughly. If they're good with the horses, we promote them from cleaners to junior grooms. Like Alejandro. He's progressed to junior trainer."

Molly glanced at her notes. "Who've we missed?"

"We have two vets. Dr. Rich Dunhill who's visiting his alma mater in Iowa, and Dr. Bill Redmond who manages semen collection, division and dispersal. He won't be here until noon."

Molly glanced up. "Anybody else?"

"Just four grounds keepers. Only the foreman speaks English."

Molly crossed her legs. "Where do they all live?"

"Some have homes here. Others live in the apartments we built alongside the sales center."

She stood. "Do you have a picture of Todd?"

"Sure. I'll get you one. Personnel files are at the house."

"Thanks. Detectives Wilson and Schmidt will check out the crime scene when they arrive. Then I think we can break it down. We'll have to interview your staff. Could you help arrange it?"

"Happy to. There's the conference room next to my office, and I'll ask Mrs. Wick if we can use a couple of rooms at the house."

"Great." She turned for the door. "I have to get something from the car."

Molly started her interviews with the trainers. Last of that group was Big Bonny. Tall and slim, she wore jeans and English boots. After preliminary questions, Molly asked, "How long have you worked here?"

"Six years. I started like, right after high school."

"You must enjoy it."

"It's an awesome job."

"You probably knew Todd quite well. Know where he went to relax?"

She shrugged. "We hang out like at the Purple Chicken. Beer's cheap. Todd sometimes mentioned the Steak 'N Ale down on Camelback."

"That's a long way from here."

Bonny nodded. "He liked his privacy."

At eleven-thirty Molly stepped out onto the porch between interviews. Wilson and Schmidt had arrived and were walking toward her. "Hey, Raines." Schmidt gave her a wave.

"Glad you're here." Molly pointed toward the barns and described the body's location. "Once you're done, you can head over to the house and take statements. Check your phones. I sent you my notes." She spotted Dan crossing the lawn with a man wearing a lab coat. She pointed to him. "The guy in the cap is Dan Halyard. He's arranged for you to work in the house. Mrs. Wick is expecting you." Molly checked the time. "Let's meet at the precinct at six."

Molly returned to the conference room to update her notes, when someone tapped on the doorjamb. She recognized him as the man she'd just seen with Dan. Somewhere shy of thirty, he was sturdily built with cropped blond hair. His lab coat hung open and bunched when he sat. He draped his latex-gloved hands over the chair's armrests. "You must be one of the vets."

"I'm Bill Redmond."

"We're investigating the death of Todd Lampell. Where were you for the past twenty-four hours?"

His brow scrunched. "I worked until seven last night, went home for dinner and turned in around ten."

"And this morning?"

"I made a client call."

"I'd like your client's name and contact info." She pointed to his hands. "Why the gloves?"

"Oh." He chuckled. "I just examined a pregnant mare and was arranging with Dan to send her home when he said I should talk to you."

Precisely at six, Molly, Wilson and Schmidt gathered around a table in an interrogation room. She asked Wilson, "Did you come up with anything?"

He shook his head. "Not much. The body had already been removed, but the ground looked like there'd been a donnybrook. I interviewed twelve people. They all said the same thing. Lampell didn't share his private life, didn't date ranch girls, and was a hard worker with flirty ways. The clients loved the guy, especially the women. Ranch girls called him hunky."

Schmidt said, "I interviewed the other eleven employees and got those same answers."

"Think they were covering for someone?" Molly asked.

"Hard to say," Wilson said.

Molly grimaced. "I spoke with all the others. Tomorrow I'll talk with the guy who delivered the horse in the middle of the night." She reached into her pocket and dropped the torn fabric with the pearl snap on the table. "I found this at the scene. It didn't come from the vic's shirt."

"Western wear?" Schmidt asked. "Nobody I saw dressed like that. Most of 'em looked like they shopped at a thrift store."

"Right. Arizona grunge seems to be the desired look these days," Wilson said.

Molly picked up her things. "I'm going to make some calls. Thanks for your help. I'll let you know when I get the M.E.'s report."

The following afternoon, Molly walked into the Steak 'N Ale. She approached the bartender, showed him Todd's picture and asked if he recognized him.

"Yep. Was here about a week ago. Came in with Nicki."

"Nicki, who?"

He shrugged. "Nicole somebody. Never heard her last name." He tapped the picture. "She and this guy are regulars. She came in with some other guy before him. He always wore western shirts and cowboy boots. Lately it's just been this guy. Because of our rowdy crowd last week, I might not have noticed them, but she'd been smacked in the mouth. Had a bandaged lower lip."

"How'd they act?"

"Extra friendly. He held her real close. She appeared to be crying. She'd pull herself together long enough to sip her drink. Then she'd break down again. It was sad."

"Did they stay long?"

"Had a couple of rounds."

Molly's next stop was John's Equine Hauling. She spoke with the owner and his wife and learned that their daughters were away attending a college preparatory school for gifted children.

When Molly asked about Todd, John's eyes grew wide. "Todd's dead?" He frowned. "Believe you me, he was alive when I left. He unloaded the mare and signed my paperwork. Who would do such a horrible thing?"

"We hope to know soon." Molly thanked them and headed back to the precinct. There she methodically went through her case file. She noticed on the shipping instructions that the horse owner's name was Eugene Billings of Harrisburg, Pennsylvania. The smudged telephone number was unreadable.

Three days later, the ME's preliminary report arrived indicating, "Cause of death was blunt-force trauma. Probable weapon was round, possibly a heavy flashlight, given the late hour." The list of broken bones included six ribs and a crushed skull besides those Molly already knew about. Dr. Barlow, the Medical Examiner, declared the mark on the vic's jaw to be a deep bruise. His equipment produced an improved image. The report read, "Possibly made by a class ring." Barlow's sketch showed the angular lines of a V. *As in veterinary?*

Molly still needed more. She called Halyard.

"Hello, detective. What's up?"

"What more can you tell me about Dr. Redmond?"

Dan hesitated. "He's an equine specialist. Came from Tennessee. He's been here about five years. Married an equitation champion, Nicole Billings, who worked for us. I understand they're getting a divorce."

"How long were they married?"

"About three years, I guess."

Molly gnawed at her cheek. "What about his work?"

"Top quality. He gets a high percentage of mares settled in foal with the first service. That's important for Wickersham."

Molly frowned. She hadn't learned much. "Thanks, Dan."

She turned again to the file on Todd Lampell and picked up the shipping invoice. The contract was signed by a Eugene Billings. *Billings? Could he be related to Nicole Redmond?*

She hit redial on her phone. Dan picked up immediately. "Hey, detective. Didya miss me?"

Molly laughed. "One more question. Is Nicole Redmond related to the man who shipped the mare from Pennsylvania?"

"He's her dad."

"Would Dr. Redmond know in advance when the mare would arrive?"

"Sure. He gets the paperwork. He has to do a vet-check on arriving mares first thing."

"What time does your night watchman arrive?"

"Juan's here. Came early to help feed."

"I'll be over."

Molly met Juan Espinosa in front of Dan's office. "What time did you find Todd's body, Mr. Espinosa?"

"Three-fifteen," he said in heavily accented English.

"Are you sure?" Molly asked.

"*Si.* A truck was at the hospital barn, and I think maybe we have a sick horse. I go to help, but he drive off, so nothing I can do. But now I am fifteen minutes behind. I always go by the last barn at three. It takes fifteen minutes to walk there from the hospital barn. *Comprende?*"

"Yes, thank you, Mr. Espinosa, you've been very helpful."

Molly called Schmidt and instructed him to get search warrants for Todd's apartment, Dr. Redmond's home and his work area, including bank records for both. "Then come to the farm as soon as possible."

A while later, they entered Todd's apartment, on the far side of the ranch. "Wilson, you search the computer and desk," Molly said. "Schmidt, you take the kitchenette, and I'll search the bedroom."

It wasn't long before Wilson shouted, "Raines, check this out." She and Schmidt both joined him. He tapped the screen. "Todd has a file on Redmond. The doc left Tennessee after losing his license for doping Walking Horses. Only then his name was Renovich. The newspaper said he shot 'em full of something called Eq4." Wilson pulled up another screen. "The vic's bank statements show he's been depositing two thousand a month in cash from an unidentified source. He also receives an automatic deposit each month of eleven hundred from the ranch. Could be a stipend that goes with free rent. Those are his only deposits."

"Two thousand in cash?" Molly rubbed her neck. "Todd may have been blackmailing Redmond after discovering the doping charge."

"And dating his wife." Wilson grinned. "Both excellent reasons for murder."

Schmidt said, "Better bring that computer. Let's head for the doc's house."

Wilson asked, "Did Redmond appear to have been in a fight when you interviewed him?"

"His face didn't show signs, but he could have attacked from behind with a weapon. He wore latex gloves on his hands and a long sleeved lab coat. I didn't see his arms."

When they reached the AI facility, the building was dark but unlocked. Once inside they split up and began their search. When they found nothing to support their suspicions, they drove to Redmond's home.

The vet opened his door, and the detectives brushed past him. Molly said, "Dr. Redmond, we have a warrant to search your home." Schmidt headed for the garage and Wilson the bedrooms. She said to Wilson. "Check all his shirts.

Redmond's jaw dropped. "Why on earth…?"

"You've been implicated in the murder of Todd Lampell," Molly said.

He gestured wildly. "I had nothing to do with that."

She squared her stance. "Well then, hold out your hands." He hesitated but did as she said. Although they were not scraped or bruised, she saw clearly the ring he wore on his right hand. She couldn't make out the logo, but the V was distinct. She snapped pictures of his hands and the ring.

Wilson approached her. "Redmond banks on line. His account shows regular cash withdrawals, each one for more than two thousand dollars."

Molly glared at Redmond. "Who were you paying off?"

He glared right back. "Take it up with my attorney. I suggest you finish your search and get out."

When Schmidt came in, he held up his palms indicating he'd come up empty.

† † †

The next morning, Molly returned to the ranch. Dan met her on the porch. She explained she wanted another look at the crime scene, but after observing him, she sought out Big Bonny instead.

"Bonny, I need more information. Did you know Nicole Billings?"

Bonny appeared ill at ease. "Yeah. Like why?"

Molly smiled her best reassuring smile. "Who'd she pal around with? Date anybody from the ranch?" Molly swapped her smile for a more intimidating glare.

Bonny studied her boots. "She dated Dan for quite a while."

Molly sharpened her tone. "And?"

"Then Dr. Redmond came. Dan and Nicki broke up. Dan couldn't control his feelings, you know, so she quit her job."

"How can you be sure that's the reason?"

Bonny smirked. "Ranch gossip. It's the worst, but usually right on."

Molly thought of the Tennessee doping charge. "There's more to it, isn't there?"

Bonny recoiled. "You mean the five missing semen vials?"

What? Molly showed no surprise. "How'd you know about that?"

"Todd heard Redmond tell Mr. Wick."

Molly thanked her and headed for Wick's home to pick up a photo of Dan. From there, she drove to the Steak 'N Ale. The bartender identified Dan as Nicki's other man. She sped to the precinct and hustled Wilson and Schmidt into an interrogation room.

"It's not Redmond! It may be Dan Halyard who murdered Todd." She turned to Schmidt, "Call for a warrant to search his home and office, bank accounts, the works."

Wilson frowned. "C'mon, Raines. How do you figure?"

Molly grinned. "Today I saw Dan in a pearl-button shirt and I'm betting he owns at least one more, minus a snap. Here's the kicker: On his right hand he wore a Masonic ring. Ever see one?" She didn't wait for an answer. "Their symbol is a V-shaped compass over a T-square." She showed them Barlow's sketch. "Big Bonny said Dan was crazy in love with Redmond's wife. I'll bet he found out Todd was romancing Nicki and went ballistic. He probably figured he'd get her back after her divorce."

† † †

Before sunrise, the detectives woke Dan and searched his home. Wilson sat down at Dan's computer while Molly and Schmidt picked through the house. The Masonic ring lay on his dresser. Schmidt found the torn shirt in a ragbag in the garage.

"Look, Molly," Wilson said. He pointed to the computer screen. "Dan's bank account lists a one-hundred thousand dollar deposit." He showed Molly a deposit entry in a small checkbook he'd found taped to the bottom of the desk drawer. It indicated the funds were received from Prince Abdul Assad.

Molly's mind whirled. She glared at Dan. "You doin' business with the Saudis? They're into Arabian horses, right?" Dan refused to comment. She glanced at Wilson and Schmidt. "At twenty thousand a pop, it's easy to figure where the five missing vials of semen ended up." She signaled Schmidt, and he immediately handcuffed Dan and took him into custody.

Molly and Wilson left for Wickersham to search Dan's office and the stallion barn. There, she found a long-barreled flashlight behind a pile of horse blankets.

A smile played on her lips. In the murder business there's little happiness, other than an arrest.

† † †

Award-winning author, **MERLE MCCANN**, is best known for her Longjohners' Mystery Series for young adults. Born in the Yukon, raised in Seattle, she has traveled the United States and Europe with her husband pursuing their Arabian horse business. With a lengthy background in ranching, she enjoys writing mysteries with an equine or farming element. Before settling down to write serious fiction, McCann worked as a scenic photographer. She lives with her husband in Scottsdale, Arizona.

MAKE THE FINAL CUT
MARGARET MORSE

Bobbi grabbed Jonathan's arm before he could pound on the balcony railing a second time. "I know you love your job. But you have to resign."

Jerking away, Jonathan clenched his fists and stared out into the night. Bobbi followed his gaze over the lake that bordered the Grand Grove Resort in Scottsdale. Lights twinkled from the mansions that edged the water.

His voice deepened to a growl. "You are not my employer."

Bobbi tightened with anger. "Right, but I'm the one who just caught you here on the balcony making out with your employer's wife." Worse, Bobbi was the one who'd dated Jonathan for six months. Jealousy burned through her. "You can't expect to stay on as my father's campaign manager. Resign. Say you're pursuing other career options."

Jonathan turned to face her. Tall and broad-shouldered, he wore a gray suit accented with a red, white, and blue striped tie that announced his patriotism. Instead of meeting her eyes, he glanced at the ballroom. Chatter and guffaws marked the party celebrating her father's nomination to the U.S. Senate.

He focused on her, his blue eyes wide. "I don't want to hurt anyone."

Fury at his betrayal hit her as hard as a slap on the face. She wanted to punch him. "Then go away."

His brow creased in a frown. "Are you going to tell your father right now? Can't you wait?"

He appeared to care more about her father's reaction and his job than his wrongful act. She dreaded the thought of telling her father about Elaine. It would break his heart. The heat of the desert night swept over her. Sweat coated her face. "Do you think I'd walk up to him at the party and tell him Elaine is sleeping with you?" Anger cleared her mind. "You have to resign."

He shook his head. "If I leave, Elaine will follow me. That

would derail your father's campaign."

Her father's election seemed assured, since his opponent had just been indicted for fraud. "Elaine is not about to give up the life of a senator's wife for a mere campaign manager."

He flinched as her words bit into him. "Okay, you're not going to say anything to your father tonight." Jonathan was not one to let go of an advantage. He slipped closer. "Why tell him at all?"

His spicy scent, sweet at first, sickened her, and she swallowed bile. She wouldn't debate ethics with a tomcat. He had to pay for being unfaithful to her. She'd start with damage to his career. "You have to quit. Leave tomorrow for Kansas. Have a family emergency. Then send in your resignation. If you stay, I'll tell Dad first thing in the morning."

His face stiffened. "I need time. I'll let you know." He turned and stomped away.

She ran ahead and blocked him. "Let me know by midnight. That's your deadline." She let him stride past her.

Bobbi wanted her heart to slow down before she went inside. As she leaned against the balcony, she took a deep breath and located her father's home, a grandiose structure of Spanish design, perched straight across the lake. Tonight, he and Elaine would be alone there, voices echoing off the marble floors.

Time to put on a party face. After she patted her chin length dark hair, she turned up her lips into a smile and planned Jonathan's removal. Fifteen years ago, her parents' divorce had taught her to meet adversity with decisive action and sardonic humor. Yanking open the door to the ballroom, she braced herself as the crowd's laughter burst at her.

Food and drink stations strategically placed kept people on the move. From the wine bar next to the door came the inviting sound of a popped cork. Promising herself a glass later, she searched for Elaine to see if her stepmother wore a guilty expression. No, Elaine beamed at the group around her husband. A red scarf decorously covered the low cut neckline of her stepmother's black sheath. A crimson tie splashed color into her father's ensemble of a white shirt and navy suit.

She scanned the room and located Jonathan, who lingered on the outer fringes instead of circulating. After he bolted down a drink, he locked his eyes on Elaine, whose blonde hair slid down her face as she hugged a dowager. Laughter erupted from the supporters around her father. He detached himself and headed for the wine bar, where the owner of vineyards near Sedona stood behind a line of bottles.

When her father picked up a glass of a brownish red wine, Bobbi tapped his arm, her smile still in place. "Dad, I need a minute."

David Montgrove accompanied her to an empty space at the side of a carving station. His tanned complexion, which photographed so well, burned with two red spots on his cheeks. Bobbi sniffed and wondered if he'd been celebrating, but couldn't detect any liquor. Instead, she inhaled the scent of beef as the carver deftly sliced off a slab of pink meat.

She knew the server well, had graduated with him from law school. Currently an attorney at the public defender's office, Zach Bancroft moonlighted for a caterer to pay off his school debts. He was good with a knife. For a delicious second Bobbi wished she had the simple job of sliding a knife through flesh.

Her father's brown eyes fixed on her with rapt attention, the focused look of a man who had rebuilt the family banking business with fast, smart decisions. "You first."

She blinked, curious about what he had to say. "Don't let on I told you, but I'm worried about Jonathan. I think he's had some bad news about his family. Just a heads-up for you."

He nodded and glanced around the ballroom, his eye on Elaine, who laughed with a bronzed older man, a wheeler-dealer in Arizona politics. "Bobbi, Elaine and I are making an announcement tonight, really good news. I wanted to give you more lead time, but she's already told her family, so the secret will soon be out." He flashed his full voltage smile. "Elaine and I are expecting a baby."

Dazed by the implications of his news, she steeled herself to act appropriately, hugging her father, careful not to rumple his suit. She made her tone perky. "I can't tell you how happy that makes me. Congratulations, Dad."

He darted off to confer with Elaine. Stiff-legged, Bobbi tottered a few steps and leaned against the carving table. Alone with Zach the carver, she tried to absorb the fact that she would have a sibling of questionable parentage. As she dug her nails into her palms, the pain sharpened her thoughts. She wanted to scream and was surprised at her level tone. "I just won the dysfunctional family contest."

The black T-shirt and slacks of the caterer's uniform elongated Zach's slender runner's build. Spiky blond hair gave him a jaunty look. He sliced off a thin piece of beef. "What've you got that beats my brother framing me for the attempted murder of our father?"

They'd played the dysfunctional family contest since the first year of law school. Zach's wicked stepbrother usually trumped her family's efforts.

She shook her head when Zach offered her the meat. She had a bad taste in her mouth. "I can't tell you now. Let's meet at Mojo's later." After all the time she'd spent listening to Zach bemoan his latest break-up, he owed her some sympathy.

"You ought to dump your crazy family and go in with me." Zach had turned in his resignation at the public defender's office and planned to start his own legal practice. For months at their lunch meetings, he'd urged her to give up her job as her father's errand girl with a law degree.

Before she could answer, a tinkling emerged amid the party's roar. Three of her father's aides tapped on wine glasses with spoons. As the chatter subsided, her father stepped onto a stage at the far end of the room.

"Friends and supporters—'' His deep voice, amplified by the microphone, vibrated through the room.

"Elaine is pregnant," she whispered to Zach. "But that's not the only news."

He leaned across the table. "Get yourself a drink. Several drinks. I'll drive. I never drink and carve."

A smile fixed on her face, she joined in the applause as her father announced Elaine's pregnancy. She stepped over to the wine bar, where the owner poured her a generous glass of Syrah and offered congratulations.

"It's impossible to express my happiness."

She enjoyed the thought that her father would be seventy-eight when this kid went to the prom. The rich flavor of the wine, with its tannic bite, pleased her as she mingled with the guests and accepted more congratulations. She returned to the wine bar for a second glass, after a half circuit of the room. Tensing all over, she watched Jonathan pick up another scotch.

She marched up to him. "Don't make me cut you off. This is your fourth."

He gulped the amber liquid. "Sixth."

"I've already hinted to Dad you might have to quit."

"What will you do if I stay on? Shoot me?" He scanned her black silk dress. "No place in that number to hide a gun."

"I left my purse—'' She stopped. She had a rule never to apologize or explain to a weasel. "How do you know I carry a gun?"

He smirked. "Elaine."

Anger spiked in her. The gun wasn't a secret, but it was a private matter. *What else had Elaine blabbed about?* "You have till midnight to decide. Text me."

Jonathan swayed sideways, then steadied. "Elaine will never give me up." He left, bumping into her Aunt Caroline.

"Bobbi, are you excited?" Caroline asked. Her bronze hair drizzled out of a topknot secured with a scarf. Caroline launched into a gruesome account of her own "I was in labor for two days" story, ending with "Tell Elaine to take all the drugs they'll give her. Where's she gone?"

Her father and Elaine had left, signaling the party's end. Bobbi longed to leave and pour out her story to Zach, but would stay on, because she did not want to leave behind any passed-out guests or lost items. She ached from her stiff stance, and the smile felt frozen on her face.

Jonathan had left the ballroom without telling her his decision, so she texted him: "Remember, you have till midnight."

After she said good-bye to the last partygoer, she retrieved her briefcase-sized purse from the front desk and found Zach in the lobby. "Coffee?"

He eyed her. "I don't know if you need further stimulation. Why don't you wait for me here and I'll bring my car around. I had to park two blocks away."

The second she sank into the chair, she remembered she hadn't checked the restrooms for left-behind items. She'd been too worried over the whole Jonathan/Elaine mess. She pictured herself searching a red-faced infant for Jonathan's nose or her father's ears.

As she stood in the entry to the women's restroom, blinking at the gleam of marble and mirror, her phone rang and showed Zach's number.

"I checked the knives when I put them in the trunk. The long one for boning is missing."

When a tingle crept down her back, she turned and looked up and down the corridor. Nothing. The place was dead. "Do you want me to search for it?"

"No, I never took it out of the case. Somebody stole it. You're still in the lobby, aren't you?"

She paused in the restroom's sitting area and peered under the satin covered chaise lounge. "No, I'm in the women's bathroom. I forgot to inspect it for lost items."

"I'd feel better if you went back to the lobby."

"Okay, be there in a minute." She disconnected and stared at the piece of fabric on the floor. The striped tie was exactly like the one Jonathan had worn. As she bent over, she thought she heard a thud outside in the corridor. Cramming the tie into the front flap of her purse, next to her gun, she checked the hall but saw nothing.

Bobbi still had to check the men's bathroom. After she knocked on the door, she waited two seconds and entered. On the white tile near the stalls lay a man's suit jacket, steel gray like Jonathan's. Had he wandered around doing a striptease, then passed out drunk and half naked? Best to get Zach to help her look for him, since she didn't relish dealing with Jonathan on her own.

She retrieved the jacket and folded it over her arm and noticed a greasy stain around the collar. Probably whatever he used to keep his hair disciplined. From the jacket wafted his scent, thick and oily.

She strode down the corridor, braking when she heard Elaine cry out, "Jonathan, don't!" Her shriek came from the Azteca Room.

Bobbi flung open the door. Jonathan sat at the head of a conference table, a knife held against his wrist. A red line an inch long showed he'd made the first cut. His rolled up shirtsleeves gave him an absurdly casual air. Elaine stood next to his chair and glared at him.

Bobbi moved slowly into the room until she was close to Elaine. "Put the knife down, Jonathan. You're a bully and a jerk," Bobbi said.

Jonathan jabbed the knife at Elaine. He missed, but made her jump backwards. When she pulled out her phone, Jonathan charged into the two women. Unable to snatch Elaine's phone from her death grip, he grabbed Bobbi's purse. Furious, Bobbi lunged and head butted him in the groin. He sprawled on his back, dropping the knife and purse.

Bobbi kicked the knife away and dove for her purse. Elaine reached it first. She pulled out the gun, came around the table and stood over Jonathan.

Elaine held the gun with both hands. "If you move, I'll shoot you."

Jonathan grimaced. "I just wanted to talk to you."

"Talk to me!" Elaine's voice was a screech. "You get me down here by lying and then threaten suicide unless I agree to run away with you?"

Bobbi, standing on the other side of Jonathan, stared at blood dripping down Elaine's arm. "Elaine, be careful with the gun. Those things go off easier than you think." She tried to keep her voice calm. "It's not serious, but you have a scratch on your left arm. I think Jonathan nicked you when he charged us."

Elaine gaped at her arm, waving the gun wildly in Bobbi's direction. She wobbled sideways toward a chair, pushed it aside, and sat on the table. To Bobbi's relief, Elaine pointed the gun at the floor.

Painted cheekbones flamed on Elaine's face. "I don't feel so good."

Sitting up, Jonathan leaned on the chair and pounded on his forehead with clenched fists. Bobbi hoped he was knocking in some sense.

Bobbi kept her voice steady, not wanting to startle Elaine. "Give me the gun."

Elaine dropped the gun on the table. Jonathan surged up and seized it. His face twisted in anger, he pointed the pistol at Bobbi. "I'm not going to wait around for you to stab me in the back and tell your father. You should not have given me the ultimatum."

Elaine slipped off the table and moved away from Jonathan. He swung the gun towards her. "Don't move. I'm doing this for you too."

"You're not doing anything for me." Elaine reached under the table and reappeared with the boning knife that Bobbi thought she'd kicked safely away. Elaine backed up until she was just past the door. "Now you'll see what it's like to have someone threaten you." Tugging off her red scarf, she pressed the knife against her exposed cleavage. "You do anything with the gun and I stab myself."

"But you're pregnant," Jonathan objected. He moved toward her and stood close to the door.

"It's not your baby, so shut up."

Jonathan reeled toward Elaine as the Azteca Room door swung open and hit him squarely. He plunged sideways, arms flying, and crashed into the conference table. Bobbi whacked him with her purse. The gun banged, and fragments of the ceiling exploded into the room. When Jonathan dropped the gun, Bobbi grabbed it.

Zach dashed into the room, yanked Jonathan up, and punched him. "You need to be careful with guns." He shoved Jonathan into a chair.

Elaine flung the knife away and threw herself on Jonathan, pummeling him and screaming, "You idiot, you've ruined everything."

Bobbi retrieved the knife and slipped it into her purse. Over their heads, she told Zach, "They're in love. That's the big secret."

"Seems to be cooling off." He pried Elaine off Jonathan, and moved her out of striking range. "Calm down, Mrs. Montgrove. You don't want to hurt yourself."

Zach's words, possibly the mention of her married name, quieted Elaine, who wilted, her face streaked with tears. Bobbi kept an eye on Jonathan, his lower lip puffed out from Zach's punch. He'd collapsed in the chair, panting as if he'd run a mile. The sound of his breathing grated on her.

Elaine was a dolt, but Dad loved her, so Bobbi was stuck with this woman. However, she could eliminate Jonathan. She spoke to Elaine in an encouraging tone. "I have a plan to get you out of this mess."

Zach checked the hallway. "I'm amazed no one has called the cops."

Bobbi stood in front of the door. "The hotel is mostly empty." She focused on Jonathan. "I'm ordering you, not asking. You'll take a leave of absence because your drinking problem spiraled out of control—"

"I don't have a drinking problem."

"You do now. You'll then resign to explore other career options. This is the story we're telling my father. You got drunk tonight and on impulse stole the boning knife." Jonathan's face reddened and he started to speak. She raised her voice. "Shut up. You were suicidal." She addressed Elaine. "How did he get you here tonight? Did he text you or actually talk to you?"

Elaine cleared her throat. "He called me." She brushed her hair back. "I've had trouble sleeping, so your dad's in a guest room."

Bobbi concentrated on the glum Jonathan. "Your call to Elaine was a cry for help. You know of her interest in mental health issues." She zeroed in on Elaine. "Foolishly, because you have a big heart," Elaine nodded gravely, "you hurried down here to try to save him. I interrupted you."

"And we disarmed Jonathan, and that's how I got this cut," Elaine finished for her.

"My father will be angry, but Elaine can persuade him to hush the whole thing up."

Elaine stroked Jonathan's shoulder. "It's for the best. You can make a new start."

Jonathan gawked at her. "You're giving me up?"

Bobbi shook her head. "How can you possibly not get it? She is totally dumping you!"

Jonathan rushed at Elaine. He grabbed her by the neck and shook her. "You betrayed me!" Teeth bared, he pressed his thumbs into her throat. Elaine choked as she clawed at him. They staggered across the room. Bobbi and Zach dived after them and yanked on Jonathan's arms.

Jonathan lost his balance and pitched forward, dragging everyone down. Zach hit his head on a chair and let go. His eyes glazed and blood dripped down his face.

Bobbi scrambled to her knees and tried to pull Jonathan off Elaine. Unable to dislodge him, she punched his nose. Jonathan released Elaine and hit Bobbi so hard she flew backwards and landed on her butt.

His blow split her lip. When she tasted blood, rage flamed through her. From her purse, she snatched out the knife and stabbed wildly. She sliced into his right arm.

Blood gushed as she removed the knife. Heart racing, she lurched back. Jonathan charged her with fists clenched. She plunged the knife upward, felt it tear cloth and slice through flesh. Jonathan grunted and swayed, but didn't collapse until Zach kicked his legs out from under him.

Her hand clamped on the knife, she jerked it out of

Jonathan's chest. A red stain spread over his shirtfront.

Elaine stumbled out of the Azteca Room. Zach tossed Bobbi the scarf Elaine had discarded. "Try to stop his bleeding," he said, pulling his cell phone from his pants pocket.

Bobbi swallowed the blood from her cut lip as she pressed the fabric on Jonathan's neck.

†   †   †

After the first group of paramedics had taken away Jonathan and Elaine, the second squad patched up Zach and Bobbi. An officer escorted her to a vacant conference room. The air conditioning chilled her to the bone. She replayed the scene of the knife thrusts into Jonathan. Had there been a moment when a better word or action would have stopped the violence?

Zach joined her in the icy chamber. "Your dad won't be here. He's meeting Elaine at the emergency room. He hired Toby Bernstein to come here to represent you. I briefed him. Toby's sure the cops will let you go while they verify your claim of self-defense."

He leaned so close his breath touched her face. When he shut his eyes and grimaced, she blurted out, "Jonathan is dead, isn't he?"

Zach nodded and slumped back in his chair. Even his spiky hair drooped. Bobbi squeezed his knee. *Strange, the killer comforts her witness and protector*

Bobbi shivered and let go of Zach. For the tenth time, she wiped her hands on her black dress.

†   †   †

MARGARET MORSE lives with her husband Duane and nine rescued dogs in South Phoenix. After working as an attorney for twenty-five years at the Maricopa County Public Defender's, she retired to begin a second career as a writer. She has completed an urban fantasy murder mystery novel. WELL DEFENDED portrays a lawyer who turns into a witch during a murder investigation. She's had five short stories published—two in *Arizona Attorney* and three in Desert Sleuths anthologies.

GRAND CANYON STANDOFF
KRIS NERI

If Tom Brewster didn't know better, he would think that one of his companions here on the Colorado River bank in the Grand Canyon, now sitting so congenially together around the campfire, was trying to kill him. But there was no reason to believe one of them wanted him dead.

Oh, there were lots of others who would love to dance on his grave. Dozens of them, if not scores. Most of his enemies were still in prison, though, and those who had gotten out would never know how to find him. But these strangers he hadn't met until three days ago? None of the people on this Grand Canyon river rafting adventure, which was made up of unattached singles traveling alone, had shown any more interest in him than they'd shown in each other. Why would any of them want him dead?

"More steak, Tom?" their river guide, Dale Flannery, asked from his place before the camping cook stove, just off to the side of the campfire circle, offering him the same friendly grin he'd shown the others.

Flannery wasn't a big man, or all that young, judging by his silver hair and the fan of wrinkles radiating out from his stony gray eyes, but his muscles seemed as strong as the canyon walls rising up around them. Given his job navigating the rapids, and working sixteen-hour days caring for the people on the tours he led, he'd have to be strong. Apart from his occasional brusque manner, though, he'd never seemed particularly threatening.

"Or another potato?" Brewster vaguely heard Flannery ask. "How about more to drink?" He was so lost in his own troubling thoughts, he didn't answer.

"Tom's off in never-never land," one of the men on their tour said. Brewster thought he remembered the fortyish bald man as having introduced himself as Doug, but he hadn't paid that much attention to any of their names.

"That happens to folks here," Flannery said. "Tom's not the first."

His name wasn't actually Tom Brewster. He didn't really have a name, unless you counted the one he was born with, but he hadn't used that in years.

By rights he should have been called Jesse James or John Dillinger. Like them, he robbed banks, and he was one of the greats. Unlike them, he remained unknown. For eighteen years, he had eluded detection with an ingenious system he had devised. Now he was in hiding after his very last job. Even bank robbers retire—the smart ones do, anyway. Once this seven-day river trip was over, he'd slowly drive across the country, and finally, fly off to his Caribbean hideaway, where he had squirreled away the millions of dollars he had taken from the dozens of banks he had robbed all over the country.

It helped that he had been born to touring actors. Throughout his youth, while being home-schooled by his mother, he was also tutored in the craft of acting and the art of creating disguises. Only he put those lessons to better use than his parents had.

His system was simple. He scoped out possible banks in a geographical area, albeit while wearing disguises, and chose the one he considered the easiest to get away from. Then he hired some local talent to carry out the job with him, but he met with them in disguise so they could never provide a genuine description of him to the police. Finally, he got one of the members of his heist crew to co-opt someone in the bank, who could tell them when the on-hand cash would be the greatest, making certain that person could never be connected to him.

Naturally, they all wore masks during the robbery. But while he made sure he left nothing of himself behind—to the extent of wearing latex gloves and a wig to prevent him from leaving hairs—he always dropped some evidence that would lead to his hired cohorts. When the police or the Feds picked them up, by virtue of his always having been disguised, their description of him led the cops off in another direction.

There was one last part of his plan. Right after the job, instead of rushing away, he hid somewhere locally. His unique hideouts were always the last places the cops would think to look. Once, he had signed on as a clown in a weeklong benefit that went on in various childhood cancer wards in local hospitals—and the best part was that event was sponsored by the Police Benevolence League. As he'd hoped, it didn't seem to occur to them to look within their own ranks, or at the guy behind the clown makeup. Another time it involved working as a security guard on a movie shooting on location in the very city where he had robbed that bank, right under the nose of the officer consulting on the film.

Now, after the successful robbery he had pulled off in Williams, right before the start of this rafting adventure, he once again did the unexpected. Who would imagine a bank robber would hide out at the base of the Grand Canyon, where he couldn't escape in a hurry? But this atypical, counter-intuitive roost would hide him just as surely as all his other outrageously inventive choices had.

It was all a matter of daring, something he had in spades. Law enforcement types expected a bank robber to make himself scarce—he didn't. They assumed the robber would feel worried about being caught—he wasn't. His genius was in choosing the perfect hiding place. His daring involved carrying it off without flinching.

In between jobs, he continually created new names, investing in high quality fake IDs. Mostly, he didn't even need those IDs, but since 9/11 everyone checking into hotels or signing onto excursions, had to present a photo ID. He counted on the name he'd chosen, Tom Brewster, to work well enough for now, and for his phony driver's license to hold up to routine scrutiny, and it had. But once the river journey ended, he would shed this identity as easily as a snake leaves his skin behind.

Eventually, the conversation around the campfire moved on to the wildlife they'd seen while rafting that day.

The young man with the beard, whose name Brewster had forgotten, said, "Did you all see that California Condor circling over us before? Do you believe how wide their wingspan is?"

Despite his urgent distraction, Brewster forced himself to join in. "They release the chicks they breed in captivity into the wild here," he said.

He didn't care in the least about the wild birds and animals they'd seen, but he needed to appear as engaged as anyone else, so as not to draw attention to himself. Thankfully, he had read up on the Grand Canyon before he arrived for the tour. Doing the research necessary to blend into whatever hideout he'd chosen was also part of his methodology.

Other people contributed their own sightings, including herds of elk and big horn sheep. Brewster continued to speak as often as he considered necessary until it seemed safe to drift back into his thoughts again.

He had to admit his system had not gone so exactly on his first job, the only other robbery he'd ever pulled here in Arizona. Everything went perfectly with the bank. The inside man told them when it would be full of cash and when the security guard would be off on his lunch break. He chose two-time losers to help him with the job, and left behind evidence that led to them as he planned. It was just his bad luck that a local police detective happened be among the customers in the bank, when they robbed it. Sure, Brewster disarmed him and made him remove his Kevlar vest, but at one point, that detective made a grab for Brewster's mask. He didn't fully pull it off, but he alone, of all the people in all the banks Brewster had robbed, got a good enough look at his face to describe him.

Naturally, that led to a momentary standoff. Brewster broke that stalemate by firing straight into the cop's chest. That was the only person he'd ever had to shoot in all these years. Fortunately for him, the detective, whose name was David Greene, had died later that same day. According to the newspaper, he only regained consciousness for a few minutes before passing away, just long enough to say goodbye to his kid.

He'd sweated that one out in the days that followed. But he kept his cool. He'd made a study of bank robberies, specifically what worked and what led to arrests. No matter how nervous he had been, he stuck to the plan. Because he had, he'd earned a life of wealth and freedom. Soon, it would be endless freedom. He came to believe he would never have another risky standoff, and he never had.

"Tom, sure you don't want anything else?" Flannery asked again.

"You're too good a cook, Dale," he said, while patting his belly and remembering to assume a friendly, easy-going manner. "I've already eaten too much."

"Not me. I'll take another one of those potatoes, Dale," the woman, Hannah, said.

Flannery stabbed a fork into one of the baked potatoes he was keeping warm on the grill and passed it to her across the circle they had formed around the fire.

Hannah, who was probably in her late twenties or early thirties, was the only woman on the tour. She was attractive enough in that girl-next-door way, although not especially memorable. Since she was also on the small side, Brewster feared she might prove to be a burden when the river got rough. She held her own, though; she was stronger than she looked. He supposed she must have been an artist or something—whenever they made camp, she was always sketching in that little journal she'd brought along in her backpack. She was pretty good, too, judging by her Grand Canyon pencil sketches and the quickie drawings she'd done of some of their tour-mates.

"Yum," Hannah said while munching on a piece of baked potato skin. "Dale, does everything just taste better out here?"

Through eighteen years, in over twenty states and more than a hundred cities and towns, Brewster's plan had always worked perfectly. Nobody had ever come looking for him.

Except maybe now.

Was it possible? Was someone finally on to him? He couldn't see how. If anyone suspected him, why would they toy with him? But if no one was trying to kill him, how could he explain everything that had happened? Hannah was the only one he didn't suspect—she was always too busy sketching. But one of them must be trying to kill him, as hard as it was to believe. Either that, or he'd become the unluckiest guy in the world. And he hadn't survived these eighteen years of brilliant thievery by being unlucky.

Their first day of cruising down the river had been uneventful. His problems didn't begin until the next morning. After their initial night of camping on the riverbank, Brewster couldn't wake up. His first awareness was of Flannery, leaning over him in his tent, shaking him hard.

"Come on, Tom. You gotta wake up. We've been ready to go for twenty minutes."

That might not have been significant for anyone else. But he never needed much sleep. Besides, this tour wasn't recreation for him, it was part of a well-planned scheme.

"You might want to cut down on the sleeping pills, Tom. Quiet as it is here in the Canyon, most people find they don't need them."

He certainly never took pills, and if he did, he sure wouldn't take them immediately after a job, when his senses needed to be keen. But maybe it was just a matter of the quiet of the Canyon, after the stress of pulling the job, lulling him into a deeper than usual sleep. He didn't jump to the conclusion that he'd been drugged. At least, not until the day wore on, when he continued to feel lethargic, and developed a strange aftertaste in his mouth.

Brewster had paid extra for a private tent. Naturally, the lone woman had her own tent, too. And Flannery also slept alone, storing all the equipment with him. The four other men bunked two-to-a-tent. John, Ted, Doug and…something odd for a first name. Rafferty, Brewster finally remembered. Four guys, of different ages, from different states—what could have brought those strangers together, apart from merely taking this trip? And they had all helped Flannery with the cooking—any one of them could have slipped something into his food that first night.

The following day of cruising the river went okay until that night, when some large boulders fell down the cliff onto his tent, barely missing flattening him. When Brewster squeezed himself out of his crushed tent, he found only one of his fellow travelers sitting on the river's edge, smoking a cigarette.

"You—Doug," Brewster shouted. "Were you up there on the canyon wall? Did you roll those boulders down on me?"

"The name's Rafferty," the bearded young man said. "Doug's my tent-mate. And I haven't been anywhere near the canyon wall."

Flannery came out of his tent. "Would you two keep it down out here? Your tour-mates are trying to sleep."

"Someone just tried to put me to sleep for good!" Brewster snapped. He had to make himself settle down, but he was trapped in that space with these people.

Flannery finally convinced him to quietly share what had happened.

Brewster dragged Flannery back to his tent. "You see, someone must have climbed above me and send those boulders down."

With a sigh, Flannery said, "Tom, why would they?"

Brewster didn't respond.

"Didn't you read the waiver you signed before you came on this trip? Boulders fall down all the time—we warned you about that. All kinds of wildlife here—animals knock rocks over the edge regularly." Flannery ran a hand through his silver hair. "You really think one of your tour-mates has it in for you?"

Brewster didn't answer that, but he did insist that Flannery check the other tents with him to make sure everyone was accounted for. They were all in their tents, including Rafferty, who had climbed into his sleeping bag by then. So much time had passed since the boulders came down, and it was so dark that whoever had climbed up there could easily have returned to his tent by now.

But after the drugging, and then the boulder crashing, at least he was sure about it. One of them was gunning for him.

For all the good that knowledge did him. Things became even worse earlier today. While they were going through the rapids, he took an elbow that knocked him out of their boat. Sure, like all of them, he'd worn a life vest, but the white water was so choppy, they didn't manage to rescue him until he'd swallowed gallons and only then because his vest caught on a fallen tree.

"Now do you believe me?" he'd hissed to Flannery, when he dragged him off alone after they made camp. "Someone knocked me out of the boat."

"Who? Tell me which one, and I'll take care of it."

How could he say? It could have been any one of them. Well, any one of the men. The woman was seated too far away from him and was surely not strong enough to push him out. She was the only one who couldn't be behind the threat against him.

Brewster struggled to stay engaged during dinner, but his fears and thoughts kept pulling him away. He also kept his backpack, which he would normally have stowed in his tent, nearby. But all hell broke loose after that, when he finally returned to his tent. He heard the sound first—an unmistakable rattle coming from the inside of his tent. He found a branch and gently lifted the flap. A rattlesnake was coiled and ready to strike precisely where he would have slipped into the tent.

"No, no, no!" Brewster shouted. He grabbed for his backpack.

Flannery came running. "Tom, what...?"

"Don't, 'Tom' me, old man. You're probably in on it."

Brewster reached into his backpack and pulled out a gun. By then the others had gathered, so they were all within range.

"One of you is trying to kill me," Brewster insisted.

Hannah took a step closer to him. "We're not *trying* to kill you, we just wanted to shake you up." She shrugged. "But we didn't really care if we did happen to kill you."

What...? "One of you must be a cop," Brewster shouted. He

knew he'd blown his well-crafted cover with that remark, but it was too late to worry about it.

Hannah's young face hardened to stone. "Actually, we're all cops of one kind or another, or were. Ted here," she said, gesturing with her thumb to the blonde man beside her, "is with the St. Louis PD. You remember St. Louis, right? You robbed the First National Bank there. And Rafferty is from California, and the L.A. County Sheriff's Department. You hit at least three banks in his jurisdiction." She went through the other male tour-members, too, until finally introducing herself. "I'm a Special Agent with the FBI, in the bank robbery division." She paused. "I'm also Hannah Greene. David Greene's daughter."

"Who?"

"David Greene. He was a detective with the Phoenix PD. You shot him in what I figure must have been your first score, if the case I've built against you is right."

Brewster tried to gather his wits, but Hannah had rattled him. Had all of his successes made him complacent?

"I don't know—"

"Don't even consider bluffing. I've got you nailed."

He had to try to brazen it out. "Assuming you're right—and we're just talking hypotheticals here—that cop only had a few minutes of consciousness before he croaked. He couldn't have told you anything useful about me."

"Funny that you'd remember that if you weren't involved," Hannah said with soft certainty.

After having walked into that trap, he felt a shiver of panic.

Hannah sighed. "My dad was a cop all the way to his core. Knowing he only had moments to live, he didn't bother telling me where to find his will or life insurance or other important papers. Instead, he told me what you looked like—and I sketched it."

This really couldn't be happening. But he held the gun, he reminded himself. None of them were armed. Though they also didn't seem worried about his weapon.

Flannery cleared his throat. "I was David's superior at the time. To my eternal regret, I made the choice not to hang my case on some sketch a kid created." He paused long enough to send a sorrowful look Hannah's way. "But I never forgot it. Now I'm retired from the Phoenix PD, and I run this river tour service. When you sent in a copy of your driver's license, which is a fake, by the way—a good fake, but I've seen too many of those not to recognize one when I see it. Anyway, as soon as I saw your photo, I remembered that sketch, and I knew we had you. We sent out the word through the law enforcement community, and we put together this little band to trap you."

"Yeah? A little premature about that, aren't you? You know I can't allow any of you to leave here alive." But it worried him that none of them seemed the least bit concerned about the gun he held on them.

Rafferty spoke up. "Dude, pull the trigger already."

The confidence in Rafferty's speech told the story. Even before Brewster squeezed the trigger, he knew it wouldn't fire.

It didn't.

"Why do you think we drugged you?" Flannery asked. "We removed the firing pin that night."

There was no way he could escape from them, but desperation spurned Brewster to try to run anyway. The four other men on that tour were faster. In moments, they had him pinned to the ground.

Flannery pulled a satellite phone he hadn't seen before, from under his shirt. "He's ready for you," he said into it. It wasn't long before Brewster heard the sound of a helicopter in the distance.

"I've been too smart for you. You'll never build a case against me," he told Hannah.

She tilted her head. "When you don't have a suspect, some cases do defy cracking. But once you have someone, they tend to come together quite well. I've actually worked through most of it already, and the rest should be a snap. You'll have left trails that we'll find. And there will be people who'll remember you, no matter how well you hid your identity."

"Why didn't you just kill me?" he asked in tone that sounded pathetic even to him.

"My dad always said, 'Never do anything yourself if you can get someone else to do it for you.' I figure the prisons are filled with men aching to get a shot at you. You'll never know when it's coming."

No! Brewster thought.

She turned to Flannery. "What do you say, Dale? You think Dad would be happy with the way this Grand Canyon standoff has turned out?"

"You can bet on it, kiddo." Flannery laughed. "What was that other thing David used to say? Oh, yeah." Flannery looked pointedly at him. "'Justice delayed isn't necessarily justice denied.'"

Brewster feared that, for him, justice wasn't going to be delayed at all.

† † †

KRIS NERI's published novels include the Tracy Eaton mysteries, the latest of which is *Revenge on Route 66*, and the Samantha Brennan & Annabelle Haggerty magical mysteries. Her novels have been nominated for such prestigious awards as the Agatha, Anthony, Macavity, International Book Award, and the Lefty Award for Best Humorous Mystery. Her novel, *Magical Alienation*, won the 2012 New Mexico-Arizona Book Award. Kris teaches writing for the UCLA Writers' Program, and co-owns The Well Red Coyote bookstore in Sedona.

MOST IMPORTANT MEAL OF THE DAY
NANCY HART NEWCOMER

Today was the day. The sun came up over the Mazatzal Mountains, glowing like an electric apricot in the turquoise sky. I rose early, made my tea and toast and reveled in the warm light streaming into the kitchen through two-story windows overlooking virgin Arizona desert.

I started the oatmeal for Dutch's breakfast. My husband loved my special oatmeal. At least he did until his appetite waned. I put water, oatmeal, salt and a nub of butter into the pan on the range. When it simmered, I added chopped toasted pecans, dried cherries, maple syrup…and, today for the first time, my secret ingredient.

Dutch had had heart problems since his double bypass surgery a couple of years ago. Lately, he'd just been feeling sickly. Old Doc Parsons ran the usual tests but he couldn't determine the cause. After all, Dutch was seventy-five and these things happen. For the last few days, he hadn't made it out to the kitchen for breakfast. I decided I'd better go to the bedroom and wake him up.

I walked in with his breakfast and saw Dutch stretched out across the bed, his breathing shallow and ragged. I shook his shoulder and he blinked his eyes open. After helping him sit up, I placed the tray table over his scrawny legs. I pulled a chair closer and began to feed him with a spoon. His mouth opened and closed like a baby's as he ate the warm, sweet cereal. Bless his heart, he ate the whole thing.

The websites I'd consulted said it might take three or four hours for my special ingredient to work but in fact, he died pretty quickly. My computer searches at my local library had revealed a cornucopia of poisonous desert plants. In the end, I selected Jimson Weed because it caused heart arrhythmia which I figured would be enough to do the trick. I liked that it was in the "Deadly Nightshade" family, too. Also, it grew in the dry wash behind our house.

The delirium set in after about thirty minutes. His eyes glazed over then he smiled and made noises that sounded like singing. After about an hour, he clutched his heart and his chest heaved up and down. Finally, he gave one last rasp and collapsed.

His eyes stared upward but I knew he saw nothing. He was quite dead, I was sure of it. Still, I needed to confirm it so I grasped his bony wrist to find a pulse. None there. I closed his eyelids and pulled the covers up over his head.

I looked over the collection of prescription pill bottles on the bedside table, mainly heart meds. He wouldn't need those any more. I glanced at the framed poster of Georgia O'Keefe's painting *Jimson Weed* over the bed and found it comforting. Then I knew just what to do. After all, I had made a checklist.

Sitting on the window seat in the den, I pulled out the list on pink paper which I kept in the inside zippered pocket of my purse. As I scanned the items, I felt a sense of accomplishment. I was really doing this. Number one: GET RID OF GROUND JIMSON WEED SEEDS. I retrieved the small jar behind the flour canister in the pantry.

Stepping into the back yard and, making sure the wind was behind me, I scattered the deadly particles over the five-foot tall bush with the white trumpet-shaped flowers. Seed to weed. Dust to dust. *Hasta la vista*, Dutch McGraw.

Back inside, I took a nice hot shower. I carefully applied makeup, adding a little pink eye shadow to make the lids look swollen, and styled my beautiful blonde-streaked hair. It costs a pretty penny but I'm worth it. Then I selected khaki jeans, the cowboy boots with the turquoise trim and a brown cashmere sweater. The neckline covered the crescent-shaped scar on my left breast. I got it the night Dutch hit me hard with his fist. His ring left a souvenir I will always carry. After he saw the torn flesh, he learned to hurt me in places where it didn't show. Tucking my hair behind my ears, I inserted gold stud earrings— the perfect touch for the new widow-in-mourning.

The next item on my list was: CALL THE DOCTOR. Old Doc Parsons arrived in about fifteen minutes. He'd taken care of my husband since Dutch and I moved to Dry Creek, Arizona, seven years ago. After feeling for a pulse, he shook his head.

"So is this how you found him?"

"Yes, Doc, except I closed his eyes."

"Did he feel sick last night?"

"He complained of some tightness in his chest but he said he could tolerate it."

"It's two years since the bypass surgery. Maybe some blockage built up again. He'd lost so much weight. His heart must have just given out." He touched my shoulder. "I'm sorry, Kirsten."

"Thanks, Doc. I know you did your best."

"Well, I guess you better call the funeral home."

"Yes. I have their number," I said, tears welling up on cue. "Thanks for all your help."

After the funeral home people came and took the body away, I had some time alone again. I consulted my checklist and found the next thing I needed to do. CALL FRIENDS AND FAMILY. Oh brother, I'm not looking forward to this part. Two ex-wives. Three mongrel offspring. However, I had to do my chores as the dutiful third and last wife...widow. I opened my address book and jotted down the names and phone numbers.

When Harry McGraw, Dutch's oldest son, appeared on my doorstep on Friday, the day before the funeral, I knew right away we were not going to get along. For one thing, he looked just like Dutch. Well, what Dutch probably looked like at twenty-five years old—tall, lanky and cocky, with the same set to his squared-off chin and a cowboy hat tilted just so.

He and Dutch hadn't seen each other often in the years after the divorce and his mother, Rachel, wife number one, didn't do much to encourage the father and son relationship. But after Dutch's bypass surgery, Harry came to visit for a couple of weeks and they got along like bosom buddies. I didn't like that at all.

When he came back last Thanksgiving, he worried about how much weight Dutch had lost. I assured him Doc Parsons took excellent care of Dutch but sometimes getting older meant getting frailer. Frankly, I don't think Harry bought it.

"Well, Harry, how nice to see you again, although I'm sorry it's under such tragic circumstances." I added a little more of my native Atlanta drawl than usual.

"Me, too. I guess he just never got better."

"He didn't," I said, looking down. "And finally his heart

gave out, the Doc said."

"Well, I'll get settled into the guest house, if it's okay." Harry nodded toward the duffle bag slung over his shoulder.

"Of course."

"I thought you could use some help going through his belongings. I can stay through next week," Harry said. "He mentioned giving me some skis and tools in the garage."

I was not craving company but what could I say? "Fine. We'll go through it together then." I hoped my smile quivered just the right amount.

From the bedroom window I watched him take his bag into the guesthouse. Then he returned and got some more things out of the back of the battered white pickup truck: a guitar case, a heavy-looking file box and a cooler. I remembered he liked his beer nice and cold. The galley kitchen in the guesthouse would accommodate him. He came out once more for a garment bag, probably his suit for the funeral.

I had to run into town to get my hair touched up and to retrieve my black Dior outfit from the dry cleaners. As I waited at the counter, Doc's wife, Betty, sidled up to me.

"Kirsten, I am so sorry to hear about dear Dutch."

"Thanks, Betty. I guess it was just his time."

"Norman says he doesn't know why he lost so much weight the last few months. He's still quite puzzled about it but says it must have had to do with the heart disease."

"Sometimes it happens."

"Yes, that's what I've heard. We'll be at the service tomorrow, of course. Do you need anything?"

"No, thanks. Maria is coming to cook. She'll make sure no one goes hungry. The only houseguest is Dutch's oldest son, Harry."

"You take care, dear."

† † †

There must have been fifty guests at the funeral, which surprised me. I guess I didn't really know much about Dutch's earlier life. Harry's mother, Rachel, decided to pass on the festivities. After all, she had Harry there to represent her interests.

However, Destiny, wife number two, did turn up with her boys, Scout, eight, and Cody, eleven. There was no love lost between her and me as I had had an affair with her husband while they were married and she didn't see fit to forgive me. I had no respect for her because she actually signed a pre-nup without even getting a lawyer to look at it. Talk about stupid. Then she blamed me when she didn't get any alimony or property. Go figure.

Destiny and Dutch's youngest two kids still lived in the backwater town in Texas near some oil fields where Dutch worked before he started making real money. Scout and Cody didn't know Dutch and that suited me fine. Already tall for their ages, they had those danged square jaws just like his. I told the ushers to seat them in one of the rows behind me at the funeral parlor and at the cemetery.

The service went fine with Reverend Crouch from the Desert Sky Methodist Church presiding. People got up and said nice things about Dutch. Too distressed to do so, I cried behind my black polka-dotted veil. I had carefully applied more pink eye shadow and mascara I knew would run. Some of Dutch's former business colleagues actually sounded sad. They'd never had him come after them in a bedroom with bourbon on his breath and rage in his eyes.

Back at the house, Maria laid out a beautiful spread on the rough hewn oak table in the dining room and her husband, José, tended bar in the kitchen. I thought the guests would never leave.

When they finally did, Maria and José tidied up and said their goodbyes. Harry and I sat in front of the fire in the massive stone fireplace watching the embers. He took a pull on a cold bottle of beer.

"Well, I guess you'll be going back to your job in L.A. at the end of the week," I said, trying not to sound too happy.

"Actually, I'm between jobs. I think I'll stick around awhile until things get settled."

"Things?"

"Yeah. You know. The Will and stuff."

"Yes, of course. The Will and stuff," I said. "Well, make yourself at home, Harry."

"Thanks." He propped his feet on the ottoman. "I'll do that."

Ten days went by before the receptionist at the law offices called and set up a time for the reading of the Last Will and Testament of Edward "Dutch" McGraw.

Harry and I had been going our separate ways and pretty

much staying out of each other's hair but I offered to drive us to the lawyer's office in Carefree. Harry, however, said he would take Dutch's car, the gray Mercedes-Benz G63 AMG. That luxury SUV cost north of six figures and sat in the triple garage. I said, "Fine," and handed him the keys. I would get there just as fast in my red Prius and use about a hundred gallons less gas.

The firm of Johnson, Keyes and Donegal was located on Easy Street in Carefree's quaint downtown. Their offices took up the entire second floor of an old brick building. The beige decor gave a contemporary look to the renovated space. The receptionist directed Harry and me to Robert Donegal's office behind the glassed-in conference room.

When we entered, who did we see but Destiny McGraw sitting there smiling at Robert as though they were old friends. Harry looked at me with raised eyebrows. I shrugged.

As I expected, the Will left the bulk of the estate to me with a few thousand going to Harry and his mother. Destiny received a big fat zero. Apparently she expected this and rose saying to Robert, "My people will be in touch with your people." She pivoted on her five-inch spike heels and left.

Harry looked at Robert with bewilderment. "He told me he wrote a new will. One leaving me half of everything," he said, jumping out of his chair.

"Half?" I said, almost choking on the word.

"Sorry, Harry," said Robert. "He talked about revising his will over the holidays but he never actually came in to do it."

"I see." A storm cloud descended on Harry's face.

"We're done here, then," I said. My smile turned into a tight-lipped grimace.

When I got back to the house, I hid my purse behind a tote bag way in the back of the top shelf of my bedroom closet. I felt claustrophobic. Harry's outburst had shaken me since I had no clue Dutch had even considered modifying his Will. Thank God he didn't get it done.

Feeling the need for fresh air, I went out to the paddock and saddled Goldie. Dutch had named her Goldwater after the Arizona senator but I preferred the diminutive name. Rascal, the aging mixed-Shepherd dog, pranced around us in anticipation of an outing.

The late afternoon sun painted the mountains with a golden

glow. I rode out to Sunset Rock, a place Dutch and I had frequented when we first became lovers. Sometimes we'd bring a picnic and champagne, back before his bad behavior started. Oh, how I wished I could return to such an innocent time.

When we reached the rock, I just sat there for a long time wondering how I had gotten to this point in my life. My first marriage was normal. I probably would still be living in the Atlanta suburbs if my husband hadn't died of cancer. But then my life went in a whole new direction. The last few years had been mostly downhill. Now this. Thank heavens I'd had time to prepare—set up bank accounts, plan my itinerary, rent a condo.

The sun grew rosy, warming all the boulders and mountains as the sky turned azure, then lavender. Rascal curled up at my feet—a rare moment of peace.

I climbed up on Goldie and we headed back to the house.

The SUV was parked at an angle in front of the garage. It was covered in dust and had Dutch's mud-encrusted ATV on a trailer behind it. Harry must have taken it north up into the mountains. I decided to be less hospitable to Harry. It was time for him to move on.

The next morning I grabbed my wallet and keys and drove into town for a hair appointment. I returned after lunch. As soon as I walked into the house, I felt something was wrong. When I reached the master bedroom, my stomach lurched. Drawers were pulled out, clothes strewn on the floor. Shoes and boots were scattered across the carpet. My mind leaped to the checklist. I grabbed the tote bag off the closet shelf and reached for my purse. It was there but when I looked inside, the zippered pocket was empty. Who said he could do such a thing?

Harry found the list. So what?

I'm sure many wives have fantasized about getting rid of their husbands. Of course, they have. You just can take so much and you have to do something. And if you can't actually do something, then you write something down you would like to do. Like poisoning your husband until he dies. But you never would really do it. Would you?

They can't actually dig him up and test for poison, can they? Aren't there laws against that? Oh, why didn't I just have him cremated?

I ran over to the guesthouse. Harry was sitting on the

veranda, sipping on a beer. He was smiling. "Looking for something?" he said.

"No, but apparently you were."

"I don't know what you're talking about," he said, then gulped more beer.

"This is over right now. I will not tolerate your going through my personal belongings. I want you out of here first thing tomorrow." My voice rose to a near scream.

"Or you'll do what? Call the Sheriff?"

"You don't want to find out who I'll call." I snorted at him and turned back toward the house. I grabbed my purse and car keys and went out to my car slamming the door and leaving a cloud of dust as I sped away. I had some more research to do.

When I returned from the library several hours later, Deputy Luke Hays called and asked my permission to exhume Dutch's body. I said, "Certainly not." He said they would go ahead and get a court order to do it then. I would have to speed up my plans.

Luckily, my research on the library's computer had been very productive, once again. There was a most interesting video by a nice man dressed in a car mechanic's uniform. He showed how easy it was to disable the Antilock Braking System in an SUV by just removing the tiny little fuse that controlled it under the hood. I knew where Dutch kept the SUV manual in his study and discovered it was fuse number six. Piece of cake.

I also found the owner's manual for Dutch's ATV with a helpful illustration showing which hose carried the brake fluid. It said how important it was to make sure the hoses were in good condition and not cracked or leaking. That would be a very bad thing. Surely, it wouldn't be long before Harry headed back up into the mountains with his toys and a case of beer.

After the ten o'clock news on TV, I saw that the light was still on in the guesthouse. I peeked in the window. Harry was passed out and snoring on the couch, a row of empty beer bottles lined up on the coffee table in front of him. The full moon made it easier for me to find the fuse and hose.

I didn't take long to pack. I would only need a few swimming suits and beach dresses in the Bahamas. I could get anything else I needed with the fat bank account I had there. I tucked the boarding pass into my purse along with my passport and enough cash to last a few weeks.

✝   ✝   ✝

The next morning bright and early, I sat on the veranda in front of the house with my purse, tote bag and roll-on suitcase. A black Lincoln town car pulled into the driveway and stopped in front of me.

"Hello, Mrs. McGraw. Nice day to travel." The driver put the luggage in the trunk and held the door as I got into the car.

"Perfect day, Walter."

We turned onto the main road leading to the highway to the airport. Just as we started up the entrance ramp, I saw two Sheriff's cars turning in the direction of my house. Harry's house now.

My stomach growled as we accelerated onto the highway. I smiled as I realized I'd forgotten to eat the most important meal of the day.

✝   ✝   ✝

NANCY HART NEWCOMER was an award-winning advertising copywriter for twenty-two years. After retiring, she turned to fiction writing and had her first short story published in the Desert Sleuths' anthology, *SoWest, So Wild* in 2011. Her second mystery story was published in last year's anthology, *SoWest: Desert Justice*. She lives in Fountain Hills, Arizona, with her husband John and gray tabbies Thelma and Louise.

WOMAN IN THE MAZE
TONI NIESEN

Cara Little Dove Rivers placed her basket, the one she toiled so hard to make with *Gaga'a*'s tutelage, next to the collection of supplies. She arranged the coils of willow and devil's claw on the shelf. Her grandmother, *Gaga'a*, as she liked to be called in her Pima language, stored her basket-making supplies carefully, everything where it belonged.

It had been much more difficult to make her basket than she'd imagined. She'd roamed the reservation gathering willow in March, collecting cattails in July while they were green, and finally harvesting devil's claw from her grandmother's garden in the fall. The project had taken more than a year to complete. Now, it would make the perfect accessory to the traditional Pima dress she planned to wear in the Miss Native America Arizona 2013 Pageant.

As she closed the door to the supply cabinet, her older brother, Michael, burst in the door of the house they shared with their father and grandmother. He carried a pile of mail in his hands. "It came!" He held a magazine high above his head. "Check this out."

"What came?" Cara asked.

"My *Indian Arts* magazine. Look at the cover. What do you see?"

Cara took the magazine from Michael's extended hand and glanced at it. Her eyes froze in place, then zoomed in for a closer look.

"It's grandmother's inheritance basket. What did you do?" Cara threw the magazine on the kitchen table. "You better not let her see this!"

"Oh yeah. Like I'm scared already. What's the big deal anyway? She should be happy her basket is famous now. It'll be worth a lot more money after the publicity."

"Michael, you're an idiot. She won't be pleased." Cara sat at the table and put her head in her hands. "Don't you see? You've ruined everything for her."

"No, I don't see. What's the use of having it if no one ever sees it? Besides, I'm hoping to talk her into selling. I could use some money to pay off my bookie. I lost my ass betting on that last Vegas fight."

Cara rolled her eyes. "First of all, the basket isn't yours to sell. It was made to pass down to the oldest daughter in the family of each generation. That's happened for six generations now, and it would have been seven except grandmother didn't have a daughter to give it to."

"Exactly, so it should go to Dad, or better yet, to us."

"It's not for you to decide what grandmother should do with her basket. She doesn't like to tell people about it. She's private that way. I think it's partly because she doesn't want it stolen and partly because not everyone, especially some of the elders of the tribe would approve of the design."

"I don't get it," Michael said. "What's not to like about the design?"

"The man-in-the-maze design holds a lot of significance for the Salt River Community. Why else would we choose it for the tribal seal? It symbolizes life and how the choices we make in life impact our ability to meet personal goals. It guides us to reach harmony."

"So don't ladies need guidance too?"

"Of course we do. That's one reason I like the basket so much. But the original man-in-the-maze is thought to have been Elder Brother, not Elder Sister. I think that's why the inheritance basket includes both a woman and the standard design. It's a matter of interpretation, and grandmother wants to avoid any controversy if others on the reservation disapprove."

Lewis Whitman, owner of Southwest Antiquities Gallery in Scottsdale, pulled his procurement agent into his office and closed the door. He pointed to the cover of the *Indian Arts* magazine on his desk.

"Here's the deal. I want that basket. I have a female Hollywood producer on the string. She's anxious to get it and will pay up to six figures. Not only does she collect Pima baskets, but she's a feminist as well. It doesn't get any better than for her to have a basket with a woman-in-the-maze motif in her collection. Besides, the workmanship is incredible, and the design even includes the female figure holding another basket with the original man-in-the-maze. It's a basket within a basket no less. It's definitely something unique."

"Have you made an offer to the grandmother?"

"I've tried, but she won't talk to me. I've written, but no answer so far. I guess it has some special family significance. Michael, the grandson says it's passed on to each generation through the eldest daughter."

"That will make negotiating tough."

"Do what you can. The grandson wants to sell it. He's desperate for money, but so far he can't convince his grandmother. I'll give you double your usual commission if you can make the deal. We're talking about one of my best clients here, and I want to keep her happy."

The following day, Cara and *Gaga'a* sat together on the sofa finishing the appliquéd border of quail that edged Cara's traditional slim front-wrap skirt. The over-blouse made of the same creamy silk was simpler with only a geometric fretwork design around the neckline and short gathered sleeves. The costume was representative, rather than an accurate reproduction of a cotton Pima dress. Silk draped better and would flatter her figure when she walked on stage at the Chandler Center for the Arts.

"Thanks for helping me, *Gaga'a*. I hate finishing at the last minute like this, but I needed to jazz up my costume after I saw how beautiful Miss Navajo Nation looked in her deep purple outfit accented with turquoise jewelry. She's my toughest competitor for the title. Her talent is amazing, and she fields the interview questions like a media pro."

Gaga'a ran her fingers through Cara's gleaming black hair and pushed it back from her face. "Little One, you think she's outstanding? No one is as outstanding as my Cara. Don't worry about the other girls, just focus on Cara. Listen to your grandmother. You will make our family proud."

Cara gave the completed skirt to her grandmother and stood. "I think I hear someone at the door."

"Probably that pesky art dealer. Tell him I don't want to sell my basket. Tell him to go home."

A few minutes later, Cara returned to take her place on the

sofa. "You were right. It was the gallery man. He wanted you to name your price for the basket."

"You told him it wasn't for sale didn't you?"

"Of course. You should have seen his face. He seemed shocked you didn't want his money."

"It's not about money. It's about family. That's why I want you to have the basket. I didn't have a daughter, but I do have a beautiful granddaughter." She got up and put her hand on Cara's shoulder. "Come with me."

They walked into the kitchen and *Gaga'a* opened the door to the freezer. She pulled out a plastic wrapped package and handed it to Cara. "Here's the basket. You carry it tonight when you wear your traditional dress. It will give you the confidence of generations of our family's women."

"Oh, *Gaga'a*! Are you certain?"

"Of course I am. I've always known I would give it to you, and this is the perfect time. Now, I'm feeling tired. I think I'll take a nap. Wake me in time to help you get ready."

"*Gaga'a*. One quick question. Why did you have it in the freezer?"

"Oh, I put it in there from time to time. Helps keep bugs from making it their home."

Cara smiled. "Pleasant dreams, *Gaga'a*."

Stepping out of his black Cadillac Escalade parked in the casino employee parking lot, Victor Veronin and his two henchmen moved to intercept Michael on his way into the casino to go to work.

Victor stopped directly in front of Michael and turned to face him. "I hope you have my money like you promised. I think you know what's going to happen if you don't."

"I just need a little more time," Michael said, his voice quaking. "Please. I gave you the ten grand I borrowed, but I didn't expect the interest to double what I owed."

"Hey, what did you expect, that I loan you my money for nothing? The price has doubled again, my friend. Time is money. You offered me your basket. Well, the picture in that magazine was good for one extension, but if you want another, you have to give me the basket and give it to me now."

"I'm trying. I searched my grandmother's house last night when she was asleep. The basket was gone. It wasn't in the cabinet where she always keeps it. With all the attention resulting from the cover of that magazine, I guess she decided to move it. Or maybe she gave in and sold it to the art gallery."

"You guess?" Victor shoved Michael against a nearby pick-up truck. "Your guesses don't cut it. Let me tell you what I guess. I guess it's time for me to get serious with you like we did with that loser from the gallery. Let's just say he's not in the picture anymore, and you won't be either unless you pay up." He motioned to the two men standing behind him. "Go ahead." Victor backed up a few feet, rocked back on his heels and crossed his arms.

The men moved in. One held Michael from behind. The other stomped on Michael's foot with his boot. Michael's sneaker offered little protection. He screamed and slumped forward, but was pulled upright by the rear guard.

The man in the boots struck again, this time punching just below Michael's sternum. Three times he slugged him. Michael gasped for air. When they finally released his arms, he fell to the ground and tried to roll under the truck.

"Mistake," Victor said. "Drag him back."

After multiple kicks to Michael's ribs, Boots turned to look at his boss.

"Enough," Victor said, looking at a white security cart angling across the lot toward them. "You have twelve hours. Consider it my gift to you. Remember this. Tonight, I get the full forty thousand or you die. Your grandmother too."

The three men jumped in their car, leaving Michael lying on the pavement. He struggled to get up, but couldn't put weight on his foot. He waved his arm, motioning to the parking valet driving the cart.

"Help!" Michael managed to croak. "I need a ride."

The valet stopped next to him. "You look terrible." He pulled out his cell phone. "Who are they? Did you get their license plate?"

"No, forget it. I'm okay. Just drive me back to my car."

Cara touched her grandmother gently on the arm. "*Gaga'a*. It's time to wake up. We have to leave for the pageant soon."

"Thanks, dear. I'll be a few minutes. You get your things together while I wash my face and comb my hair."

Cara carefully placed her traditional costume, evening gown

and talent outfit in a full-length garment bag. At the last minute she'd changed her mind and decided to wear her original traditional costume for her talent presentation. It seemed appropriate since she was singing "America the Beautiful" in both the Pima and Maricopa languages. She'd decided on this approach because her reservation represented both tribes.

Opening a small suitcase, Cara packed her sandals with fiber straps to tie around her ankles and a pouch containing multiple strands of beads and shells to accent her dress. She added her carefully wrapped eagle feathers and her face paint and went to check on *Gaga'a*. She was surprised to see her grandmother still sitting on her bed.

"What's wrong? Aren't you going?"

"I don't think so, Little One. I'm not feeling well, and I don't want to spoil your evening. Your cousin Jerry promised to make a DVD of your performance so I can still watch you shine."

"Oh, *Gaga'a*. I'll miss you being there, but I want you to be well. Take good care while we're gone." Cara pulled a fleecy afghan from a drawer. "Here, you can snuggle up in this."

"Thanks. I'll just rest a little longer."

"Do you feel well enough to help me get ready before I leave?"

"What can I do?"

"Well, the traditional event comes first. I can't tie the eagle feather spray in my hair like you do, and you have a special flair with the face paint."

"Bring them here. It'll just take a minute." *Gaga'a* tossed the afghan aside and struggled to sit up.

Cara sat on the bed while her grandmother applied a few strategic white dots to Cara's face and attached the fan of feathers with a thin leather thong to strands of hair on the back of her head.

"There, that should do nicely. These feathers are almost as old as your basket. They've been in the family longer than I've been alive."

"I know I feel blessed to wear them. Thank you."

"They'll bring you luck," *Gaga'a* said as she lay back on the bed and closed her eyes.

Michael, his foot in a cast, hobbled into the Center for the Arts and hurried back stage to find Cara and *Gaga'a*. Two security guards blocked his way.

"Sorry, sir. No one is allowed back stage before the program.

"But I'm family," Michael protested.

"Sorry. We have strict orders. Space is limited."

Michael retreated and spotted his father in the audience. He limped over to sit beside him. He checked his watch again. Out of time, he thought. His father started to speak to him. Michael's phone chimed and he checked the text.

TIME'S UP. WE HAVE YOUR GRANDMA.
MEET AT THE HOUSE.

Michael left his seat without a word.

Michael spotted Victor's car outside the house. He parked and pushed through the broken front door. He had to make *Gaga'a* understand. She had to cooperate with Victor. He didn't want to think about what would happen if she didn't.

No one was in the living room so he headed for the bedrooms. Victor stood in Cara's room holding *Gaga'a* at gunpoint. One of his thugs held her by one arm.

"Look who's here," Victor said. "Okay Michael, tell your grandma what will happen if she doesn't hand over the basket."

"*Gaga'a*, please tell him where it is. I'm sorry I got us into this mess, but he'll hurt you if you don't do as he says."

"Michael, he can't hurt me enough to make me tell him. It would just lead to others being hurt."

Victor raised his gun and pointed it at Michael's midsection. "Maybe this will get your attention old lady. Do you want me to shoot your grandson?"

Gaga'a yanked her arm away from the guard and jumped for the gun.

Victor dodged, swung the gun at her head, knocking her down against the frame of the bed. "You're fast for an old woman, but not fast enough." He jerked his head toward his henchman. "Get her on her feet."

"Boss," he said, kneeling over her crumpled form on the floor. "I think she's dead."

"*Gaga'a!*" Michael leaped at Victor.

Victor sidestepped, the gun went off. Michael collapsed.

"Check one last time for that damned basket and let's get out of here," Victor ordered.

The men upturned furniture, pulled out vents and rummaged through the pantry and refrigerator. One man grabbed Cara's basket out of the cabinet and held it up. "I think I found it!"

"No, you fool, that's not it. But take it anyway. It's the best we can do for now."

Cara straightened the winner's crown on her head and drew Miss Navajo Nation and Miss San Carlos Apache closer so they could pose for the cameras together. She couldn't believe she'd won, and she couldn't remember when she'd been so happy. She called for her dad to take her flowers so she could pose for the final photos holding the inheritance basket. She would always associate this night with *Gaga'a* and the basket.

After the last picture was taken, Cara headed for her dad's car. "Where's Michael?" she asked. "I haven't seen him since I went back stage."

"I'm not sure," her dad said. "He limped in wearing a walking cast and sat next to me at the beginning of the program. He got a text and left."

Cara tried calling Michael, but he didn't answer. She tried calling her grandmother hoping if she were feeling better she would join them for a celebratory dinner. Again, no answer, "We need to get back to the house to check on grandmother. Maybe Michael's there too."

They arrived at the house fifteen minutes later. Something was wrong. The front door hung crookedly on its hinges, partially open. A lamp and her grandmother's laptop lay on the ground below her broken bedroom window. Cara and her dad ran inside.

"*Gaga'a*. Are you here?" Cara called out. She searched the rooms of the house.

"Over here," her dad shouted.

Michael lay on the floor in the hallway, bleeding from a wound in his chest, with a trail of blood behind him. Her dad bent over him, calling 911 on his cell phone. "He's unconscious."

"I've got to find *Gaga'a*!" Cara ran to her grandmother's bedroom. The room was ransacked like the rest of the house, but there was no sign of *Gaga'a*. She followed the blood leading from Michael to her own room where *Gaga'a* lay sprawled on the floor, one leg bent beneath her. Her head rested in a pool of blood at the foot of the bed.

"*Gaga'a, Gaga'a!* Please wake up." Cara knelt beside her and checked for a pulse. Feeling nothing, she lowered her head to her grandmother's chest, listened for a heartbeat, and started compressions. "No, no, no. You can't be gone.*"*

Cara didn't know what to do. CPR wasn't working.

"Dad! I need help."

Her father came into the room and watched for a moment before putting his hand on her shoulder. "I can't help, Cara. No one can. Not even the paramedics when they arrive. It's just too late. You can't bring her back."

Cara clung to his neck and sobbed into his shoulder. "Who would do this to her?" She raised her head and looked into his eyes. "Is Michael...?"

"Unconscious, but he's breathing. The ambulance will be here soon."

They returned to the hallway, and Cara bent over her brother. "Michael, help is coming. Just hang on. Can you hear me? Please tell us who did this..."

Michael's eyelids opened part way. "Victor did it. My fault. I'm sorry." His eyes faded out again, and his slowed breathing became even more ragged.

The tribal police arrived at the same time as the paramedics. The house was surrounded by official vehicles, their lights flashing. The paramedics confirmed they could do nothing for *Gaga'a*. They started an IV for Michael and loaded him into the ambulance.

"Please, I want to go with him to the hospital," Cara said.

"Sorry, can't allow it," the officer said. "We've got a homicide here. Otherwise, I'd send you to the hospital with an officer." He paused and raised his eyes from his notebook. "I've called the homicide detectives, the Bureau of Indian Affairs and the FBI. They'll all need to talk to you." He glanced at her gown and the ribbon that went with her title, still draped across her chest. "Sorry. It looks like you've had quite an evening."

Cara came home from her grandmother's funeral service and changed into jeans. Although emotionally drained and physically exhausted, there was something she had to do before she could say her final goodbye.

Michael wouldn't understand. She'd wait to tell him until

after he was able to leave the hospital. At least he could relax now that Victor and his cohorts were in custody. The police found them with both the gun and her basket still in their possession.

She went to the freezer and pulled out the inheritance basket. She clutched it to her chest as she remembered how much it meant to *Gaga'a*. Blinking back her tears, she wrapped the basket in multiple layers of bubble wrap, added a letter of explanation and double boxed it. She taped the boxes closed and attached a mailing label addressed to the National Museum of the American Indian in Washington, D.C.

Even though *Gaga'a* had wanted the basket to continue to be passed through the generations of their family, she wouldn't want future families torn apart because of it. This way many generations from many families could ponder the meaning of the woman-in-the-maze basket.

She knew *Gaga'a* would approve.

†   †   †

TONI NIESEN was born in Arizona. She lived in Alaska for two decades before returning to live in Scottsdale with her husband and grandson. She has written newspaper columns and several short stories including two published in previous *SoWest* anthologies.

LUCKY IN CARDS
R K OLSON

Big John raised his Scotch. "To Tony. Rest in peace, man." The annual toast. Our fifth or sixth of the night.

A chorus of "Tony," clink "Tony," clink, clink, followed by a slurred refrain of "Rest in peace…"

I tossed my shot and wiped my mouth with the back of my hand. "He can't rest in peace until we figure out who really killed him."

Grant scowled at me. "Goddamn it, Dewey. You say that every year. Let it go. It's been five years. He killed himself, okay?" Grant gave my right shoulder a little squeeze, harder than necessary. "There's nothing more to say." He slapped the deck down in front of me. "It's your deal."

I grabbed the cards letting one slip from the deck. As I leaned forward to snatch it off Big John's kitchen floor, all eyes focused on my cleavage. I sat up and did my best to look indignant.

"I just think we overlooked something," I said, shuffling. They lost interest in my chest and glared at me. If looks could kill.

Until Tony's death, every Monday night since high school I had joined Big John, Bobby, Grant and Tony in a game of five card stud, or some variation, four studs and one lady. Me. Kassandra Dewey. We'd shared drinks and stories for more than ten years. After Tony died what had been a weekly tradition became an annual ritual, minus the laughs, the four of us now getting together only on the anniversary of Tony's death.

We still gathered around the same table in Big John's kitchen. It seemed the three guys had moved on long ago, leaving me behind when it came to the subject of Tony's unfortunate demise.

The town sheriff, in what was his first official case and the single suspicious death of 2008, still stands by his original conclusion. It went something like this. In the early morning hours, after a night of heavy drinking at our tenth class reunion, Tony, my high school sweetheart, regular occupant of my bed, love of my life (or at least the only one who mattered) somehow made his way to the desert a few miles outside of town, put a .45 to his own head and pulled the trigger. Case closed.

Shuffling once more, I tapped the deck twice and dealt each player one card, face down. "Ante up boys."

The worst night of my life, and the last night of Tony's, began five years ago at our reunion, held at the recently remodeled Piñon Bar & Grill.

After a few drinks, dances, and banter with people I never really knew or liked, I lost track of Tony. I spotted him across the room, dancing with Marisa Cleator, class skank, whose various skills had landed her the coveted position of dispatcher for the Cajetan County Sheriff's Office.

I followed when Tony trailed Marissa to the parking lot and watched as he leaned against the trunk of her yellow Corolla. Her hand cupped his as he lit her cigarette. The hushed tones, furtive glances, vapor lights draining color from their faces, it was like a scene from some goddamn B movie. I watched for a moment.

But I'd seen this show before and knew the ending. I turned and walked back inside under the CLASS OF '98 banner, to strains of Garth Brooks, and half of my former classmates, singing "Two Piña Coladas."

I found Big John, Bobby and Grant at their booth in the bar. Along with Tony they had moved as a pack since fourth grade, with Big John as Alpha dog. Emphasis on dog.

"Umm, I'm really worried." I showed them my most innocent face...and lied. "The cops keep talking to Tony. He hasn't been himself lately. I just heard him talking to Marissa saying he would see her first thing on Monday morning. Do you think he's in any trouble?"

Big John stared into his glass of Scotch. "You hear anything else he said?" He raised an eyebrow.

"Not really. But I don't know why he would go to the Sheriff's office, do you?"

"Don't worry about it, honey. Tony's cool." Big John patted my back. "Anyway, none of us got anything to hide, right boys?" He and Grant exchanged glances then looked at Bobby, who nodded blindly.

I sighed. "I sure hope you're right." I felt confident that if Tony had a brief chat with his best pals they'd warn him off any further contact with Marisa Cleator. I hummed as I trotted off to powder my nose. A girl should look her best when she's fighting for her man.

Breathing deeply, I took a long look across the table, now stained and scarred and littered with peanuts and poker chips. I had known these guys for most of my life. It took a long time for me to understand I was never part of the posse. In the beginning they tolerated me. Then they used me. Hell, maybe I used them too. But they were Tony's friends, never mine. Depending on your definition of friends.

You spend so much time with a bunch of guys, you learn a few things. Number one, you can't trust 'em. You are simply the sum of your parts, if you are female. Number two, you can't trust 'em. And the aforementioned parts do not include your brain. Number three, you can't trust 'em.

Once I put all the pieces together about what really happened after the reunion, I realized I had all the tools I needed to even the score for Tony and me, and beat these guys at their own game.

I tapped a manicured fingertip on my lower lip, and then dealt the next round face up. I hit Bobby with the queen of diamonds, Big John with the king of spades, and Grant with the nine of clubs. "Grant, you show low." He threw in a chip and we all followed. I turned over a seven of clubs to Bobby, flipped Big John the ten of spades and Grant the ace of spades.

I remembered how as the reunion dragged on, I kept a close eye on the front door and spotted Tony as soon as he walked back in, his anxiety obvious as he scanned the room. He spotted me, and made his way through the crowd, giving me that hangdog grin I'd seen too many times before.

"Marisa Cleator? Are you that hard up?"

His smile evaporated. "We were only talking."

"I can hear the conversation in my mind." I turned on my heel.

"Kass, listen to me."

Looking over my shoulder as I walked away, I saw Grant

and Big John draw him into their huddle.

That night Tony was as handsome as the first day I saw him. My mother and I had moved to backwoods Arizona, right next door to Tony's house, just in time to start sixth grade. It was love at first sight, Tony and me.

By high school I had carved out my place in the group, sort of a good luck charm. And I charmed the pants off a couple of them. More than once. But by our senior year Tony and I had become inseparable. When we weren't bickering. At some point we reached an understanding. I understood we were exclusive, he understood he better not let me catch him with any more women. At least I thought he did.

He had a talent for love, let's call it a huge talent, and a brain for business. A girl could learn a lot from him. He excelled in school. He retained facts and figures. He should have been the best poker player, but he lacked a certain social awareness. Gullible and easy to read, I would spot Big John studying him and I could swear he knew every card Tony drew.

As I sat in Big John's kitchen, my mind slid back to a more simple time when five unsophisticated kids sat around this table, smelling of sweat and dust, John's mother pouring glasses of lemonade. "Kassandra," she said, "you grab those cookies I just bought and put them on a plate, will you? We need to feed these growing boys."

When she later remarried and moved to LA, Big John kept the house. To all appearances the guys hadn't changed much since then. John was bigger, much bigger, but you could still see the boy in Grant and Bobby. I had transformed from a tomboy into a woman who had learned how to use all of her assets.

I poured myself one more shot, and ran my fingers down the side of the perspiring glass with more than a trace of suggestion. "Grant you're high."

He tossed in two chips and I added three to the pile. By the time we got to this hand we'd been playing for almost two hours and as usual, Big John's stack had grown while the rest of ours shrank.

"She's upping the ante boys," Big John joked as he and Bobby each tossed their chips in the pot. He enjoyed making little digs at my expense. Nothing new. "I wonder what she's hiding."

I raised my palms and stretched my bare arms. "Nothin' up my sleeve." I laughed, just a little, smiling at Big John, then dealt the next round. "Seven of clubs to Bobby, nine of spades to Big John, and the two of hearts for Grant." I gave myself the jack of hearts.

Jack of hearts. I'd called Tony that more than once. Not that I felt insecure, but the man had an eye for the ladies. So I kept an eye on him.

Which is why it surprised me that he had gotten away from me that final night. At times since Tony's death it has crossed my mind that he really was meeting with Marissa to give up the operation, and I hadn't simply made that up. I'm still not sure.

What began as high school kids passing out a few grams of weed for pocket change had become an operation that included meth and a lot of stuff I'd never heard of. If it was illegal and you wanted it, Big John and the boys could probably get it. They stopped using but continued dealing, keeping themselves at arm's length from any transaction.

Turns out they weren't above removing anyone or anything that got in their way. I wish I had known that on the night of our tenth reunion.

Tony had known how much money they had stockpiled. And anything Tony knew, I knew. I had always thought it was small-time stuff until he showed me the books one night in early 2008. Their little operation had matured right along with all of us. I assumed their small fortune had multiplied since then.

"Last round." I placed a fifth card, face down, in front of each man.

I snuck a peak at my hand, like I couldn't remember what I was holding. "Show and tell time boys. Who's in?"

Grant stacked his cards and threw them to the center. "Fold."

Bobby stared at his hand. He looked from me to Big John and tossed them in. "Fold."

Clasping my hands in my lap I said, "Listen John, let's make this interesting." He raised his eyes and I flashed my purest smile. "What say I take over your little side business if I win this hand?"

Big John guffawed. "That's a little extreme isn't it Dewey? Especially from a girl who has never mastered the game of poker?"

Grant chimed in. "Anyway, what's in it for us? You got something of equal value to wager?"

I chewed on my lip. "If I lose, I will drop the subject of Tony's death forever."

The boys whooped as Big John shoved all of his chips to the center. "All righty then. I bet this nice big pile of chips plus," he winked at Grant and Bobby, "the deed to our very own, highly successful, uh…retail enterprise. I'm all in."

I matched him, repositioning my much smaller pile to the center. "So am I."

Big John sighed. "Ya know Dewey, since you are about to lose your stake for the ten thousandth time, I'm feeling generous. Here's a little tip. Stop chewing your lip when you're bluffing. It's a tell, and we all recognize it." One by one he rolled four more spades over his thick fingers. "Straight flush, king high."

I tapped my next card then laid the king of hearts on the table. "Maybe my tell is a bluff."

Big John laughed and took a swig of Scotch. "Kassandra, honey, you do know there's only one hand that can beat this?"

I flipped over a queen. Hearts again. Big John stopped laughing.

I showed my last card. Ace of hearts. All three men gasped. "Read 'em and weep, isn't that what you always say?"

Big John jumped to his feet, nearly flipping the table. "Now listen, Dewey. If this is some kind of joke, you need a better punch line. I'm not sure how you pulled this off, but there is no way you are taking over our business."

"I'm not joking. I won the hand."

He raised a fist then glanced at Grant and relaxed a little. "All right. We'll let you have the win. You can keep the kitty." He pushed the pile toward me. "Now, cash in your chips and go home before I lose my sense of humor, little lady."

I stared hard. "I don't think so."

His hand went to his hip, where I knew he holstered his gun.

I pulled my right hand up and pointed my small but deadly Hellcat pistol which I had pulled from my boot when I dropped the card. "Don't move."

His hand went to the holster. I fired, nicking his pinky. Big John screamed. I laughed.

Wincing, he shook his hand, scattering droplets of blood on

the cards. "What the hell, Dewey? You are some crazy bitch. You really think you are gonna milk our little cash cow for yourself."

"I do."

"Are we gonna let that happen, boys?"

I looked from Grant to Bobby. "Boys?"

Grant stared at me in disbelief. "Now just a...Take the money, Dewey. Let's all settle down. Last time I checked we were all friends."

I took a step back and tilted the gun toward them, one at a time. "Friends? Friends? You think you were Tony's 'friends?'" Ignoring the smirk on John's face I said, "It never crossed my mind that you'd kill him. You really thought he would give you guys up?" I kept my tears in check. For once. "You didn't give him a chance."

Bobby made a move. I took out his glass with a quick shot. Bourbon and glass shards pelted his right arm.

I shifted my weapon toward Grant and Big John. "Friends?" I hissed.

I wondered how long it would take them to realize Bobby had unburdened himself to me after last year's game. When he followed me home that night, it didn't take much to see Bobby was looking to come clean. I heard his confession. I said I forgave him. He believed me.

As Bobby told it, Big John laid out the plan for them while the reunion was winding down. He knew Tony held every detail about their operation in his mind. Tony could take them all down. Never one to get his hands dirty, Big John sent Grant and Bobby to do the deed. I knew they had made Bobby the triggerman to keep him quiet. Unlike the others, Bobby was saddled with a conscience. Killing his lifelong friend chafed like a burr.

Keeping an eye on all of them, I nodded to Grant. "You. *Friend.* You drove Tony home from the reunion after he and I argued and I left alone."

Grant took a quick look at Bobby who studied the beads of blood on his forearm, then said, "I...yeah, but I didn't drive him home..."

"No. No you didn't. Tony thought you were driving him home. But you drove him out to the desert."

Bobby glanced up at Big John.

Big John gave a slight shrug. "What are you saying, Dewey? You think Grant here killed Tony and made it look like a suicide? I can't picture that."

I fought the slight twitch in my gun hand as my impatience grew. "Can you picture Grant driving Tony to the open desert, where Bobby does the deed? Can you picture yourself as the mastermind who needs to get rid of Tony before he tells all to the new Sheriff? I can."

Big John leaned over the table. "Now. Hold on…" My next shot ricocheted off the souvenir Grand Canyon ashtray in front of him and dinged his silver belt buckle as he jumped back.

I suppressed the urge to blow on the end of my gun.

Grant, ever cautious, held his hands in the air. "It's your word against ours, Kass. Let's just take it easy here."

When Grant went for his pocket, I shot him. Dead. Revenge, for Tony.

"That's for driving the car."

Bobby screamed. Tears ran down his cheeks, he wiped his face on his shirt sleeve, leaving fine, red scratches on his cheek. He looked across the table at the body, then at me. "You killed Grant."

"Oops." I eyed Big John, shrugged, and chewed my lip. "Now, I'm gonna need all your paperwork. Clients, suppliers…supplies."

"Is this about Tony? Or are you just greedy?"

"Both." I swallowed hard. This was no time to get sentimental. "I only wanted you to warn him off Marissa…"

Bobby looked from Big John to me; tears flowed into little red-tinged rivulets rolling down his cheek.

"But you said he was gonna snitch."

"I didn't *say* he was about to snitch, I hinted at it. I wanted you boys to scare him, not take him out and kill him, you stupid…"

Bobby let out a yelp of pure anguish and hit his head on the table. Big John saw his opportunity and drew on me. Not unexpected. I aimed to kill. The big guy fell hard. Revenge, for Tony. And me.

Bobby went for Big John's gun when it hit the table. I let him. I couldn't picture him shooting me. I understood the remorse in his eyes. No surprise when the shot rang out and he ended his own misery.

I surveyed the damage. It turned out to be a bit more complicated than I had anticipated, but I felt certain I could clean it up and turn it into something that looked like a drunken suicide pact on the anniversary of their best friend's death.

I tucked the pistol back into my boot, heaving a sigh. "Looks like I'll have to find that paperwork myself."

† † †

A transplanted native of the Pacific Northwest, author **R K (RONI) OLSON** enjoys a downsized life in Scottsdale, AZ with her very good dog, Jemima. Visit her blog at http://ronisays.com. Roni is a former President of the Sisters in Crime Desert Sleuths Chapter.

WOMAN'S WORK
CATHY ANN ROGERS

Sipping her coffee and watching the other five around the table doing the same, Josefina was startled when she heard the soft wind rattle the water bucket hanging outside the kitchen door. Winter in Flagstaff was harsh compared to the temperate climate of her León in Mexico, and by its bleak nature, propelled her further into a sense of isolation and nervousness. Before she recovered, she heard another gust of wind whistle through the Ponderosa pines before slamming metal tools against the wood rack where they hung outside the garden shed.

The familiar sounds fueled an already tense atmosphere that Josefina saw on the faces of her husband, Ricardo, and their friends. In the nearby distance, she heard the comforting gentle snorts of the horses stabled in the structure across the yard.

Kerosene lamps scattered around the room and centered on the table, they leaned inward as if to keep warm even though the parlor stove was the primary heat source. The cooking stove upstairs in the kitchen and the parlor stove in the front room made the ground floor cozy this time of year, but down here in the basement, the penetrating coldness of the earth left a chill that made her bones ache.

"Are we all agreed to leave everything as it is for now?" The sound of her husband's voice brought her to the moment. "It's nineteen twenty. Times have changed. Not as easy to rob the stagecoaches and trains as it once was." Nodding in agreement, she knew she should pay more attention, but with the three men making all the decisions for their wives, she wondered what was the point.

Life had grown dull and her apathy had increased during the last couple of years. Compared to fighting with the *Soldaderas* in Mexico and supporting the soldiers behind the lines during the Revolution, the safe life of an American wife and mother in modern day Flagstaff was tame. No reason to run out in a fire spray of bullets to rescue soldiers, to shoot at the enemy with the two *pistolas* she had always carried, or to dress up as a man and fight in direct combat with the enemy. The security of her new life was to her a prison instead of a safe haven. At least the thrill of their daylight robberies of the stagecoaches and trains, made her feel alive. Now, as Ricardo had promised, that would stop and the six, with their children, would forget that life and settle into comfortable positions in this community.

Grinning at her own imagination, she found that visualizing shooting out Ricardo's kneecaps for sticking her here gave her a sense of justice and lightened her mood. At least enough to be civil after the others went home.

"What are you thinking about now, woman? I don't trust that sneaky smile you get sometimes," Ricardo said.

"Remembering the old days, that's all."

"The old days from two years ago, you mean. When we barely got out with our lives and had to sleep on dirt holding our guns? We did what we had to do and now we don't need to live like that anymore. I think the real problem is you got used to having that power and you miss it," he said pointing his forefinger between her eyes. "Well, society women are pampered and delicate and make their concerns the needs of their men and their children. They don't shoot people and ride horses bareback, and they sure don't rob stagecoaches. You need to get over that and get on with what God intended for you as a woman."

"Women are going to get the vote any day now. That is what God intended or it would not happen."

"It hasn't happened yet, has it? What a world that would be. Every woman cancelling out her husband's vote. That's not moral. I want to know what those Suffragists are up to anyway, taking over the world?"

"Yes. We want to take over the world and when we do, you'll be the first to go!"

Her next thought was how handy her pistol was hanging inside the cold closet, followed by the amusement of his shocked face when she shot him. As pleasing as the fantasy was, she would never kill him. Her children were not going to suffer the humiliation of knowing their mother was hanged for anything, much less for killing their father. He was right about one thing. The person she hid inside had no place in society now. Maybe things would change in her lifetime.

Waking up the next day, Josefina opened her eyes to a clear, crisp morning. Even with the brisk temperature, the sun was strong and warming. With Ricardo packing up to head to Phoenix for banking and the children sent to school in San Francisco for the winter, Josefina speculated that the day before her could be a soothing break or a monotonous bore. Icy windowpanes stung her fingers when she leaned in to survey her property and the surrounding neighborhood. A dusting of early morning snow deadened sounds on the street surfaces until the sun reached down to melt it, while the other homes seemed to draw themselves inward out of defense from the frigid winds.

"Leavin'," Ricardo said.

Smiling, she followed him downstairs to the kitchen and down the stairs to the basement door where they said their goodbyes. Her eyes followed him as he rode off down the hill and out of her sight. One day, she thought, they would get a horseless carriage. Then she could go with him on these trips.

Alone in the house, enjoying coffee before the morning chores, she had a start when she heard the basement door leading to the back yard open and shut. An unfamiliar pierce of fear shot through her midsection and froze her. Could Ricardo have returned? Before she had time to react, a man burst through the door in the kitchen that led to the basement stairs, aiming a gun at her.

"What do you want?" Josefina's dark eyes glassy with the jolt of adrenaline held his glare.

"Don't ask questions. Fix me something to eat."

"You break into my house for food?"

"Shut up, and get to cookin'."

His eyes, his manner, his agitation, the face of desperation, was familiar to Josefina. She had seen it before in Mexican soldiers. A need to escape from someone scarier than themselves meant they were reckless and dangerous, willing to do whatever they had to do to get out alive. She understood because she had lived it and knew the last thing she should do was to antagonize him. Suspicious eyes followed her as she went to the icebox and opened its right door to get eggs and bacon.

"What's in the other door? Open it." He used his pistol to point to the left side of the oak cabinet.

Moving to the right side of the icebox, she reached over to swing open the oak door that concealed the ice cabinet and drip pan.

"Never saw one of them fancy iceboxes. Okay, get on with it."

Using the cast iron skillet resting on the back burner, she dropped several slices of bacon to its warmed surface before turning to him. "Fire's low this time of day. Not hot enough to make a meal. I need more wood for the cook stove. It's outside the back door." With watchful eyes and his gun trained on her, she said, "Need more for the parlor stove too or this house will be as cold as it is outside."

"Get it and don't try nothing." He watched as she carried in an armful of logs, tossed one inside the cook stove, and the rest in a basket in the corner.

"Quit stalling and get on with it," he said.

Turning her attention to him from time to time, she continued cooking. Her advantage here was he probably assumed she was ordinary. With her five-foot frame, dark skin and round brown eyes, he would expect a feminine reaction. Taking solace in the belief she was too terrified to run, he would be confident that he could frighten her into submission. To keep him calm, she pretended to be afraid and intimidated. That would give him the feeling of dominance and would give her time to figure out how to handle him.

That Ruger pistol hidden in the cold closet was her best bet. Her problem was getting to the closet, grabbing the gun, pulling back on the hammer, all before he had time to react. If she were clumsy about it, she would not make it across the room before he shot her in the back.

While she took the bacon out of the skillet, she glanced over to find him looking not at her but out the window. So, she figured, he must be waiting for someone or was afraid of someone coming for him. This gave her a sense of urgency. One way or another, she had to deal with him before someone else showed up, and left her to subdue two men instead of the one.

Once the eggs had cooked, she dished up the food onto a tin plate and headed to the table. Keeping his gun aimed in her direction, his red-rimmed eyes darted from his plate to her as he started shoveling in food, swallowing without chewing.

"What's your name, woman?"

"Josefina."

"Where's your husband?"

"In town tending to business."

"You're a liar, Josefina," he said, speaking her name as a vulgar sound.

"He *is* tending to business."

"I saw him ride off, packed for a longer trip. It don't matter anyhow."

"Why did you pick my house? Why come up the hill when you could've stopped somewhere else."

"Simple. I saw your man leaving. Easier to handle a woman on her own."

Repressing an urge to laugh, Josefina kept her face soft and averted her eyes. She remembered Ricardo telling her she had dangerous eyes, and maybe she did. Dark, round, and piercing, the downward slant of her eyebrows expressed a deliberate sadness that could turn to anger in a flash.

An answer was not coming to her about what to do. Eventually, she would have to show her hand.

"Give me some of that coffee you got brewing there," he said, pushing away his empty plate and placing his gun in front of him. She poured his coffee and carried the large handled metal cup to the table. "Don't try anything with that boiling coffee or you won't live the seconds it takes to set it down."

"We're out of milk," she said, careful not to spill the hot liquid.

"Thought you'd be more scared. You're fair steady for a woman. Why is that?"

"Being careful, that's all. I don't want you to hurt me."

She continued avoiding eye contact with him and retreated to her place by the stove. She imagined that the old cur would think she was keeping her woman's place ever ready to serve the menfolk, and saw she was right when he relaxed long enough to sip the hot liquid. Sure he felt in control of her and the house, she waited for an opportunity to use that against him. First, she had to get her pistol from the cold closet.

"We might have milk in the cold closet over there."

"Okay. Git it."

Opening the door that concealed the cold closet, she reached in for a glass bottle of milk. Inside to the left, on a long nail hung her pistol that she kept loaded for emergencies. She turned her hip inside and knocked the Ruger into her apron pocket. A movement so swift, the only discernible clue was a new weightiness in her apron. When she brought out the milk, she walked to the stove and grabbed the dishtowel that she tucked into the waist of her apron, covering the sagging pocket. First step done, she thought, as she splashed milk into his cup.

As time passed, she developed a growing sense of urgency. Not knowing why he had to hide here and who or what he waited for, she started to give in to anxiety. Before she let that happen, she had to catch him off guard or take his mind off her long enough for her to get a shot. Do something that only a half-witted woman would do facing danger and sure death. Take some action to make him believe she behaved like a desperate female who acted without thinking of the consequences.

As if she had lost her mind, she started screaming for help at the top of her lungs. The impact had the effect she wanted. He lost his concentration and his temper, rushed over to her stumbling against the chair. He grabbed her by the arm, and slapped her across the face with, she was certain, the full force of his rage.

The blow sent her sliding across the floor. "Stupid woman," he said as he turned his back on her. Good, she thought, feeling the sting on her face from his rough hand. The assault made it easier to do what she had to do.

Rolling onto her back, she reached into her apron pocket and brought out the gun. Using both hands, she straightened her arms, locked her elbows, aimed, and pulled back the hammer. She saw him flinch in recognition as he heard the double-click the same time she did, but he could not react fast enough before she pulled the trigger.

Josefina watched the bullet make contact between his eyes, and then fired again in his left shoulder to make her shots appear wild for the benefit of the sheriff. The first shot jerked his head backward. The second shot dropped him in a heap.

A moment later, a dead man at her feet, she heard the sound of a single horse approaching fast, followed by an abrupt stop. After the sound of dismount, she heard her basement door open and shut for the third time that day. Annoyance mingled with anxiety, the adrenaline rush set her heart pounding and sharpened her mental acuity. She bent down to pick up the dead man's gun. She hid behind her kitchen's basement door and held his gun in firing stance. Heavy footsteps on the stairs grew louder. Tense, almost without breathing, she stood motionless as the door opened slowly.

The man coming through the door was cautious, but he moved with purpose into the kitchen without looking behind him. Josefina saw him recoil when he saw the dead man and raise his hand to his gun. Coming out from the back of the door, she slammed it closed with the bottom of her foot, took aim, and fired. A well-worn veteran of the outlaw class swung around in time for her to watch his surprised expression at the oncoming bullet.

Keeping her concentration and her calm, Josefina took his gun from its holster, and let it drop to the floor at his side. Rushing over to the first intruder, she returned his gun next to his hand. Her heart pounded through her clothes, and for the first time in hours, she felt cold.

Expecting the law to arrive any minute, she grabbed her thickest shawl before opening the kitchen door. Relieved to hear horse hooves on the snow-covered roads, she leaned against the wooden porch posts and hoped she looked like a convincing victim. If the sheriff knew the truth, he might start to figure out that none of the six were what they seemed.

After the sheriff and the undertaker had come and gone, Josefina sat at her kitchen table. Adding more wood to the cooking stove, she left its door open to feel the heat on her skin. Her worry about how to tell her story had been unnecessary, and she was amused at how they put it all together on their own. The two men, gentle and caring, had applauded her heroics. Portraying her as a defenseless woman lucky enough to know where her husband kept his gun and gutsy enough to use it to defend her home and her honor, neither bothered to ask the penetrating questions they would have asked a man under the same circumstances.

At one point, she started to laugh, hiding her face in her hands, leaving the sheriff to believe she was crying. For what it was worth, she was positive she had been taught a great lesson about complaining that her life no longer had adventure and danger. At the same time too, she thought maybe it is a great advantage to be underestimated.

† † †

Born and raised an only child in Cincinnati, Ohio, CATHY ANN ROGERS spent her early years listening to vivid stories by parents, relatives and other elders. After establishing her accounting and tax business, she resurrected her writing career with various short stories and her first novel, which presented the opportunity to showcase her interest in history. In the arid climate of the Arizona desert, she shares her home with two Bichon Frises, Whitney and Sophie.

FACES OF TIME
MARTIN ROSELIUS

Phoenix, Arizona, August 1953

Oscar Kruger inserted the iron key and unlocked the aged wooden door set flush against the adobe brick facade. The stuffy air in his clock shop provided little relief from the mid-morning sun that already sizzled. He glanced at the wall. The needle on the Mason's Root Beer thermometer pointed to ninety-three degrees. He shook his head and removed his green Alpine hat with the decorative feather. Closing his eyes, he fanned himself and took a deep breath.

The rhythmic ticking of more than a hundred clocks swept over him like a soothing breeze from the high country. One hundred ticks a second. Six thousand ticks a minute, 360,000 ticks an hour. Followed by a burst of one hundred bells, whistles, gongs and like-minded cuckoos.

This cacophony of chaos would burrow deep into the consciousness of any sane man, pushing him toward life's edge, but to Oscar, a bachelor and man of few words, it was the voice of his being and the pulse of his creative inspiration.

He allowed himself a rare half-smile, then stepped over to stand beneath the dusty ceiling fan, looked up and yanked on the frayed cord.

Having emigrated from Germany just after the Great War, Oscar had settled in Arizona and established Phoenix Clocks on the corner of Central and Osborn, in a weathered building that had been treated rather harshly by the passage of time. Despite his brusque demeanor and surly disposition, he had built, and for thirty-two years maintained a reputation for dependable timepieces with precision pendulum movements. His most popular clocks, imported from the old country, bore the traditional design of Bavarian cuckoos that appealed to America's growing middle class. But his passion and genius would be found in the back room where he displayed his western collection of pricey museum quality timepieces. A creative achievement of clock making never before seen in the world of modern horology.

Uninspired, and deeply but secretly tired of the traditional Bavarian theme originating from his birthplace, Oscar had embraced the icons of the American West, creating instruments of time measurement that featured custom woodwork surrounding each clock face. Exquisitely detailed reliefs of six-shooters, ten-gallon hats, horseshoes, lassos and bucking broncos created by a skilled Navajo woodcarver from the nearby reservation.

Though the expertly carved western detailing on the wood case made his clocks unique and highly prized, it was the faces that made Oscar an acknowledged master and captured the imagination of his discriminating admirers.

Astonishing life-size faces of craggy gold miners, slick card sharks, common horse thieves and bawdy saloon girls that seemed so alive, floating motionless in space, staring outward with haunting eyes from behind the clear crystal dial with the copper numerals.

The face behind the face.

The curious were often startled by the chilling accuracy of detail. The encapsulation of reality. "The face seems so lifelike," they would whisper.

Collectors were captivated by the incredible realism. "Truly genius," they would say.

Inspired by sculptures observed in European museums during his youth, Oscar had long envisioned integrating facial sculptures into his clocks, experimenting for years without success, until unexpectedly, a stray cat slipped into his shop, curled up and fell asleep in one of his clocks under assembly. He stared at the fuzzy feline through the glass pane and realized that in this case, art could not imitate life. Only life could imitate life.

At first, it was a bit of a moral struggle. But just a bit. Eventually he convinced himself he was simply helping out poor unfortunates whose lives had little meaning. Misguided souls. Drunks. Unemployables. Undesirables. Hobos, tramps and vagabonds whom he'd met along the railroad tracks, were lured back to his shop with the promise of rye whiskey and then doped with a mystery concoction that slipped them into a paralyzing sleep from which they'd never awake. Those with no hope of a future, who if asked, would surely surrender their lives for the sake of art, science, and immortality.

But Oscar didn't bother to ask.

After years of experimentation, filling a secret journal of notes, Oscar had the process down to a science, although it was as much an art as a science. His art could find a place for him in the finest museum; his science, the finest penitentiary.

His shop opened at 10:00 a.m. and closed at 4 p.m. Monday through Friday. The evenings and weekends were spent working on his creations. The basement, concealed beneath his business, served as his studio, fabrication workshop and laboratory. There he assembled the intricately hand-carved twenty-inch square clock case and five-foot tall base cabinet with the mechanical movements, and of course, memorialized the face in what might be called, a horological death mask.

His secret process required Oscar to master the varied skills of a surgeon, embalmer and taxidermist.

Two or three times a year an order from one of the far corners of the globe reached his mailbox as a result of the small advertisement he renewed monthly in *Clock Time* magazine, the world's leading horological publication. The text never changed.

UNIQUE CLOCK FACES
CUSTOM ORDERS ONLY
WRITE FOR DETAILS

The ad displayed a black and white photo of one of Oscar's unique creations to showcase his style and craftsmanship, although the grainy picture never did his work justice.

On this particular morning the postman dropped off a handwritten envelope with a return address postmarked, London, England. The letter went on to identify the sender as a scholar of world history and a passionate admirer of the American West. A wealthy industrialist, he inquired about commissioning a clock that might showcase the face of an American Indian warrior surrounded by appropriate Indian cultural artifacts. He would pay whatever Oscar deemed appropriate.

Oscar held the letter in his hand and settled into deep thought. *An Indian warrior? Hmmm, a small challenge certainly, but with my genius, and for the money, I will find a way.*

† † †

Navajo Indian Reservation, NE Arizona, three months later

Billy Snow-on-Mountain Johnson raised his head up as Ajei, his wife, stepped through the door of his workshop, a wood-sided shack with a corrugated tin roof and wood burning stove that smelled of raw wood chips, earth and sweat. She moved closer as his fist, gripping a mallet, hesitated in mid-air. She leaned down, examined his work with a look of contempt. "Why do you do this for the man?"

Billy glanced back down, dropped the wooden hammer, striking the chisel handle with a thud. A small wood chip flew up, flipped over and dropped to the ground where it joined a large gathering of similar shavings. "He pays me."

"Not enough."

"It is steady work."

"I do not like this man. He carries *Tchin'dih*, an evil spirit with him."

"He is an artist like me."

"No. He works with the devil spirit. I feel it when he comes. I see it when I go to the shop with the timepieces. This work you do will lead to bad things."

Billy rested the tools in his lap. He paused a moment. Looked up and studied Ajei's eyes. He glanced down at the piece he was working on for Oscar the clockmaker. A bow and arrow. A spearhead with feathers. Warrior's weapons. The intricate carvings of the frame to be mounted on the case surrounding the clock dial. He, like Ajei, had felt the evil too. He asked himself, *Who will be the face of the warrior? Whose spirit will live in the face of the white man's clock?*

† † †

Two weeks later

Oscar paced back and forth in the showroom of his clock shop, occasionally stepping to the window, pulling the curtain and staring out. *Dammit, these people are never on time.* He had been expecting the Indian wood carver, Billy Johnson, to drop off his latest work. Oscar pulled a handkerchief from his pocket. Wiped his brow. He felt a twinge. Pain shot down his left arm. He grimaced at the sharp sting, a recurring discomfort that had overcome him the past few days. He shook it off as weather related. It was the first of winter, the temperatures had cooled but the shop remained warm and stuffy on this late Saturday afternoon.

A battered pickup the color of rust, the motor clacking with a staccato beat, pulled to the curb. The driver silenced the engine and a moment later stepped out clutching a package wrapped in a burlap sack. As Billy approached the entrance, Oscar moved from the window, slid the hand-bolt and pulled the door open. Billy hesitated. With a nod, Oscar urged him to enter before closing and locking the door behind him.

Oscar led him to the back room where he pointed to a table he had cleared. "Let me see what you have, my friend."

Billy stood in the doorway, his eyes scanning the collection of clocks. The faces that peered from behind.

Oscar noticed his interest, but it was not unusual. Billy had always seemed in awe of his masterful work. One artist admiring another. Yes, Billy was in awe of the master. Oscar nodded. "Come. Come quickly. I am anxious to see this latest piece."

Billy shifted his eyes to Oscar and moved with cautious steps toward the table where he gently set down the package held tight with a manila cord. Oscar brushed him back with his hand as he stepped up. His fingers worked the knot then pulled away the multiple layers of burlap, exposing the wooden carving of the Indian warrior motif. Oscar's eyes widened. He licked his dry lips and ran his hand through his silver beard. "Magnificent. Your best work yet."

He rubbed his fingers along the edges, feeling every crevice. Following every detail. He began to hum as he often did when excited, and beneath his breath mumbled, *"Wunderbar! Ahh, fantastisch, mein Freund."*

After admiring the work, Oscar covered the piece with the burlap once again and turned to Billy. "Come. Let us sit and have a drink. We must celebrate."

Oscar walked over to his wooden desk in a corner of the front room. The place where transactions were handled, money collected, bills paid. Billy still seemed hesitant. "Come. Come. I have the finest rye whiskey in the West. We must have a toast to celebrate."

Billy took a few slow steps.

Oscar sat down in the leather chair behind the desk, pulled

open the right-side bottom drawer, and retrieved a dark bottle with an ornate label and two ceramic cups.

He pointed to a wooden side chair. "Sit, my friend. Let us enjoy a drink."

Oscar poured a shot in each cup, pushed one toward Billy and gestured with his open palm. Billy hesitated a moment, watched as Oscar tipped his own glass, then sat down and reached out.

A soothing burn ignited Billy's throat as the dark liquid warmed his chest. He set the cup down and stared at Oscar. He had known this man for nearly ten years. Though he admitted to himself, he didn't really know him. He was not one to befriend easily, let alone trust. Billy knew Oscar took advantage of him. Paid him little for the fine work he produced. But there was not much of a market for his woodcarvings. Navajo weavings, yes. Ceramics and jewelry, yes. But tourists were not interested in his carvings. He had to make a living. Even if it hardly supported his family.

He glanced toward the back room and the collection of museum quality timepieces. The hands moving forward with each tick even as the faces remained frozen in time. Ajei was right. Oscar carried *Tchin'dih* with him. And it was strongest in the room with the faces.

Oscar leaned forward as if studying him. Squinting, he grinned. "You have the perfect warrior face, my friend." The two men raised their cups and drained the last drop. Oscar lifted the bottle of dark liquid. "How about another?"

Billy shook his head. "No. I must go. I have a long journey ahead."

Oscar stared at Billy a moment. Hesitating. "Before I pay you for your services, and because I am so pleased with your latest work, we must seal our deal with a special elixir. It is from the old country. I have been saving it for just the right time." Oscar leaned back down and pulled out another bottle, capped with a cork. He removed the plug with a twist, and set the bottle on the desk. "One drink of this and you will feel like a new man. All your troubles will be forgotten."

Billy glanced from Oscar to the bottle but said nothing.

Oscar lifted it, reached over and poured a full shot into both mugs. Gray milky liquid gurgled out and splashed against the curved ceramic surface, leaving a dark stain as it settled into a pool at the bottom. A bitter odor rose from the cup: white man's medicine, tinted with the scent of acrid chemicals like those found under the hood of his pickup. Billy stared down at the mixture.

Oscar gestured with his open palm. "Come, my friend. We can't finalize the deal until you drink. Think of this like one of those spirit ceremonies you people do."

Billy reached out, gripped the mug. Lifted. Touched it to his lips. The smell nearly made him gag but he wanted to appease Oscar. He wanted his money. He wanted to get home to his family.

As Oscar's cup sat on the desk, he urged Billy on. "Chug it, Billy. It'll do you good."

Billy tipped the cup. The liquid burned his lips. But not like the whiskey. A few drops settled on his tongue, hit his throat. He lowered the cup to his lap, hidden from Oscar, then, as he gave out a whoop, he discretely poured the remaining liquid into his boot where it was quickly absorbed by his wool sock. He then raised the empty cup to his lips and feigned a quick chug, relinquishing a loud gasp as he wiped his mouth with the back of his hand.

"See, that wasn't so bad, now was it."

Billy swiveled toward the voice. His head felt like it would explode. His eyelids heavy, began to droop. Oscar's face became a blur. His mouth was open. Wide. So wide. Billy grabbed his ears as a thunderous laugh rocked in his head. The room tilted left. Then right. Billy reached for the desktop, knocked over his mug. It crashed to the floor and shattered. He tried to grip the edge of the desk. His arms slipped against the wood surface. His body, too heavy to hold upright. He slid further to the side. His head thumped against his shoulder. His world went black.

Oscar chuckled as he lifted the rye whiskey bottle by the neck and took a long chug, setting the now empty container down on the desk with a satisfied clunk. "I'm sorry my friend, but the Englishman made me an offer I couldn't pass up. You did good work, but I can find another wood carver." Oscar chuckled again. "Maybe even from among your own people."

Thirty minutes later Oscar had moved the body down a hidden stairway to his studio/laboratory located directly below his shop. A maneuver that as the years passed and Oscar aged, had become more difficult and left him exhausted. Though the room was cool, his shirt had soaked through with sweat. He sat down on a chair, next to the table where Billy lay, took a few deep breaths and removed his glasses to rest his eyes.

CUCKOO! CUCKOO! BONG! TWEET! TWEET! DING! CLANG! BONG! CUCKOO! DING! CLANG! BONG!

A dozen clockworks erupted to announce the hour. The sudden outburst surprised Oscar as his mind had drifted from exhaustion and the warm whiskey. He flew out of the chair. Tried to steady himself as his eyeglasses toppled to the floor. The room appeared a blur, but through his fuzzy vision he caught sight of a figure. A man. The man was sitting upright on the table next to him, staring. The face, though distorted, seemed familiar.

Oscar's heart pounded. "Ah...ah..." He gasped for breath, stumbled, his shoe crunching something beneath it. He dropped to his knees and brushed his hands in a frantic circular motion, searching for his eyeglasses. He felt with his fingers, touched something cold, wiry. Yes. He slipped them on, blinked through one shattered lens. He lifted his head. His eyes shot upward. The vision of the figure had become clear. "Ah...ah...you're... you're supposed to be..."

Billy shook his head back and forth, rubbed his face. Blinked. He stared down, his deep dark eyes penetrating, his lips white, crusty. "No, my friend. I am not dead. But I think it is time we continue with the spirit ceremony."

A sharp pain gripped Oscar's chest and shot down his left arm, leaving it dangling. His eyes bulged. He gasped. Sucking in air, he reached out with his right arm. "My...God! Help...me..."

Billy slipped off the table, steadied himself then glanced toward the stairway. Leaning down, he whispered. "I will go to your desk and return with your special elixir from the old country. The cup you never brought to your lips. One swig and you will feel like a new man. All your troubles will be forgotten."

Oscar collapsed to the floor, and watched helplessly as Billy turned, walked away and disappeared up the stairs.

† † †

Five weeks later

The two patrolmen sat in their squad car passing idle chat as the locksmith pulled his panel truck to the curb. All three men stepped out of their vehicles and walked to the locked door of Phoenix Clocks.

"Can you open it?" The first officer asked.

The locksmith turned to them with a sly grin. "Haven't found one I couldn't."

The officers glanced at each other with raised eyebrows.

The locksmith rummaged through his tool kit and retrieved a small cloth bag. He selected one thin rod with a hook and inserted it into the lock. After a bit of wiggling and jiggling, the lock clicked, and he pushed on the door.

The patrolmen exchanged another look, then the first officer stepped in. A beam of sunlight bathed the entrance, but the corners of the room remained in darkness. He removed his flashlight from his belt and swept the room. Finding a light switch, he flipped it, but no power existed. The room was cast in silence. The clocks had sounded their last tick and the hands had come to rest at random times as the weights had halted from the lack of gravity and the pendulums had come to a complete standstill.

He took a few steps, leading the way for the second officer and the locksmith. Bright beams of light swept the room, highlighting individual clocks mounted on walls and sitting on shelves. The first officer wiped his finger across a shelf leaving a glossy streak of underlying wood beneath the thin layer of dust.

The locksmith stayed close to the second officer, following his steps. "Whatcha looking for?" he whispered.

"Missing persons report. Apparently no one's seen the owner for weeks. Mail hasn't been picked up. Bills aren't being paid. Had numerous inquiries from concerned citizens."

"You think he's dead?"

"That's what we're here to find out."

The locksmith stopped. Turned to look behind him. "Ah . . . hey, why don't I just wait outside?"

"Good idea. But don't leave until we tell ya to. Got it?"

"Yes, sir."

The officers continued on, passing through a doorway into

the back room, their lights sweeping a clear path. "Jeez, would ya look at this."

The second officer stepped in. "Holy cow. Look at them clocks."

"Yeah, and those freaky faces."

"Creepy as all get-out, ain't it?"

They stood side by side, their flashlights scanning the room, bouncing from one masterful clock to another, soon landing on one in the back row. It was unlike any of the others as the surrounding hand-carved wood frame didn't have a western motif, but rather displayed the traditional design of Bavarian cuckoos: a Black Forrest chalet, oak leaves, acorns and an Alpine hat with a small decorative feather. "Check this one out."

"Jesus. The eyeglasses have a shattered lens in them."

"Yeah, and check out that pained expression on that face. Looks so real."

The officers continued to stare with a growing sense of unease before the first officer spoke up. "Come on, Frank. Let's get going. File our report. Ain't no one here."

†   †   †

One year to the day later

Billy Snow-on-Mountain Johnson glanced at the Mason's Root Beer thermometer attached to the wall of his new studio, a hogan set behind his home on the Navajo reservation. The needle pointed to seventy-three degrees. Today would be a warm one on the high plateau tucked into northeast Arizona.

Ajei, his wife, opened the door. "The buyer from the art gallery is here."

Billy stood and stretched. He'd been working long hours over the past few days polishing and applying the finishing touches on his latest sculpture after picking up the bronze casting from the foundry. The first in a new series after completing a group of seven icons of the American West: bronze busts of craggy gold miners, slick card sharks, common horse thieves and bawdy saloon girls. Faces sculpted in clay by an up-and-coming master. Cast in bronze, they seemed so alive they captured the imagination of his discriminating admirers, those who shopped the galleries in the fast growing art district in Scottsdale, Arizona.

The gentleman stepped into the studio and the two men shook hands. "Hello Billy, good to see you again."

"And you, Mr. Steinberg."

"So, what have you got for me? I must say, I'm a little curious, as you haven't mentioned what it is you're working on."

"Yes. This one is special. Although it may not be typical of my sculptures of the past. It is a new direction for me. A new series I call Craftsmen of the West."

"Craftsmen?"

"Yes. Merchants, shopkeepers and craftsmen. Those who helped build and settle the towns and communities in the American West."

"Hmmm." The buyer paused a moment as he glanced around the studio. "Okay, Billy. Let's see what you've got."

Billy stepped over to the table and in one quick motion lifted the white sheet that had been draped over a bulky object.

The buyer moved closer, leaned down and studied the masterful work. "Magnificent, Billy. Your best work yet. And the realism." He rubbed his hand over the smooth bronze face, like a caring grandfather. "What do you call this one?"

"I call it 'The Face of Time'." Billy glanced at the thermometer mounted on the wall, then back to the sculpture. He leaned against the table, crossed his arms and allowed a rare half-smile to slip across his face. Yes, this was his best work yet, the authenticity, the realism, right down to the cracked lens in the clockmaker's eyeglasses.

† † †

Following a career in graphic design/illustration, **MARTIN ROSELIUS** channeled his creative energies into the art of writing, having completed an espionage thriller, YELLOW BLOOD, RED FEVER, and a suspense novel, LAST SHADOW OF THE CROWN, set in Esfahan, Iran, where he lived in the late '70s. His publishing credits include: *Caribbean Travel+Life* magazine, *Mystery Readers Journal*, short stories published in three SinC Desert Sleuths anthologies and 3rd place winner in the 2010 Society of Southwestern Authors writing contest.

THE SUN CITY ZONE
AMY SCHUSTER

You're travelling through another dimension, a dimension not only of failing sight and unyielding sound, but of collapsing minds, a journey into a geriatric land whose boundaries are that of an addled imagination. Your next stop: The Sun City Zone.

Meet Delores Finch your average octogenarian, wife, mother, grandmother. She knits, plays bridge, drives a Lincoln Town Car real slow, makes only right hand turns and never goes to a restaurant without a coupon. Her ordinary twilight years are about to unravel as she desperately clings to the faded memories of a glorious youth. A desire for revenge takes center stage shattering her moral compass and igniting the dark side that lurks within.

The rubber soles of her orthopedic shoes made little noise as she shuffled along the path behind Tabitha the tiny Maltese who was tethered by a pink leash. Their pace was slow, the years bearing down on both of them as they passed the repetitive themed, low maintenance yards with green rocks and citrus trees. Her mind wandered as the periwinkle hovered above them, but a foul mood festered, as she dwelt on the bitter loss she'd suffered almost two months ago. It was a heavy weight inside her. She wished she could cut it out and be done with the agony slowly eating her alive but it wasn't that simple. She shook her head trying to rattle loose the evil thoughts driven by revenge and blind jealousy. She sighed, releasing a heady breath as the little dog paused to sniff the air before continuing on.

The duo turned up the drive toward the red door of home, the little dog's nails clicking along the concrete in perfect time.

Inside, Mel was seated at the round table covered with daisy print vinyl pouring over the sports page, readers settled on the bridge of his nose. The smell of boiled eggs and instant coffee hung in the air. "How was your walk?" he asked over the lenses as she unleashed the dog.

"All right," she said in a dull voice.

"You don't sound all right."

She sat down and picked up her cold cup of tea from earlier and took a sip. "You know I was robbed," she said out loud setting the cup down and avoiding his glance. She loved him like nobody's business. He was the peanuts in her Crackerjacks but she was lost to him right now, unable to let go of the raw emotions that boiled inside of her.

"Dee Dee don't. Let it go, it's been months," he said as he scooped up Tabitha and nuzzled his face to hers. "I hired a man to paint the shed. He's out there now," he said. "Why don't you make him some lunch, take your mind off things. He looks like he could use a good meal."

"Where did you find him?"

"He knocked on the door while you were out walking. Said he needed some work so I offered up the shed. Lord knows I didn't want to paint it. I better run or I'll be late for my tee time," he said standing slowly, hitching his pants up over his pot belly.

She washed up the dishes and dried them by hand before putting them away. Then she sat down at the kitchen table to consider the crossword puzzle. "An eleven letter word for physical beauty, starts with P," she said aloud before tapping her pen lightly on her temple. "Pulchritude." Then she laughed as she inked in the word nodding her head.

Through the window she saw the man painting the shed. She watched him from the quiet of the room as the clock ticked softly. He was young maybe thirty, and moved slow for his age she thought. His hair was in need of a cut, the copper ends curling around his neck. There was a red and white bandana hanging from the back pocket of his jeans which were baggy on his frame. His skin was dark from the sun, t-shirt faded blue, lips set in a line while he concentrated on the steady, bold stokes of his work. She felt that odd sensation of watching someone who wasn't aware, like stealing. Tabitha clawed her leg lightly before jumping up into her lap. Delores worked her fingers over the dog's silky fur while she watched the man. "Maybe he can help me right this wrong," she said as she raised her generous behind out of the wooden chair to make his lunch.

Delores stepped out onto the patio carrying a tray and set it on the table under the awning. "I've made you some lunch, liverwurst on toasted white with sweet gherkins, potato salad and homemade chocolate chip cookies. I bet you could use a break, come on over and sit down." She motioned toward the table.

"That's mighty nice of you ma'am," he said pulling out the bandana to wipe his hands as he sat down in front of the tray. "Wow, this looks great!"

"Go ahead, dig in. I've already eaten. I bet that's like your mother used to make."

"No, she was more of a pop tart sort of mom and I'm not talking Brittany Spears. She did the best she could, being section eight and all."

"Section eight?"

"You know, crazy," he said raising both of his hands in the air and shaking them.

"Where is she now?"

"A halfway house in Yuma, she's been there for years. They tell me she isn't ever going make it more than half way. You know what I mean?"

His question hung in the air between them without reply as he ate. She paused in the silence, sizing up the content of his character, noting the heavily tattooed forearms and the deep scar through his right eyebrow.

"What's your name?"

"Bo."

"It's nice to meet you. Are you from around here?"

"No, just passing through. I'm on my way to Vegas," he said raising the glass of sweet iced tea. "Man that's good."

"I wonder, no, it's probably too much to ask," she said twisting her wedding band with the fingers of her right hand.

"What?"

"Well, someone stole something from me and I'm wondering if you'd be willing to get it back," she said batting her drooping eyelids, a slight smile right where she needed it, revealing yellowed teeth, she palmed her jowls on a propped elbow.

"Who?"

"Phyllis Keats."

"And what did she steal?" he asked.

Reaching into the pocket of her apron she pulled out a recent photograph of herself and another old woman wearing bedazzled evening dresses, satin sashes and pasted on smiles. She laid it on the table in front of him. "That crown."

"But it's on her head. Possession is nine-tenths of the law."

"Exactly and it shouldn't be. We both competed in the Miss Sun City Beauty pageant, I was the runner-up. I am a seasoned pageant veteran with three titles to my name: Miss Wall Drug nineteen forty-six, Miss Corn Shucking Queen nineteen forty-seven, and Miss Road Kill nineteen fifty-one sponsored by the Maine Taxidermy Association, which I'm obligated to mention for trademark reasons. I had it all sewn up," she said with a despondent wail.

"Don't the judges decide?" he asked.

"Look at that dress she's wearing, it's clearly against pageant protocol to expose that much flesh. I was robbed of the crown by her salacious ways. She's a cheat. First of all, I think she doctored her birth certificate. The contest rules clearly state that you must be at least eighty years old. Frankly, I don't think she's a day over seventy-five. Then there was her mysterious absence during the canasta tournament. Rumor has it she was down in Mexico getting 'the works' done," she said as she made quote signals in the air with her fingers. I saw her bribing the judges with gifts of her peach preserves and heavy-handed pours of apricot cordial. I'm no racist but she is Canadian. I clogged circles around her in the talent competition. Since when is hoola-hoopin' a talent anyway? She dropped it twice before Doris Day finished the final chorus of "*Que Sera, Sera*". I had a lock on that competition I tell you. It's mine," she yelled pounding her fist on the table and making everything on it tremble.

"What is it you want me to do?"

"Go to her house tomorrow, it's down the street from here. There won't be anyone around, it's Senior Day at the casino, free hotdogs and ice cream cones. You can walk right in, no one locks their doors. She keeps the crown in a curio cabinet in the dining room. After you bring it to me, I want you to go back and start a fire in her bedroom. I stuffed my old support hose with excelsior that I've collected from fruit cake gifts over the years for you to use as an accelerant. Start the fire and run."

"What's in it for me?" he asked, his head cocked upward, black pupils holding a steady bead on her.

"I'll give you this ring. It's a family heirloom. It belonged to the other Mrs. Finch, my mother-in-law, old ironsides. It's valued at ten thousand dollars. Not bad for a few hours' work."

She laid the magnificent bauble on the table top between

them. The center stone was a five karat pear shaped ruby surrounded by row after row of cascading diamonds that flowed away from the center like water.

"Why burn the place? Isn't getting the crown enough for you?" he asked leaning back into his seat, tenting his fingers.

"If you burn her house down, chances are she won't have the energy to enter the competition next year. Call it preventative," she said.

"Some might call it evil. Are you sure you want to go down that road?"

"Look at you all smug in your youth. You think you're so smart. Well take a good look around pal because this is where you're headed," she said with a sweeping gesture, her upper arm flab fluttering.

"I didn't want to be old at all, but time struts like a pimp through the ages sparing no one. Your skin won't fit, your muscles will ache, your spine will curve, hair will grow everywhere except on your head. You wake up one morning and you're long in the tooth, barnacles are bursting forth all over your body, thin skin that tears like tissue paper. Your willie won't work and you're reduced to begging your primary care doctor for Viagra samples."

"All right, stop. I'll do it. Just shut up, you're freaking me out," he said trying to shake free the images of her words. "Let me see that ring. Since I'm heading to Vegas, maybe it's hot enough to get me on Pawn Stars."

Delores held the crown gazing at the spiraled prongs adorned by diamonds that sparkled in the vanity lights shining down from above. Her eyes misted as she settled it on top of the Kitty Carlisle wig that graced her head. She lowered her gnarled hands and folded them together as she drank in the beauty of her reflection. She was young again, a mirage as real as that of a thirsting man in the desert. She skimmed her fingertips over the velvety softness of her face, tears trembling, hypnotized by the vision of yesteryear that she thought she would never see again. She took out her tube of ruby red lipstick and laid it on thick blowing kisses in the mirror. Off in the distance the siren of a fire engine blared.

Later that day she was sweeping the kitchen floor, her nylon knee highs bunched down around her ankles, the crown and wig still holding court atop her head when the doorbell rang.

"Afternoon Ma'am," the officer said removing his hat.

"Can I help you?" she asked.

"Depends. Is your last name Finch?"

"Yes, that's my last name. Why?"

"There was a house fire up the street. We saved the house but not before a young man died of smoke inhalation inside. It looks like the highly combustible nature of Queen-size pantyhose and excelsior surprised the naive arsonist. We found this ring in the pocket of his jeans. The name Finch is engraved inside the band. The homeowner's also reported a crown missing. You wouldn't happen to know anything about that, would you?" he said as his eyes darted toward the top of her head.

Delores Finch pleaded no contest to the charges. Considering her advanced age and feeble mind the judge remanded her to a different sort of institution. She resides in a semi-private cell that smells of old skin and urine. It's approximately ten by ten with a thin curtain down the middle separating the shared space. She's free to roam the halls lined with the dilapidated bodies of yesterday's beauty queens and the virile men that turned them to mush once upon a time. The outer doors are locked keeping the detritus hidden inside from those who would rather not see their future.

Her husband Mel visits every day, pinning a crown onto her head before she shuffles along the linoleum perfecting her parade wave, as the chanting voices of the other inmates cry out "Queeny, Queeny," in the Sun City Zone.

† † †

Amy Schuster is a native of Phoenix, She loves to read, write and people watch, not necessarily in that order. She dabbles in a multitude of genres with an emphasis on humor. "The Sun City Zone" is her third short story published in Desert Sleuths anthologies. She lives in Scottsdale with her husband and their four children.

LI AND THE DAUGHTERS OF JOY
JACKIE SERENO

The thunderous noise prevented Li from hearing the curses, "Outta the way, you filthy chinee," but the earth shaking under the hooves of animals warned him just in time to step to the side of the rugged track. A mule train carrying water to the camp rushed past him, whipped mercilessly by a dirty, grizzled old man in a floppy hat. Dust and the smell of sweating animals swallowed Li.

He looked up the mountain. *This must be the famous Cleopatra Hill.* From a distance, the traffic on the slope reminded him of a trail of busy ants. He surmised these were the latest arrivals trying their luck at mining for ore in this desolate Arizona land. They came from Europe, and China, and Mexico. Many of them had passed him on the way, on foot or on pack burros, anxious to make their fortunes in this new El Dorado.

He resumed his journey. His feet bare, toughened up after weeks of walking, he hardly felt the cuts from the small rocks that sometimes rolled down the slope and caused him to slip and fall. It was harder to breathe at this altitude and the heat felt intense under the bright blue sky. But Li had to go on, trying to avoid stepping on the animal droppings littering the trail. He carried his few belongings in a canvas satchel on his back. Underneath the conical straw hat he wore tied under his chin for protection against the sun, his long braid bounced as he limped up the rugged path.

He had been a worker on the railroad that was about to reach the community of Flagstaff, Arizona Territory, when a careless or drunken worker had set off an explosion too early, killing two men and seriously injuring Li. He'd lost some of his hearing and it had taken months for his leg to recover from a piece of rock that had embedded in his calf. He limped but at least the surgeon had removed the rock and saved his leg when it became infected. He was alive. However, he'd also dropped a great deal of weight and his strength failed him, so railroad work was out of the question for the present.

While he recuperated from his injury in Flagstaff, he'd found out about the discovery some distance away of a large deposit of copper. He inquired about this Cleopatra Hill in his broken English, and managed to get directions. There were bound to be opportunities for a hard working man to earn a living. He decided to seek his fortune in the newly booming camp.

A huge, mule-drawn freight wagon forced him again out of the way and he stood stoically aside while the vehicle passed. A buggy followed closely behind, driven by a woman in a gold shawl over a red and white satin striped outfit. Li was surprised when the buggy stopped.

"Hey, China Man," the woman called. "C'm here."

He frowned slightly and approached the vehicle.

"Miss?"

"Wanna ride?"

"No, Miss. Me fine."

"C'mon. I've got a proposal for you. You're looking for work, ain't you?"

"Yes, Miss. Look for work wash clothes miners."

The woman, a heavily made up busty blond with fluffy hair, laughed. "Ah! Miners don't wash their clothes. They wear them until they're so filthy they're stiff. Just dump them and buy new ones. But me, I have a job for you. What's your name?"

"Name is Li Zhi, Miss. Can call me Li."

"Well, Li, they call me 'Dutch Bettie' and I own a fine establishment in town, a boarding house. Get in, I'll explain."

Li hesitated, but the thought of sparing his tired legs the rest of the way was too enticing, plus he was curious about what the woman had in mind. A boarding house was a fancy term for a bordello. He learned that much on the railroad. He obeyed Dutch Bettie, careful not to sit too close to her for the cloying sweetness of her cheap Jasmine perfume overwhelmed all other smells and nauseated him. This was a very improper situation and he kept his eyes down.

The woman got the horses moving again and said, "Like I told you, I run this fine establishment, not in one of these tents the miners live in, mind you, but in a fancy brick building. I have four girls you'll meet and one that's due here soon. I keep a very clean place. Water is hard to come by, has to be transported, but sheets are washed once a day and the customers have to clean their private parts when they visit the girls. I could use a man to start the fire in the morning, do the laundry and carry water upstairs. To keep an eye on the girls, too. Maybe even cook. You know how to cook, Li?"

"Me not much cook, Miss. Rice and fish."

"Well, I can teach you. You'd get room and board and good pay. Easy work. What d'you say?"

Li wasn't sure what to say. Dutch Bettie steered her horses through the throng of carts, workers and animals bottlenecked at the entrance to the camp. Men in various states of dress and cleanliness did minor chores in front of dozens of tents aligned on each side of the dirt track passing for a road.

"Make way, make way."

The buggy passed the tents and turned left. There were rows upon rows of canvas dwellings struggling to fit on the hilly terrain. On a ledge above these, Li noticed some brick buildings in different stages of construction. After they'd climbed up a dirt track, the horses stopped, breathing hard, flanks covered with dust and sweat. A young boy came out of one of the two-story buildings and led the animals and buggy away. Li remove his hat and limped behind Dutch Bettie, through a red painted door, into a foyer and then to a large parlor. She whistled once, a loud, masculine sound, and three women came down an elaborate staircase.

Dressed in various states of provocative attire, they observed Li with curiosity and made lewd comments, before Dutch Bettie introduced them. "These are the girls. The Mexican one is Santa Fe Queen, the skinny blond is Wicked Mary and the fat redhead is Irish Fanny. The last one, Belle, went to the apothecary to get some laudanum. She's had a bad pain in her belly. I don't think she'll...well." She flicked her hand, dismissing the thought. "Never mind. I'll be getting one of your kind, too, from a woman called Dah Toy, all the way from San Francisco. Some men really like these China girls. To each their own, I say, hey Li?"

She slapped his back, laughing. Li remained silent, running his hands on the brim of his hat, his eyes down.

Dutch Bettie continued. "Girls, this here is Li. He's gonna keep this place clean. Don't you give him no guff. It's hard to find good help. Li, Humpback Joe will show you what you need to do and where you can sleep. We'll discuss wages after supper."

She whistled again, this time twice, and the little boy he'd seen earlier rushed from a side door. Li didn't see a hump, but the child was bowing under the weight of too much work for a malnourished body. Joe motioned to Li with some impatience.

Li sighed, wondering if he'd be able to work in this place. He would like to know if his wages would be equal to the thirty-five dollars a month he earned on the railroad, but decided he could wait to find out. For now, he'd follow the boy.

† † †

Summer passed. Li had made up his mind to stay though he found the women shocking in their behavior, clothing and vulgarity. He knew that came with the job and besides, the wages Dutch Bettie offered were on a par with his railroad pay. He'd found other Chinese workers in town and they socialized in whatever spare time they had. At work he spoke little, remained humble and avoided the customers whenever possible, but he was always aware of his surroundings. He took his meals of rice and fish alone and retired to the small area under the staircase to sleep on a pallet where he hid his satchel. No one paid much attention to him after the women noticed he didn't seem to hear them very well, and so their initial teasing of him stopped quickly. He was an unobtrusive, efficient ghost in a palace of fake pleasure and noisy greed.

Belle, the sick woman he hadn't met right away, was discharged. Dutch Bettie wasn't entirely heartless; she only docked pay for actual sick days rather than for entire weeks. She quietly gave Belle some extra money, but she was a businesswoman first. If she regretted losing the woman, Li didn't see it. While cleaning Belle's room, he found a bottle of laudanum and stored it with his belongings. A man never knew what might come in handy.

One morning, as Li brought an armful of firewood to the kitchen, voices in the parlor startled him. This was unusual, for the whole household slept late and Li was first to get up and work, enjoying his quiet musing time. He took a peek into the parlor. A very elegant Asian woman conversed with Dutch Bettie. Her exquisite grooming, hairstyle and clothing spoke of wealth. Behind her cowered a young girl who couldn't be more than fourteen years old. She too was Asian and wore delicate silk pants and long, high-necked jacket. Her black hair, parted in the middle, fell in long strands and hid her face, which she kept down. The woman turned around and nudged her toward the blonde Madam.

"Let me see you, China Doll," Dutch Bettie said, reaching for the girl's chin. The young lady pulled away from the heavily ringed hand. "Is she going to be a challenge, this girl? She looks terrified. What's her name?"

"She understan' some English," Dah Toy replied. "All she need. She can answer." She shook the girl's arm. "Tell her your name."

"Lotus Moon," whispered the child.

"What a pretty name," Dutch Bettie said. "Well, Lotus Moon, you're going to meet my girls, and they'll tell you I'm not one to abuse them." She patted the girl's arm. "But you'll need to do as you're told." A whistle from Dutch Bettie brought the prostitutes downstairs. Noticing Li, she motioned. "C'mere, Li. Maybe you can speak to her since you're both from Canton."

"Yes, Miss. Lots Chinee from Canton."

"Well, tell this girl I don't bite."

Li approached Lotus Moon, bowed and translated. At the Chinese words, she lifted her face, obviously surprised. He wanted to tell her he understood, not to worry, he'd help her escape, but he was sure Dah Toy also knew Cantonese. He'd have to wait for the right time.

Then Dah Toy spoke harshly to the girl who cried out, turned and ran toward the door. Dah Toy quickly caught her and slapped her, all the while yelling in Cantonese. Anger flamed in Li's chest, anger so hot it took all his self-control to hide it. Defeated, Lotus Moon simply bowed her head, tears running down her face.

"Look, Dah Toy, maybe this is a mistake," Dutch Bettie said. "This girl is not ready."

"Yes, she ready, she broken in, don' worry. You'll see. I go now to other mine town, come back in week. You lock her up for while. If you not happy, I take her back."

Dutch Bettie hesitated then nodded. It was settled, then. "Irish, you prepare her and lock her up in Belle's old crib. Li, you go with them in case she needs translation. Go on," she said with a gesture of dismissal.

While Dutch Bettie and Dah Toy finished their business, Li and Irish Fanny fetched the young girl and took her to Belle's former room. "This will be your crib," Irish Fanny said. The girl attempted to resist but was overcome. "Look," the redhead added, "tell her there's no point in fighting this. Easier on her if she don't. Dutch Bettie don't like to whip us, but she will if she don't listen."

Li bowed and conveyed the message adding, "Do not despair, I will be back in a while and I will help you."

"It is too late," she murmured. "I am dishonored. I wish to die."

"What did she say?" Fanny wanted to know.

"She is ashamed."

"Ah, we all were at one time. But we are what we are. And here, at least, Dutch Bettie makes sure the Johns clean themselves and don't hit us too bad. She could be a lot worse off. Tell her that."

He gave Lotus Moon an abbreviated version, repeating that he would check up on her. With regret he locked the door as he left with Irish Fanny and they both lingered in the hallway.

He could see the door knob move, but he knew it was in vain. He heard the girl scream and kick the door. He thought about the window, but it was barred, so she couldn't escape. He understood her frustration. It must have shown on his face because Irish Fanny tried to reassure him. "She'll settle down, don't worry Li."

An hour later, Li unlocked her door and went in. Her eyes were closed. He guessed she'd tried to shut off her mind, too. He explained to her that she would have to "work" tonight and Wicked Mary would come and instruct her. After checking that no one was around, he gave the distressed girl the small flask of laudanum he'd stashed in his satchel. "Take three drops of this," he advised in Cantonese. "It will make it a little easier on you. All the girls use it. But don't take more than three drops, for it is dangerous." Looking over his shoulder once more, he handed her something wrapped in a piece of cloth. "And this is a good knife for your protection. You can use it if a John hurts you. You must hide this. If they find it, don't say I gave it to you. Tell them you found it in your crib."

The girl held the flask and the bundle against her chest. "Thank you. What happens now?"

"Wait for Wicked Mary, she'll explain. You need to know that Miss Bettie will be watching from this peephole, here, see?

So be sure to do as you are told. If you do not, or if a customer complains, she will dock your pay and maybe beat you. Do you understand?"

The girl nodded. "Why are you in this place of shame?"

"I was hurt on the railroad. I wanted to find a job washing clothes for the miners, but this is what I found instead. I have been here too long, all summer. I shall be leaving soon. Maybe we can go together. I have to think of a way. In the meantime, do not despair. You have a friend. I will free you."

Lotus Moon smiled sadly, and took his hand in hers. "Thank you for your kindness."

"Do not thank me. I am sorry I cannot do more for you now. You go to the kitchen, they will feed you. Follow me."

"I am not hungry."

Li hesitated. "Then you should rest while you wait for Mary. The bed is pretty comfortable. I am sorry I must lock you up again."

She smiled, and Li's heart thundered in his chest. She said, "It is not important, now." He looked at her, uncertain, uneasy, not knowing what else he could do or say to comfort her, then left her in the gaudy crib.

† † †

"Oh! Hell!" Dutch Bettie cursed and ran to the hallway leading to Lotus Moon's room. Her shrill whistle alerted Li who forgot the pain in his leg to run up the stairs. It was late at night.

"Li, the Chinese girl...I was watching her through the peephole..." Dutch Bettie said, out of breath, as she tied the belt on her robe, "She stabbed her John. She stabbed young Peter Morton. Damn it! Get some bandages quick, then get the doc. Hurry. Hurry."

The Madam entered the room, went to Lotus Moon who sat shock-still, covered in blood, on the only chair, and slapped her with both hands. "Fool girl, I knew you'd be trouble. I'll have words with Dah Toy when she comes back."

She knelt by the man who lay on the bed. He was still breathing but a torrent of blood escaped from a slash in his neck and ran down his shoulder, saturating the bedding. Li delivered the bandages that Dutch Bettie applied with an efficiency that bespoke of experience. Peter Morton tried to speak, but it was clearly hopeless and by the time the doctor came up, the man had died.

The other women had heard the commotion and were out of their rooms, trying to find out what was going on. The doctor, irritated, thundered: "Well, don't just stand there! One of you go get the sheriff, and you, Chinaman, go get the undertaker."

"Bring him through the back door, Li," the Madam instructed.

When Li reached the undertaker's shop, it was closed, which didn't surprise him. He didn't want to go back to the horror in the house and started down the hill under the moonlight. He thought of Lotus Moon's delicate face and soft voice, of the sadness of her smile. Li had heard about the terribly humiliating ordeal the young girls destined for prostitution endured in San Francisco. He thought she had suffered through too much and could not accept the kind of life she'd been forced into. She was a brave girl.

After a while, he slowly walked back, until he heard people coming his way. He hid behind a boulder and waited. Then he saw her. Her hands were bound and the Sheriff was guiding her roughly down the path to his office, but she maintained a quiet dignity. He heard the man grumble, "It's the rope for you, gal. Why d'you have to kill young Morton? Heck, now we're gonna have to hang you. Don't like hangin' females." Li let them pass, and only released his breath when he was sure they'd gone. He needed to pick up his belongings.

† † †

Li took refuge with a Chinese friend, in one of the dozens of tents in town. He wouldn't leave until he'd made plans but didn't want to go back to Dutch Bettie's place. He knew Dah Toy was coming in a few days and so he waited for her. In his imagination, he sometimes strangled her, sometimes he stabbed her, but always as he thought of killing her he was conscious it would mean a hanging for him. At thirty-two, he wasn't ready to die, so he decided it would have to be an accident.

He anticipated her arrival at Dutch Bettie's place. There would be recriminations. Dah Toy would be upset, both at Lotus Moon and at her foiled plans. She would likely leave soon thereafter, alone in her buggy. She'd be most vulnerable on her way out of town, where a very sharp turn on the narrow way leading down steep Cleopatra Hill was often fatal to careless drivers.

He investigated the so-called road, a track on the edge of the mountain. A small cave on the slope just below was accessible and close enough to perhaps be of use. A few dozen yards away stood a vacant shack, which he explored. Another possibility? He continued walking on the slope and found a gully full of rocks and lined with brush. A hiding place?

He thought about her horses. Could he approach them? Humpback Joe often slept in the stable, but during the day he would be inside the main residence. Li should be able to sneak in and...do what? He wondered about Dah Toy's buggy. Would he have time to tamper with an axle, or the reins? The harness?

In the meantime, his friend told him they were looking for workers to blast rock. Since his accident, Li was wary about working with dynamite and he hesitated. Then it came to him. He smiled. He would take a job at the mine.

The Arizona night sky was dark and moonless and Li stumbled on his way to the cave he'd spied on the slope below the road. Inside the narrow opening, he took precautions to insert the stick of dynamite he'd stolen from the mine. Scattered campfires burned on the hillside, but no one could see him. There was an eerie beauty to this rugged site. He retraced his steps, covering with brush and dirt the length of detonating cord that reached into the vacant shack. This would be his hideout when the time came.

The next day he saw elegant Dah Toy whipping her horses to encourage them up the hill. He had no regrets about what he was about to do. He sat outside the shack so he could see her on the way back from town. An hour later, he watched her slowing her pace to negotiate a narrow turn. His heart pounding in his chest, he lit the cord. The small flame seemed to take forever to reach the dynamite in the cave, but with his years of experience the timing was perfect. Li saw the woman fly up in the air in a hellish dance as debris and rock and a portion of the road lifted under her and fell back down, burying her as the sound and the wave of the blast reached him. Flat on his face, he heard the earth groan and shake in anger, full of menace and he felt the heat reaching out to consume him.

Momentarily stunned by the power he'd unleashed, he

recovered slowly and looked around. Even from a distance he could see the gap that split the road into two sections. They would have to make some kind of bridge to get into town, or to leave for that matter. Men were hurrying to the area, too focused to see him get up, pick up his satchel and his hat. He dusted them with his hand and headed across the slope to slip into the gully he'd explored previously.

Perhaps they would catch him and hang him like Lotus Moon. So be it. But he hoped that, somehow, she knew she was avenged.

† † †

JACKIE SERENO, a transplant from the Loire Valley region in France, is a retired educator married to a member of the Pascua Yaqui Tribe of Arizona. She has lived in Scottsdale, Arizona for over thirty years and is particularly interested in the fascinating characters who moved to or through this unforgiving region in the 19th century.

ABIGAIL'S CAT
LOUISE M. SIGNORELLI

"Abigail's cat is just sitting here, staring at me," I said to Carrie. "And I'm starting to get really spooked."

The gray cat had never paid any attention to me and I'd always ignored him, but tonight he sat on the windowsill, staring, yellow eyes reflecting the moonlight, those weird cat pupils narrowed to slits.

Carrie, my best friend, had phoned to let me know she was home. She had come over tonight to watch *Twilight* with me for maybe the fifth time. We were both in love with Edward.

"Gotta go. Bye," I told her.

My mom, Abigail, would kill me if she knew I called her Abigail instead of Mother. She's so proper. And a control freak, who never lets me think for myself. About anything.

She had gone to Mund's Park, about thirty miles south of our home near Flagstaff, to help a friend who'd had a miscarriage. It had taken me forever to persuade her that I could stay home alone this weekend, even though I'd just had my fourteenth birthday.

I surveyed the mess we'd made of the living room with our snacks, and picked up the dishes and soda cans. Better get it cleaned up before Abigail found out we'd been eating in there.

Her perfect gray velvet couch and chairs went with her perfect gray-and-white wallpaper and her perfect dark gray carpet. An Oriental rug broke up the dull color scheme, and it had faded with age. Abigail said it was an antique. I thought it should be in the back hall for wiping our muddy boots. And she had gotten that gray cat to decorate the place, but then bitched about him leaving his gray hair on her gray furniture.

The cat twined around my legs as I took the dishes to the kitchen. He'd trip me up if he kept on, and he'd probably enjoy it. I stacked our dishes and the ones that had been left on the gray granite countertop and loaded them into the dishwasher.

Abigail was nothing if not consistent. She had stained the

original hardwood floor to look like driftwood and painted the cabinets a darker shade of gray, and then topped the look off with brushed stainless steel appliances. Charming.

"Meow."

I looked down at the cat, who sat there, doing nothing. "What? What do you want? Quit staring at me."

I grabbed the trash and trudged the few paces from the kitchen of our old three-story mountain cabin to the trash cans next to the garage. No need for shoes. It wasn't snowing yet. But the wind gusted and the temperature must have dropped to near freezing. The air smelled of fresh snow. Clouds tumbled past the fingernail moon and blanked out the little light it threw. Tree branches lashed back and forth, seeming to threaten the impending storm.

Inside again, a cup of coffee seemed in order.

"Meow."

"What now? You've been fed."

"Meow."

"All right." Irritated by the cat's begging, I poured half-and-half into a saucer and set it on the floor.

Once the cat shut up, I ground some coffee beans for myself. The aroma filled the kitchen as it brewed. Coffee smells so much better than it tastes, but we were out of tea. And hot chocolate is a kid's drink.

I brought my coffee to the living room, plunked into the recliner, and turned on the big-screen TV. The wind moaned in intermittent fits and the chill seeped in through the warped window frames. Abigail's remodeling projects were aimed at style rather than structure, which, considering Flagstaff's weather, wasn't the world's greatest idea.

The ten o'clock nightly news said another winter storm was howling in, then reported an armed home invasion. The guy had shot and killed the homeowner, stolen a Jeep, and escaped north on 180, but then he went off-road and the cops lost him.

I live north off Highway 180. And houses are far apart. Ours sat on forty acres.

Better make sure everything's locked. I made the rounds of the main floor, checked the locks on the doors and windows. All okay and shut up tight.

When I returned to the living room, a news update squawked that the cops were still looking for the killer. Barricades were up on all roads leading north. Worried, I ran upstairs to lock all the windows.

The cat followed me.

"Meow."

I checked Abigail's bedroom. Of course, her windows were locked. Her bathroom window was also locked. Abigail Perfect wouldn't leave something like an unlocked window to chance.

Her room was gray and utterly boring. Before my dad left, it had looked lived-in, like human beings inhabited it.

Dad finally couldn't take Abigail's perfectionism and nagging. He had taken me aside right before he left and apologized. He also had some advice for me. "Keep your head down and remember, it's only a few more years till you'll be out of here. You'll survive this."

Yeah, maybe.

Up another flight of stairs to my rooms. This was the only area in the house that hadn't been redecorated. Abigail said she'd redo it all when I was old enough to appreciate it.

Actually, I was glad she'd left my space alone. I loved my clawfoot bathtub. I didn't want her to replace that. The bedroom had a bit of life and color. The previous owners, who had probably been on acid, had left a crazy orange shag carpet. I'd removed the psychedelic tie-dye wallpaper and painted the walls a soft daffodil yellow. My old walnut bed and dresser had character. The massive bedposts spiraled almost to the ceiling, and I'd found a bedspread in shades of blue with a brushstroked rainbow in, well, a rainbow of colors. I thought it looked spectacular with the yellow walls and the orange shag.

The room also had the same ancient windows and leaky window frames. Drafts year-round. Cold in winter, hot in summer. I so wished Abigail had paid attention to something other than paint colors.

Since it was December, I had no reason to open my windows, but I checked them anyway. Murderers on the loose scared me. Much as I wished, I knew there was no hunky vampire around the corner to save me.

I sat on my bed, feeling sorry for myself, until I heard a sound like nails screeching on a blackboard. Alarmed, I ran downstairs to see what was broken. The sound, more a grating now, seemed to originate in the front hall. I edged towards it, and flipped the light switch. Nothing there.

Then a *thunk*.

Scared that the guy the cops were chasing was trying to get in, I peered out a front window. A Ponderosa pine branch scraped against the wall. Nothing but trees and that awful wind.

What a relief.

"Meow!" the cat said behind me, in the hall. Insistent, like he wanted something from me.

I watched as new snow fell, and then backed away from the window.

"Meow."

The cat sat at the entrance to the hall.

I wanted someone home with me, but I wouldn't humiliate myself by calling my mommy because I was scared of the dark. Plus, it was after eleven o'clock, and she'd be so pissed at me if she had to drive home this late. And it would be the end of me ever getting another privilege. To say nothing of the endless nagging I'd have to endure.

I'd rather die of terror.

I took my shower, brushed my teeth, and got into a flannel shirt and sweats, much warmer than pajamas. I crawled into bed, under the down comforter. The cat hopped up on the bed and lay down by my shoulder.

"Meow."

"I guess you're not so bad, are you, cat? Abigail never calls you anything but 'Cat.' I don't even know if she named you. You're just Abigail's cat."

"Meow."

The cat purred and slung himself across my left arm.

His purr was kind of peaceful, and I forgot my fears and drifted off.

The crash of breaking glass jolted me awake. I sat up and listened, holding my breath. A noise, like a footstep, then silence.

Like a fool, I'd left my cell phone downstairs in my jacket pocket. I stifled a panicked scream. There was no way to lock my bedroom door. Not that it would do much good. Anyone could break that flimsy door down.

The cat jumped off the bed, probably to check out the noise. I slid out of bed as silently as I could and grabbed him, and closed my bedroom door. But not before I saw a light down the staircase, moving around. It looked like a flashlight beam.

I sat on the bed, clutching the cat, and tried to think. All that came to mind was the old school drill, stop, drop and roll. That only worked if you were on fire. Not helpful here.

My throat ached with the effort not to scream.

I heard a crash in the kitchen. The murderer dumping the silverware drawer? Maybe he didn't know anyone was here. Maybe he would ransack the downstairs and leave for another house.

The cat squirmed out of my arms and leaped onto the windowsill.

"Meow."

"You must be nuts," I whispered. "We'd freeze out there, before we could get help. And I'd break my neck trying to get down."

Okay, think. Years of straight A's in school never prepared me for anything like this. I had always done lousy in gym classes and had no idea how to climb things. I'd taken some useless ballet lessons when I was little. Big deal.

I needed my jacket. If I could get it, I would have my cell phone. I pulled on thick socks and my sneakers. I couldn't face anything barefoot.

Noise from downstairs sounded like something being dragged down the front hall. Was the guy stealing something big?

Cold seeped under my door. Draft from the broken window, maybe the open front door.

Joists creaked and I heard the murmur of voices. Two killers? Footsteps on the stairs.

I had to get out, now. I so didn't want to climb out that window. But I opened it anyway, set the cat out on the narrow ledge, and crawled out.

The cold slapped me and took my breath away. I fumbled for something to hold onto, found a niche in the decorative trim, and hung on for dear life with one hand while I shoved the window closed with the other. And hoped the noise hadn't attracted attention.

If the murderers were going out the front door, I didn't dare crawl over to the front porch and jump onto the overhang. The old maple tree at the back of the house was about the only way down.

I stood from my crouch on the ledge, aware that it was only

about eight inches wide. And slippery with snow. It could give way any minute and dump me onto the ground, which would leave me with broken bones and the killers running to find the noise.

I shuffled along the ledge, inch by inch, toward the back of the house. The cat, leading the way, walked a foot or so ahead. Easy for him. He could balance on that ledge and jump into the tree or even jump to the ground without a problem.

Shuffled a bit more, felt for a new handhold. It took forever to get past my bedroom windows. Chills shook me and my hands went numb. A rush of wind threatened to knock me from my perch. I flattened myself against the wall and held my breath. It seemed like it took a year to cover another few feet.

The cat sat next to my foot.

"Move," I whispered. He looked up at me. We'd reached the corner of the house. I couldn't go back. I couldn't go on. I couldn't shove him forward without losing my balance. "Move, damn it. Around the corner. Keep going."

He sat and stared.

"Meow."

Then he crept around the corner to the back of the house. His progress was all but imperceptible. The ledge cracked and sagged. He stepped back.

I couldn't swallow. A lump in my throat wanted to choke me. I shivered with cold, but sweat dripped into my eyes. That ledge had almost given way under a ten-pound cat.

The cat stood at the edge of the crack and reached a paw across.

"No, cat."

The cat placed his weight on the outstretched paw. The ledge cracked again. I held my breath.

He covered about three feet with his leap across the weak part of the ledge. There was no way I could follow.

The cat leaped back and leaned against my leg, looking up.

"Meow."

"Yeah."

The cat eyed the narrow trim on the corner. What good did that do us?

The cat climbed up a few feet, then dropped back to my ledge and sat.

No way. That trim might hold a cat, but it would never hold

me.

The cat stared at me.

"No way, cat." But I couldn't go forward and I was damned if I'd go back.

I felt for a handhold on the trim and examined it for a place to put my feet. I remembered kids climbing ropes, but they wrapped their legs around the ropes. I couldn't do that here.

The front door slammed, and I could see a beam of light sweeping the corner of the front porch. If they had any idea someone was home, and they found me, I was sure the intruder—or intruders—would kill me.

Hand over hand, I pulled myself up, bracing my feet on the wall on either side. I hoped my arms held out. I hoped the trim didn't break free.

A snail had nothing on me. I didn't think about what I'd do when I got to the roof.

I heard voices, but in the blowing wind, couldn't make out their words. And couldn't tell which direction the sound came from.

My hands and feet hurt from the cold. I could feel frostbite starting in my fingers. Snow blew into my face. My gloves were in the back hall closet. Why hadn't I at least grabbed a sweater to wear over my flannel shirt?

After an eternity, I reached the roof. I had to figure out how to get on to it. My arms were breaking from the strain of hauling myself up. Climbing onto that roof, with its steep pitch, and now covered with an inch of snow, looked close to impossible.

If I could get up there, I could sprawl flat, like a face-down snow angel, and brace my feet against the gutter while I edged around to the tree. But what handholds did a roof offer? I reached up with one hand and brushed snow away. Thick cedar shingles met my fingers. It might be possible after all. I brushed more snow away and grabbed on to something that felt sort of substantial.

With fingers and toes aching from the cold and from the strain, I clung on for all I was worth, and inched my other hand off the trim and onto the roof. I found another handhold and crept. And did it again, one hand after the other. I wanted to scream. But I kept going.

Soon I was able to get my right knee over the gutter and on to the roof. I bent my leg as far as it would bend, and got my toes onto the gutter.

I stayed still and gasped for breath for a few moments. Then started again. I fumbled for a handhold a few inches higher, grabbed it, felt for one for the other hand, pulled up, pushed with my right foot.

At long last, I rested my left foot on the gutter. And lay with my face in the snow and shivered.

The cat sat next to my head.

"Meow."

"Yeah. So far, so good," I whispered. "I want to move in with Dad in California, and forget that cold and snow even exist."

I brushed snow away and felt for my next handhold. I had no idea how long ago I'd left my bedroom, with no coat and no gloves. It felt like hours. My shivers made the climb so much harder, and so much scarier. That maple seemed miles away.

I crept sideways, inches at a time.

A little more and I sprawled under the maple, where a new worry hit me. How would I move from this position and grab onto a branch? The cat could leap. I couldn't. I couldn't turn around. Even if I could, no way would I jump for a branch. I'd reached the end of the line. I might as well lay here and freeze to death, or wait for the killers to come for me and shoot me. Or jump to my death.

But then I got mad, found a spark of myself. I wouldn't die without a fight. Abigail hadn't snuffed out all of me.

If I got out of this, I'd travel to California somehow, and beg Dad to take me in. In a few years I'd enter college. Grandpa's trust fund took care of tuition and room and board, and Dad would no longer have the responsibility for me. He could deal with that.

I moved my right foot over my left and moved my butt just a bit, so I was more on my hip than on my stomach. I moved my right hand close to my left and grabbed on to a new handhold in the roof, and inched a bit more.

My right foot slipped. I managed to stifle a scream.

"Meow."

Got my right foot back on the gutter, and gasped for breath. I couldn't do this. What choice did I have, though?

I moved my hip forward. The next step would be to reach over my left hand and twist around and grab with my right, behind my left and behind where my head was. But bodies don't twist like that.

The gutter was a few inches wide. I angled my left foot in slightly. Rested. My arms and legs shook from effort. I might shake myself right off this roof.

I turned my body, and flopped on my back, breaking my hold with my right hand.

My left hand held, even though my wrist felt close to snapping. And my feet held. I was still alive and still on the roof.

"Meow."

"Yeah, thanks."

I studied the maple. A sturdy enough branch hung within reach. I had solid footing with my left foot turned out on the gutter. My right heel remained on the gutter. I felt as set as I'd ever be. My right arm was free. My left arm screamed in agony. I bent my knees as far as they'd go while still holding on to the roof, pushed off, and threw my arms around that branch.

I had it. I held on for dear life and stood on the gutter as slowly as I could. I said a prayer and stepped onto a limb just below the roof line. The branches swayed. I gasped and clung to my branch, now at head level, for all I was worth.

For the first time, I had hopes that I would live. I managed to get to the trunk, which was too big to throw my arms around. I loved that maple tree.

My footrest bounced. Then the cat jumped past me and grabbed on to the trunk.

"Don't scare me like that. Can't you wait at least till we're on the ground?"

"Meow."

He backed down the tree. I lowered myself and sat on my footrest branch. The climb down looked straightforward, but I had been too scared too long to relax.

I almost enjoyed the easy parts. I swung from one branch to reach another, then hung by my arms and dropped to a lower branch. I'd take the tree any time over navigating that roof.

That last drop to the ground felt better than anything, in spite of my frozen feet screaming in agony as I landed.

I heard voices from the front of the house. The killer and his buddy were still here.

One of them said, "Come on, we've got it all. Let's get out of here before the cops show up."

"Someone was in the house," the other answered. "I want to find them. No witnesses, remember."

"No one was in the house. Let's go."

"No, let's search for him. And there's a garage."

I stood right in front the garage. Behind me was the locked back door.

A flashlight beam swept the area to my left. I sprinted to the right for the open meadow past the garage. If I got far enough away, and lay flat, maybe they wouldn't see me. Not much else I could do out here.

I heard a screech and the men yelling. Then a gunshot. I burrowed into the few inches of snow covering the dead grass. The wind, calmer now, carried the gunshot stench.

One of the men said, "It was a damned cat."

"Did you get it?"

"I think so. Friggin' thing. See the blood?"

"Let's get out of here. Someone is bound to have heard that shot."

Oh, no! Abigail's cat!

I lay stunned. He'd distracted them so I could get away.

A car engine cranked over, and car doors slammed. I saw a Jeep that looked gray in the moonlight peel out of our driveway.

I was safe, but where was the cat? My cat now, if he lived. The thought drifted through my mind that he still needed a name. And a proper burial. I didn't want to think about that.

I plodded through the snow back to the house, and around to the front.

The cat sat on the porch by the front door.

"Meow."

I picked him up and hugged him. "Are you all right, cat?"

He purred and licked my chin.

I couldn't find a mark on him. I carried him around the side where the burglars had shot at him. A trail of blood led to a rabbit crumpled dead next to a juniper bush.

"Poor bunny. You picked the wrong time to come out of hiding, didn't you?"

But my cat was safe. *My* cat.

The killers had left the front door unlocked.

I carried the cat inside and sat in the recliner, shaking. The filth on my clothes would be all over it. Abigail would just have to suck it up. I didn't care. She'd be more pissed about that than worried about me or any of the other stuff that had happened.

I made my decision.

Got my down parka and purse from the back closet. Took out my cell phone and called Dad.

"Dad, I'm coming to stay with you. I'll tell you about it when I get there. Will you get me a ticket for the next flight? I'll pick it up at the airport."

I listened.

"No, I can't stay here one minute longer. I'm not asking, I'm telling."

"Meow."

"And I'm bringing a cat. No, the cat and I are a package deal. I don't care what Abigail says. If you want to argue with her, fine. She's not my problem any more."

I called a cab and, followed by my cat, went upstairs to pack.

At the age of twelve, **LOUISE M. SIGNORELLI** fell in love with Sherlock Holmes, joined the Baker Street Irregulars, and has been devouring mysteries and thrillers ever since. Louise's son-in-law challenged her one day as she walked around the house engrossed in a book: "You read so many whodunits; why don't you write one?" Louise earns her keep programming computers, but she'd rather spend her time telling stories, especially tales mired in murder and mayhem.

THE MAKE-BELIEVE WIVES CLUB
KATE JOY STEELE

The knots of anxiety in my muscles loosened with every mile the tires hummed along the pavement. I could hear almost no other sound. Nothing distracted me from my respite except the raw beauty of the desert and the magnificent blue sky. *I will not feel guilty for not inviting Jack Johnson to this conference.*

Five days at a conference without my husband, Jack, sounded like a nice break. Instead, it was a revelation. People I had lost touch with welcomed me, included me in their lively discussions and gossip over wine and dinner every evening. I felt awake, alive and appreciated after months of loneliness and torpor.

The fourth night of the conference, I finally realized and admitted—at least to myself—that I was relieved not to be at home, happy not to be with my husband. I felt more relaxed than before Jack and I were married. He must have heard something in my voice during our evening call because his usual sarcastic banter turned nasty; he insinuated that I must be having an affair. He wanted to know the "poor guy's" name.

I did not answer his phone calls for the rest of the conference.

I took Arizona Highway 96 from Tucson back home to Surprise. Mid-October lighted the desert in magic. The red rocks glowed purple as the sun set, their shadows flowing eastward, shrouding the flat arid ground. The sky darkened, revealing the stars high and remote above the empty desert. I felt as alone as I ever had in my life.

The headlights of a car coming toward me looked smeared. *Damn. I wasn't going to cry again today.* I pulled over, fumbled in the console for a packet of tissues. I wiped my eyes, blew my nose and got out of the car. Some small animal's skittering rattled the dry brush. An image of me as a vigilant, frightened critter popped into my mind. *How could I have let him manipulate and isolate me so completely?* I dreaded the confrontation with Jack I knew had to come.

It was dark when I arrived at the house we had chosen together. *This was supposed to be "our" house, one we'd buy together. I sold my little home I loved and put most of the money into this place, because when it was time to make the down payment, he said he'd have to wait until his business was more profitable. Yeah, right.*

I was surprised that the security lights didn't come on when I swung the car into the driveway and clicked the garage door opener. I walked into the kitchen and stopped, stunned.

The rooms I could see were stripped of every stick of furniture. No draperies, no blinds or rugs. The kitchen appliances, large and small, were gone. The pot rack hung empty.

I checked the rest of the house. Everything, right down to the shower curtains and rods in the bathrooms, was gone. My books, my paintings, my family treasures were nowhere to be seen. My clothes closet was empty, as was the small wall safe that had held the few pieces of family jewelry I had inherited.

I stood in the empty silence for several moments, until my simmering anger exploded into rage so hot and raw I called Jack every filthy epithet I knew. I marched back into the kitchen, fetched my cell phone and called the police, my voice echoing off the bare walls and floors.

Two police officers arrived an hour later. "I'm Sergeant Hennessey, Mrs. Johnson," she said. "This is Officer Olivera. What happened?"

"I'll show you," I said, and walked them through the house. "My husband isn't here."

"So, are you reporting your husband missing?" Sergeant Hennessey asked, watching me.

"Well, that's a possibility," I said, "but I've never heard of kidnapping someone and taking the contents of the house too. We're not wealthy, so I can't imagine anyone hoping to ransom him."

"But let's err on the side of 'innocent until proven guilty' and see if we can find him," Hennessey said.

"I don't remember the plate number on his car," I said, "but it's a three-year-old BMW, dark blue, with a ding in the right front fender."

"We'll talk to your neighbors and start the search for his car," Officer Olivera said, and left.

"Now, tell me about your husband," Hennessey said.

"Jack owns a photography business in Peoria. We met at a friend's barbecue about eighteen months ago. We got married six months ago."

"Why do you think he emptied the house?" Hennessey asked. She sounded skeptical.

"I...umm...I've been at a conference in Tucson for a week. Being away from him, around other people I like and respect, made me realize he's a bully. I guess it took some space to snap me out of my fog."

"Describe his bullying," Hennessey said.

"It's hard to pin down. At first, he was charming and affectionate and funny. I liked being with him. But after we were married, he was like a different person. He either ignored me or acted possessive. He became secretive, too—paranoid, maybe. I took my car to my cousin Mack's garage for servicing. Mack found a GPS tracker hidden under the dash. I asked Jack if he knew about the GPS. He just glared at me and said, "I'll decide how best to keep you safe. Take your car to the dealership next time.""

"Did you remove the GPS?"

"No. I didn't want a scene and I didn't have anything to hide." I flushed so hot my skin stung.

"So why do you think he emptied the house and left?"

"Nothing else makes sense. When we first met, I thought he was just a private person, but a lot of the things he told me about himself didn't ring true. I didn't exactly catch him in lies, but he was evasive if I asked for details. A few times, he said he was offended that I could doubt him, or he'd sort of laugh it off, but his behavior didn't feel...genuine. I wondered if he *wanted* me to be off-balance around him. He pulled away the last month or so. Left at dawn and got home very late."

"What do you know about his history?" Hennessey asked.

"He said he got a business degree from U of A. He said he's been a photographer since he was in junior high. He never seemed to be concerned about money when we were dating or choosing the house to buy together. He said he'd pay half the down payment, but when it came due, he didn't have the cash.

That seemed to bother him. I convinced myself it was male pride because I had more money than he did."

"Anything else?"

"Well, I thought it odd that a photographer would avoid having his picture taken. He was reluctant even to be in our wedding photos." I thought for a moment. "They were all here, and now they're gone, except the one I have on my desk at work."

Sergeant Hennessey nodded and frowned. "I think we'll need a copy."

Officer Olivera came back into the house. "The neighbors say they saw two guys loading the moving truck, but not your husband."

Sergeant Hennessey handed me her card. "The house will be considered a crime scene for a few days since we don't know if he left of his own accord. Where will you stay?"

I handed her my own business card. "The Quality Inn in Sun City is close to work. I'll call you tomorrow."

My credit card was declined at the hotel. I used my company card to check in, knowing I'd have to explain the charge to my boss. I was fuming by the time I got to the room. I set up my laptop. My hands shook as I logged on to look at my credit card balance. *Damn! Maxed out!* I checked my bank account next. Zero balance. Same with our joint account. I called the twenty-four-hour customer service number, my heart pounding.

The bank representative said, "Yes, ma'am, the withdrawals were made at ATMs in Surprise, Peoria, Glendale and Goodyear, starting a week ago, mostly in four- to five-hundred-dollar amounts, totaling six thousand dollars."

"Yes, I can see that online. Problem is, I didn't make the withdrawals. My debit card is the same one I've had since it was issued four years ago," I said, trying not to snap at the representative. "Do your ATMs have cameras? Is there any way to know who made the withdrawals?"

"I'll check for you." Six radio commercials later, the representative finally said, "Sorry that took so long, but yes, three of the ATMs do have cameras. I've requested that our security department investigate right away. In the meantime, do you want to put a hold on your accounts?"

"Absolutely. Now, can you check the balance of my savings

account?"

"Yes, ma'am. I see no activity since your last automatic deposit a week ago." I closed my eyes, relieved, as I ended the call.

That rotten jerk took my clothes, my jewelry and nearly everything else I own and maxed-out my credit card. How could I be so stupid?

The police did not find Jack Johnson, his car, or the moving truck. His cell phone number was actually registered to Jim Jansen. None of the BMWs licensed in Arizona belonged to Jack Johnson.

So that's why he insisted on keeping his own insurance policy. He would have had to explain why his car was registered under another name or on some list of stolen cars somewhere.

Sergeant Hennessey told me that the address for the portrait studio was real, but the business was owned by a different photographer entirely. *Of course the studio address is real. Jack had keys and knew the security codes. He took me there after hours when we were dating. So if it wasn't Jack's business, where did he get the money he put in our joint account? What was he doing when he said he was working?*

None of the credit reporting agencies had any records of a Jack Johnson who fit the description of the man I had married.

I told Sergeant Hennessey about the missing money. Her comment, "You've been had by a pretty slick operator," didn't make me feel any less stupid. "The equipment to clone an ATM or credit card is available online for about two hundred bucks. It only takes a little knowhow and a computer."

"So all he had to do was 'borrow' my cards for a few minutes when I wasn't looking."

† † †

Two days later, I decided I wouldn't depend on the police to find him. Betraying me was a property crime, after all, not a high priority for overworked detectives. I hired a private investigator, Tara Holmes. Her specialty was financial fraud and tracking identity thieves.

Straightening out my financial mess took four long months. The police and credit agency reports showing that the "Jack Johnson" I married, who helped me get cash from my homeowner's insurance, did not exist. I remembered him telling me having his name on the policy wasn't important because, he'd said, "Most of the things here are yours, sweetheart." The bank refunded the money he took from my personal account. I petitioned the court to annul the marriage, only to discover that the license "Jack Johnson" had procured, was a forgery. *A make-believe husband. Just what every woman wants.*

Regaining my self-confidence was simpler than I expected. After my initial shock wore off, each time I dealt with an insurance adjuster, a bank investigator, a credit reporting agency, the police or a judge, I became stronger. Anger carried me forward at first, but when I realized that he was probably already doing the same things to some other woman, my intent on revenge bordered on obsession.

Tara Holmes used the wedding photo and the social security number Jack gave the bank, to track him. She found enough small discrepancies to identify a dozen aliases and build a dossier for each one. She found records of four other marriages.

Finding the courage to call those four other women was hard. I had no idea how they would react and dreaded the drama. Gina, the first wife Tara found, was happy to know someone else was looking for "Joseph James," whose pattern of winning her over with his charm and stealing everything he could from her, was nearly identical to my experience with "Jack Johnson."

Janet and Callie, wives two and three, were still struggling financially after "Jon Josephs" and "Jan Jansen" emptied their bank accounts and their homes. Maggie, wife number four, was still so angry after five years, she had difficulty talking about "James Johnson" without swearing. "I just want to know why he took my damn clothes!" she said.

All five of us lived within about a one-hundred-mile radius of the metro-Phoenix area. We met as a group the first time at Gina's home in Glendale a few weeks after I contacted each one. I like all of them immediately. "Do you think it ever occurred to the bastard the five of us would be in the same room together?" I asked.

"Not a chance," Maggie said. "He probably figured we'd all be too broken up to think straight."

"Yeah," Callie said, "and too busy trying to climb out of the mess he left to look for him."

"If he thought about us at all," Gina said. "He manages to hide in plain sight. We have to 'out' him so he can't keep reinventing himself and finding more women he can fool."

We agreed to pool our resources to find him. We started by sending his photo and aliases to every business and social networking site we could find on the Internet, asking them to contact Sergeant Hennessey if the bastard registered on their sites. We put "Wanted" posters on our Facebook pages, referring to him as "Greedy Bastard," since we weren't sure of his real name. We called him "GB" among ourselves.

Gina called one Saturday morning, nearly a year after he left me. "Sarah, I think I saw GB today in the Chandler Mall."

"What was he doing?" I asked.

Gina laughed. "Being a photographer, what else? He was handing out coupons for a special on family portraits. He gave my niece one. She thought she recognized him and called me. I went to see for myself."

"Gina, that's terrific!"

"Look, why don't you drive down here and we'll both go look to make sure it's not his twin or something. He has a beard now and I'm pretty sure he touched up the color of his whiskers, probably his hair, too. It's been years since I've seen him up close, but I'm positive it's him," she said.

"I'll leave right away. Should I wear a disguise?" I asked, laughing.

"Well, I'm wearing sunglasses and a hat," she said.

"Okay. I'll be there by eleven-thirty. Meet you at the west entrance."

"Are you ready to do this?" Gina asked when I found her.

We both grinned as we bumped fists.

I lowered the bill of my blue ball cap as we walked toward the children's clothing store, pretending to window shop while we looked for him. I felt a little silly with the big sunglasses on inside, but other people were wearing theirs, so I didn't think we were conspicuous. I hoped my anxiety didn't show, and marveled at how calm Gina seemed.

Keeping my head down, I pretended to be interested in the window displays of onesies and cute little bonnets. Gina scanned the store surreptitiously. She nudged my arm. "Take a look, two o'clock."

He was standing near the photography studio entrance inside the store, a big smile on his face as he spoke to a young couple, the proud mommy holding her chubby little girl all dressed up for her first portrait.

I nodded to Gina. We left the store. It was all I could do not to shriek and attack him. I was trembling, and rage bubbled in my gut. I feared I would disintegrate on the spot.

Gina and I found a bench where we could watch the store entrance. "Okay, what next—that's legal, I mean," she said. "We'd get arrested if we punched him in the nose."

"Call Sergeant Hennessey and tell her where to find him."

"Right. And then what?"

"Notify the rest of The Make-Believe Wives Club so they can participate in making his life miserable, what else?"

Gina nodded, a wicked grin on her face.

I looked up the phone number for the store we had spotted him in and called. "We were in the store today. The loveliest man took pictures of our baby. I wanted to send him a thank-you note but I don't know his name. He's about six-four, curly reddish-brown hair and beard..."

"Jacob Janek," the store clerk said, cutting me off.

"That's J-a-c-o-b J-a-n-u-k?" I asked.

"No. It's spelled J-a-n-e-k," the clerk said.

When I clicked off, Gina said, "Well, he's true to pattern."

"Yeah. Tara Holmes said that a lot of crooks use the same initials for their aliases. Easier to remember their lies."

"Probably saves money on monogramming, too," Gina said.

Sergeant Hennessey happened to be at her desk when I called. "We'll work with the Chandler police and mall security to pick him up and question him."

I thanked her and said we'd wait for her outside the store entrance.

"Now, the fun begins," I said to Gina, punching in a number from memory. "Tara, we found him. He's using the name Jacob Janek. I don't know if he works for that children's clothing store or a private photography studio. Please find out everything else you can."

Sergeant Hennessey, accompanied by a pair of Chandler police officers, led "Jacob Janek" out of the store in handcuffs, reciting his rights as they walked. Gina and I made no effort to hide our faces as we used our phones to video his long, very public walk through the crowded mall.

We followed the patrol car to the Surprise police station, where we gleefully identified him. He didn't seem concerned, even when Sergeant Hennessey asked another officer to escort him to booking.

"Arrogant jerk thinks he'll be able to talk his way out of this," Gina said.

Tara located his residence and Gina and I went for a look-see. The neighborhood was typical of the parts of Arizona that were overbuilt during the housing boom. Half the houses were empty and others had foreclosure signs in the yards. A car was parked in the driveway, so we went to the door and rang the bell.

A very pretty young woman answered. "Can I help you?"

"Are you Mrs. Janek?" I asked.

"Yes, I am!" she said, smiling, flashing my grandmother's diamond and emerald engagement ring and my mother's diamond wedding band. "Amanda Hodges Janek, as of one month ago today."

Gina put her hand on my shoulder and squeezed gently. "We need to talk, Amanda."

I took a deep breath. "May we come in?" I stuffed my hands in my jeans pockets so I wouldn't snatch the rings right off her hand.

"Oh, yes, please. What's this about?"

"So, you've been married a month?" I said. "How long have you known…uh…Jacob?"

She blushed. "Seven months, but I knew we were soul mates from the beginning," she said. "He's a wonderful husband."

"I'm sorry to have to tell you this, but your husband is in Surprise, in jail. I don't know what all the charges will be, but I doubt he will be granted bail," Gina said.

"I have to go to him! I'm sure this is all a misunderstanding."

"No, it isn't. That's why we're here," I said, a little surprised that I was so calm. I had expected to feel triumphant that he was in jail, but I didn't. "Do you recognize the man in these photos?" I handed her a copy of the wedding picture from my office and a copy of a picture of him and Gina at a party.

"I don't understand," she said, confusion and pain clear on her face.

Gina said, "Let's sit down, and we'll explain." She kept her voice quiet, leaned toward Amanda and patted her hand gently.

After Gina and I left Amanda's house, I went home and sent an email to the other three members of The Make-Believe Wives Club.

> THE SURPRISE POLICE ARRESTED GB TODAY IN CHANDLER.
>
> The video of his "perp walk" is attached for your viewing pleasure.
>
> Tara is working on his latest alias-Jacob Janek.
>
> Gina and I went to visit his bride of one month, who was wearing my grandmother's engagement ring and my mom's wedding band. I'm pretty sure Callie's antique desk was in the living room.
>
> Hope you can all be there for the bail hearing. Any ideas who he'll call to represent him? We can prove he can afford a lawyer. My attorney will be at the bail hearing to try to make sure he doesn't get out of jail.
>
> Sergeant Hennessey wants to talk to all of us again. Please get in touch with her at your earliest.
>
> Think about how much we want to say to the reporters.
>
> Thanks, ladies!

† † †

A public defender accompanied GB to his bail hearing Tuesday morning. The shocked expression on his face when he saw the six of us—including Amanda—was truly gratifying. He actually turned quite pale.

Judge Penelope Massie was scowling fiercely by the time my attorney finished presenting evidence that Jack/Jim/Joseph/Jon/Jan/James/Jacob was not entitled to a public defender and was skilled at disappearing. "You will remain in custody. You will arrange and pay for your own defense. There will be severe consequences if you misrepresent yourself in any fashion to this court." Judge Massie banged her gavel and said, "Next!"

The "perp walk" video was a hit on YouTube after it was mentioned on the local TV and radio news.

† † †

On the four-year anniversary of the day I found my house emptied, I celebrated by driving to Tucson to spend a long weekend visiting friends. I stopped to watch the sun rise over the desert. A glorious sight.

Did we make his punishment fit his crimes? I'd like to believe that the public exposure of his thievery and deception will dog him for the rest of his life.

Was justice done? If justice means he went to jail and the judge ordered him to make restitution to Gina, Janet, Callie, Maggie, Amanda and me, then the answer is "yes."

The jury found GB guilty of every count of theft and fraud.

Was it right to pursue him because I wanted revenge? Justice and revenge are mutually exclusive, so if I wanted justice, I was wrong to seek revenge. But I'm not sorry.

Reclaiming control of my own life required that I stand up to him. But the coward ran away, literally a thief in the night, looking for a new victim to cheat and abandon without regret.

He has a parole hearing coming up next year.

All six of us will be there.

† † †

KATE JOY STEELE lives in the Pacific Northwest with her husband Paul. After working as a business consultant, writer and editor for many years, she retired and is diligently working her way through a demanding reading list compiled over forty years and making time to write fiction, paint, sew and learn new crafts. This is her second short story to be published in a Desert Sleuths anthology.

THE GOOD NEIGHBOR
KARI WAINWRIGHT

Flames flickered upward toward the patio cover like evil sprites set to devour their surroundings. The simple charcoal grill was never meant to hold a fire so large, certainly not an unsupervised one.

Mabel stared out her window at the tacky doublewide across the street, its patio crammed with outdoor chairs held together by duct tape, a shopping cart brimming over with empty beer bottles, and the grill roaring away with orange, red, and yellow flames.

Her chubby face puckered in fear until she resembled a dried-up apple doll. Where the heck was Ralphie, her drug-dealing, foul-mouthed, beer-guzzling neighbor? Why did he start the fire if he wasn't going to stay outside with it?

The flames climbed dangerously close to the metal awning. Mabel broke her mesmerized gaze from the orange glow and strode to her phone, punching in the well-known number of the HOA's volunteer security posse. It took her three times to key in the entire number correctly.

"Hello, hello," she said after a man answered. "Is this Desert Resthaven Security?"

"Yes, ma'am. Larry Tims on duty. How can I help you?"

"My neighbor's built a fire on his patio. It's out of control."

"Sounds bad, ma'am. What's your name and address?"

She knew this was the rule, but normally when she turned someone in for an HOA violation, she wasn't worried about her safety. With Ralphie, this was a concern. "Do I have to give my name? Can't I just tell you his?"

"Yes, I need your name. Sorry if this is a problem."

She didn't really care if Ralphie's place burned down. After all, it belonged to his father, not him. And his dad was in a nursing home, unlikely to return to Desert Resthaven ever again.

But Mabel considered herself to be the caretaker for the properties on either side of Ralphie's place when the owners weren't here. So she must be brave. People counted on her. Her voice lowered until it was almost a whisper. "I'm Mabel Dickerson and I live at thirty-four ninety-eight Cactus Lane. The fire is directly across the street. Ralphie lives there now, but the real owner is his father, Stanley Willis. Please hurry. I'm afraid a neighbor's house might burn down."

"I'll be there in a jiff, Mrs. Dickerson. Don't you worry none." He hung up.

But she did worry. She couldn't help it. It was just something she did. Especially when Ralphie was up to his usual no-good tricks. Like driving too fast through the neighborhood. Or hanging out with his druggie friends. Or starting fires. It was too bad his tawdry place hadn't been torn down and replaced with a nice, new stick-built, like so many other properties in the retirement community, she thought. Then there might be a different family living there and she wouldn't have to worry so much about the neighborhood.

She crouched at the window, lights turned out so she wouldn't be seen. A widow couldn't be too careful. Time clicked by, literally, as her clock's second hand moved methodically along. Finally, the security guard showed up. In his golf cart.

For crying out loud, Mabel thought. How intimidating is a guy in a golf cart? Why hadn't he at least used the security car with the community logo on it? Something official. After all, the posse had staged several fundraisers to buy the car for their volunteer staff.

He parked his vehicle in front of the patio where the fire blazed, looked at Mabel's house, then got out and walked to Ralphie's door. Mabel saw him knock then speak to someone inside the residence. After a few moments Ralphie shuffled out, no shirt or shoes, but wearing grimy denims. Gingerly, from the side, he slid a round metal lid on top of the flames. The orange glow skimmed out the other side, then disappeared as the lid covered the grill completely.

The security guard shook Ralphie's hand then headed toward Mabel's house. *What in the world is he doing? What in the world is he thinking?* Mabel stepped back from the window.

She heard a business-like rap on her front door. The security guy stood there in the pool of bright yellow from her porch light. Mabel didn't answer his knock. He tried again. Of course, he knew she was home, she realized. She snuck a glance out her window. Across the street, Ralphie stood, arms akimbo like some malicious pirate, watching and waiting.

Mabel fumed. This Larry fellow was going to get her into trouble. She pulled her white cotton robe closer around her sturdy shape, then marched to the door and wrenched it open. "What do you want?" she hissed.

"Reporting in, Mrs. Dickerson. Just wanted you to know that the fire situation is taken care of."

"You've let Ralphie know I'm the one who complained. He'll be right mad at me."

"Don't worry, ma'am. Mr. Willis apologized and said he won't have any more unsupervised fires."

"But that's what he always does. He starts a fire, stands there a few minutes and then goes inside. He *never* supervises them. Surely there's more you can do. Especially since this was the biggest one yet."

"Outdoor burning is okay according to the Home Owners Association, so unless there's a no burn day in the county, there's really nothing I can do. There's no more danger of things getting out of hand now. I'm sure Mr. Willis doesn't want to burn down his own place."

"But what about the neighbors' homes? I know for a fact that Betty Fleming, who lives next to that patio, worries. Why, she's taken pictures of her possessions in case a fire spreads to her place. I keep them for her. And the Hewlitts on the other side, worry, too. They're all snowbirds, so while they're gone for the summer, I'm the one who watches out for their places."

"Sounds like you're a good neighbor, ma'am. They're lucky to have you."

"But they're unlucky enough to have Ralphie living next to them." A thought creased her forehead. "Could you check to see if Ralphie's old enough to live here? Maybe he isn't fifty-years-old yet. That didn't matter when his father lived here, but I doubt that Stan is ever going to return." She pictured her elderly neighbor withering away in diapers and neglect and wondered if his son ever visited.

"Sorry, ma'am. He showed me his ID. He's legit."

She sighed. There must be some way to protect her neighbors' lovely places from that stupid pyromaniac.

Larry's cell phone rang and he pulled it off his belt to study the number. "Gotta go now. You take care, Mrs. Dickerson." He strode to his golf cart and drove off, the phone plastered to his ear.

She slammed the door shut. But not before she saw Ralphie's middle finger salute. Goosebumps peppered her arms as she wondered what he might do.

She stomped down the hall to her bedroom, her backless slippers slapping angrily against the tile floor. She was so infuriated she almost choked on her bedtime pills. After she finished her nightly rituals, she pulled back her floral sheets and got into bed. Leaning against the pillows, she clasped her hands together.

"Dear Lord," she prayed, "help me protect the decent people in Desert Resthaven. They don't deserve a neighbor like Ralphie. Please help me come up with a way to get rid of him." *Was that the prayer of a good Christian woman?* She wasn't sure. She raised her eyes toward Heaven. "Dear Lord, help the poor people whose homes were destroyed by that tornado in Oklahoma last week." There, that was better, she reasoned. That should balance things out.

She nestled down under the covers, worn out with worry, but sleep eluded her, remaining stubbornly out of reach. After forty minutes of trying every conceivable position, she thrust the covers off and got out of bed.

Maybe some warm milk will help. Back in the kitchen she didn't turn on the light, just used the refrigerator's beam to grab the carton of lactose-free, fat-free milk. She couldn't remember the last time she'd been able to enjoy *real* milk without suffering digestive problems or worrying about calories. Getting old was a real pain. Or in most cases, several pains.

Turning toward the stove across the room, she noticed a brightness coming from outside. At her front window once again, she saw a new fire in Ralphie's grill. This time it wasn't as high and it wasn't unsupervised. How long would that last? She wanted to rush across the street and throw the milk on the flames.

Then she saw headlights and heard the approach of a vehicle. Larry had returned in his golf cart. Maybe this time he'd play the part of the conquering cavalry. Hope rose in Mabel's chest like an answered prayer.

Larry slowed down, paused as he seemed to study the situation, then he nodded to Ralphie and drove off again.

Why, that chicken-livered no-goodnik of a security guy. What use is he?

She watched as Ralphie stood there in the ghastly glow of the flames, his malevolent smile reflected in the light. Mabel's hands squeezed the slender box of milk. Some of the thin, white liquid sputtered out and splattered her feet, slippers and carpet.

"Hell's bells!"

Mabel didn't normally curse, but sometimes a person was simply driven to distraction. She put the dented milk carton back in the refrigerator and dabbed up the small spills. Warm milk wouldn't help her now.

She needed a diversion while she stayed up to keep an eye on her neighbor. She turned on the light, no longer caring if Ralphie could see her watching him. She reached into a drawer in her dining room hutch and pulled out a bag full of medicine bottles. Mabel was the church coordinator for unused medicine to be sent to a third world country to help the indigent. It always made her feel good to handle the bottles, crossing out the patients' names and prescription numbers. Many came from churchgoers who'd either recovered from their illnesses or had succumbed to them. Through missions in poor countries, these pills could still serve a purpose.

Usually taking care of this task made her feel virtuous. Tonight good feelings evaded her just as sleep had earlier. Her stomach clenched. So did her jaw. More than anything she wanted to wipe that evil smile off Ralphie's face. To see him gone.

She recalled the last time he was away for a few months. She'd heard he'd been arrested for drug dealing. She'd never learned what drugs they were, but she hadn't cared. She'd just enjoyed the peaceful neighborhood.

She wondered if he'd committed any crimes since he'd returned. Too bad she couldn't catch him dealing dope or something. She looked over at his place again. The fire still spluttered, but Ralphie was nowhere in sight.

She gripped the last bottle in her collection, her rage and fear transferred to her pudgy fingers. Finally, she loosened them and glanced at the label. Oxycodone. Wasn't that one of those risky drugs, ones that people could easily become addicted to? Surely, it would be illegal to have those pills in your possession if they weren't prescribed to you.

An idea materialized in her mind, almost blotting out the image of flames across the street. What if a known drug dealer were to be found with someone else's medicine in his possession? She bet he'd go to jail for a while. And once again there would be peace in her corner of Desert Resthaven. Mabel went back to bed, smiling to herself. She had a plan.

She didn't get to sleep until three a.m. When she stretched herself awake around ten, she was stunned when she saw the bright digits on her clock. She wasn't used to late-night vigils. Groggy, she hauled herself out of bed, feeling like a vampire stabbed in the eyes by the mid-morning sun.

She blundered down the hallway. "Coffee," she mumbled. "Must have coffee."

Her dining room light still burned. Pill bottles still scattered across the table. Chaos ruled the area. She turned out the unneeded light and swept the bottles into a bag.

She remembered her final thoughts from last night. Put the drugs into Ralphie's possession. Get him caught with them. He'd go to jail and peace would reign again. She studied the sack in her hand, then shook her head. *What had she been thinking? She must have been insane.* She stuck the bag back into its drawer then fixed her coffee and breakfast.

Sitting at the table with her poached egg, whole-wheat toast, and a cup of hot coffee, she glanced across the street at Ralphie's place. It didn't seem so bad in the daylight.

Shortly after breakfast, she saw the mail truck rumble to a stop in front of her house and the postman get out to stuff things into her box. Maybe there'd be a letter for her, not just the usual flyers.

As she gathered the mail and shuffled back to her front door, she heard another door slam, then a string of loud curses.

"You interfering old bitch," Ralphie yelled.

More invectives followed, but she didn't hang around. With the air of a displeased royal, she huffed her way into the house. Once she shut her door, she leaned against it, her heart palpitating like a demented drummer.

Even inside, she heard his final words. "You'll be sorry!"

Fear shuddered through her. Her trembling hands released the mail. It scattered on the carpet. On weakened legs, she wobbled across the room to her recliner. Time passed and rage replaced the fear in a tsunami of emotion.

With renewed strength, she tottered to the drawer full of drugs. She'd show Ralphie who was going to be sorry. She wasn't taking any more threats from him. Or dealing with any more fires. The Bible says, "Vengeance is mine, sayeth the Lord," but sometimes she figured the Lord could use some help.

She spilled the bag's contents on the table once again. Rummaging through them, she found the bottle of oxycodone. She hadn't gotten around to crossing out the name of the patient the drugs were prescribed to, William Petersen. A truck driver, he'd been injured in a bad accident and forced to retire. She'd heard from a mutual friend that he felt useless when he could no longer work. Maybe his death from pneumonia and the donation of his pills could serve as his last useful act.

Mabel put that pill bottle aside and tossed the others back into the drawer, then gathered cleaning gloves, a can of furniture polish, and a dust cloth. After donning the gloves, she soaked the cloth with the polish, liberally wiping off her prints—she hoped. She wasn't sure what removed fingerprints, but she had to try. Maybe she should have watched some of those forensics TV shows more closely, but she didn't like the sight of blood.

She wrapped the bottle in a clean hankie and put it in her dress pocket. Now she just had to find the right time and means to get it into Ralphie's possession. She looked across the street. Ralphie paced the sidewalk in front of his house, yelling into a cell phone and swigging beer. She couldn't hear his exact words, but clearly, she wasn't the only person he was angry with. He slung the beer bottle into the shopping cart, then staggered to his car and pulled open the door. Surely he didn't plan on driving.

A plan sparked in her brain. She toddled with all haste through the house to the side door by her driveway. She grabbed her car keys, jerked open the door and rushed to her car as fast as her matronly form would allow.

She fumbled the key into the ignition and started the car. Ralphie was half in, half out of his vehicle. Maybe he wasn't going anywhere right now.

Mabel watched through her rearview mirror. She hoped this would be her chance to frame him because she didn't know if she'd be able to gather the strength to try again. She put her seat belt on. Then she put the sedan in reverse. She'd be ready.

Ralphie climbed in his car and shut the door. In a couple of seconds, the rear lights brightened and he started backing out.

This was it, now or never. She gunned the accelerator. The car lurched backwards. A grinding crunch followed. Mabel's body pitched back and forth. Her neck whipped her head about. She was going to hurt later, but so was her poor car. It had been her husband's last automobile purchase and she was sure he'd be rolling over in his grave right now if his ashes weren't in an urn on the living room mantle.

Ralphie wasn't happy either. "Dammit all to hell!" He staggered out of his car wearing a dark glare.

Mabel got out of hers. "I'm so sorry," she stuttered. She put a hand to her head. "I felt dizzy for a moment and lost focus." She peeked between her fingers. He still looked furious. "Oh, dear, I think I feel dizzy again."

"Sit in your car," he said gruffly. "It ain't going nowhere."

That wouldn't help. She needed to get the oxycodone into his car, not hers. For once she understood the saying about something burning a hole in one's pocket. She needed another distraction.

She lowered her hands and studied their wrecked vehicles. "It doesn't seem too bad, but we are rather blocking the street. We should call the police." She pulled a cell phone from her other pocket.

Ralphie smacked it out of her hand and it clattered to the street. He kicked it away. "No police."

"But Ralphie," Mabel said sweetly. "We need to report the accident. I don't think you need to worry. I'll tell them it was my fault."

"No police!" he roared.

A couple walking nearby stopped to stare. The woman asked, "Need any help?"

"No," Ralphie said, but he lowered his volume to a mere shout.

Mabel's gaze locked with the other woman's. She watched as the stranger pulled a cell phone from her pocket. If she called the cops, Mabel would have to work fast or this opportunity would be wasted.

A golf cart rattled toward them, stopped close-by and Larry got out. He scrutinized the cars tangled in the middle of the road. He looked the two neighbors up and down. "Anybody hurt?"

Both drivers shook their heads.

Larry stepped to the back of the cars, where shattered

taillights blinked. Ralphie's trunk latch had broken, leaving the dented trunk lid creased into a crooked grin. He took out his cell phone.

"No police," Ralphie said again.

"This is just a fender bender," Larry said. "But if I document it with pictures, you'll have them for your insurance companies."

Ralphie muttered, "No insurance."

Mabel rolled her eyes. "Since it was my fault, don't worry about that." She forced the words out through gritted teeth.

The security guard took several pictures from both sides, as well as close-ups of the damaged parts. He reached for the trunk lid and wrenched it upward.

"Stop," Ralphie yelled. He shoved Mabel aside.

She stumbled backward. Fell against the car door. She gasped as her bare arm connected with hot metal.

"What the heck you got here, Mr. Willis?" Larry asked, studying the trunk's contents.

Mabel peered around the men and glimpsed plastic bags full of what looked like dark weeds. An elbow struck her chest hard as Ralphie drew back to punch Larry.

The men scuffled, Larry older and bulkier, Ralphie younger and leaner—and meaner. Ralphie bit the other man's ear. While Larry screamed and tried to get Ralphie off him, Mabel ran to the cart to grab one of the golf clubs.

She swung the nine iron at Ralphie's back. It hardly seemed to faze him. Ralphie released Larry's ear, only to strike him in the nose. Larry collapsed. Ralphie turned on Mabel. He grabbed her by the throat with both hands. The vice-like grip was unbreakable. When he increased the pressure on her larynx, she dropped the club and clawed at his thumbs. She couldn't loosen his grip. She couldn't get any air. She couldn't believe the pain.

As the world started to darken, she barely heard the sirens. Or the shouts from the police to let her go. Or even the shot that followed.

The side of Ralphie's head exploded in front of her. But instead of releasing her, his grip tightened even more. When he fell, so did she. She almost passed out.

Stretched out on the hard, rough pavement, she felt the imprint of the incriminating pills in her pocket. The ones meant to frame Ralphie. She had to get rid of them. They could not be found in her possession. Easing a hand over them when attention was on Larry for a moment, she slid the pills into Ralphie's jeans' pocket. Mission accomplished. Her head fell back to the pavement while she waited for the paramedics.

At the hospital she learned the cop had been close-by when he got the call. That was lucky. But she also found out there would be a full investigation of the entire incident. Not so lucky. She'd turned several shades of pale when she considered the possible ramifications of that.

She arrived home after dark. The only outdoor lighting streamed from the streetlamps dotting the neighborhood as she stared at Ralphie's place. She wondered why he'd felt the need to build those stupid fires in the first place. Now she'd never know, but at least there wouldn't be any more of them. There would be peace.

But Mabel didn't feel peaceful. She gently massaged her neck. It ached fiercely, but hurt nothing like the wrenching remorse she felt about Ralphie's death. She hadn't planned for him to die, just go away for a while. Sure, he was strangling her. A part of her could reconcile his death because of that. But another part, a much bigger one, knew he wouldn't have been doing that if she hadn't caused the accident while trying to frame him. His death was all her fault.

Guilt shuddered through her in a tidal wave of bile. She barely made it to the bathroom before the vomit volcanoed through her rasping throat.

Later, Mabel shakily turned on a small lamp in her bedroom. She didn't want to be totally in the dark. She tried to pray, but couldn't think of the right words. She blamed her sore throat. Maybe when it was better, prayers could come again.

† † †

KARI WAINWRIGHT divides her time between her Colorado mountain home and an Arizona desert residence near her sister, Ronda, and her dog, Willow. Kari tries to spend the seasons in the place with the best weather, but doesn't always succeed. Wherever she lives, she shares her life with husband Tom, son Travis, and Shih-Tzu lapdog, Oscar Wilde. She writes book reviews for *Suspense Magazine* and publishers, Simon & Schuster, and is currently working on a traditional mystery.

EDITOR BIOGRAPHIES

Lead editor, DEBORAH J LEDFORD, is a professional content editor specializing in crime fiction. She is the author of the Steven Hawk/Inola Walela thriller series, including: *CRESCENDO*, *STACCATO* and The Hillerman Sky Award Finalist, *SNARE*. Three-time nominee for the Pushcart Prize in the short story category, her award-winning stories appear in numerous print publications. She is the current president of the Sisters in Crime Desert Sleuths Chapter. DeborahJLedford.com.

NANCY MCCURRY is a freelance editor of long and short form fiction, a college instructor of research and creative writing, a mom of two grown sons, and a reader of many fabulous subjects. Published since 1993, she's an award-winning writer of short fiction, flash fiction and essay. Nancy holds a Master of Fine Arts degree and now writes and studies anything and everything from abasia to zoophilism. NancyMcCurry.com.

SUSAN BUDAVARI has written over thirty short stories and co-edited several award-winning anthologies, including three from Red Coyote Press: *Medley of Murder*, *Map of Murder*, and *Medium of Murder* and three from Desert Sleuths. Previously, she worked in chemical research and scientific information management in the pharmaceutical industry and was Editor of *The Merck Index*, a best-selling encyclopedia of chemicals, drugs and biologicals.

MERLE MCCANN is best known for her award-winning Longjohners' Mystery Series for young adults and recently took top honors in Louisiana's Dixie Kane Memorial writers contest. Long-time member of Desert Sleuths, McCann was co-editor of the first DS Chapter anthology. Born in the Yukon, raised in Seattle, she has traveled the US and Europe with her husband pursuing their Arabian horse business and worked as a scenic photographer.

Praise For Sisters in Crime Desert Sleuths Chapter *SoWest* Anthologies from DS Publishing

SOWEST: DESERT JUSTICE

† *Suspense Magazine*'s Best Anthology of 2012 Finalist
† New Mexico-Arizona Book Awards Finalist - Best Anthology 2012

"Arizonans and all who love their mountains and deserts spiced with danger are in for a treat. The Sisters in Crime Desert Sleuths have put together another anthology of stories that powerfully evoke all the beautiful (and deadly) aspects of their state: white water rivers, hidden caves, steep mountain trails, blast-furnace deserts and yes, diamondback rattlers. Visit at your own risk!"

~MARGARET MARON, award-winning author of
Three-Day Town and *The Buzzard Table*

SOWEST, SO WILD

Suspense Magazine's Best Anthology of 2011 Finalist

"Arizona proves hot, dry, and deadly in this anthology. There's something for everyone to enjoy here, in tales of murder ranging from the humorous to the macabre."

~MEG GARDINER, Edgar Award winning author of
The Nightmare Thief

"An old time sheriff only had six bullets loaded into his gun to take care of the bad guys—with *SoWest So Wild*, twenty different authors take aim and each one hits the bulls-eye. You'll never look at the Wild West the same way again."

~TONI L.P. KELNER, co-editor of the *New York Times* bestselling anthology *Death's Excellent Vacation*

SoWest: Desert Justice, SoWest So Wild and
SoWest: Crime Time
are now available from Amazon.

Praise For Sisters in Crime Desert Sleuths Chapter Previous Anthologies from DS Publishing

How NOT to Survive a Vacation (2009)

"Smart, fresh and fast-paced with twist endings worthy of master storytellers."
~SOPHIE LITTLEFIELD, author of *A Bad Day for Sorry*

"Like a macabre travel brochure, these chilling mystery stories take you on a grisly tour of choice vacation spots, except instead of Mai Tais, they serve murder."
~REBECCA CANTRELL, award-winning author of
A Night of Long Knives

"A fabulous anthology of murder and mayhem from ship to shore and mountain to desert. The collection will leave you double checking with your travel agent…and begging for more!"
~KELLI STANLEY, award-winning author of
City of Dragons

How NOT to Survive the Holidays (2010)

"Stuff your stocking with this string of holiday sparkles, ranging from the chilling to the decidedly wacky."
~RHYS BOWEN, Agatha and Anthony award-winning author of the *Molly Murphy* and *Royal Spyness* mysteries.

"The holidays will never be the same! This collection of twisted, talented authors make sure of that."
~SHEILA LOWE author of the *Forensic Handwriting* mysteries

"There's no place like home for the holidays. That is, unless somebody in the family wants to kill you…It seems there's a lot of skullduggery going on during the Christmas season."
~DONIS CASEY, author of the award-winning *Alafair Tucker* mysteries

www.ingramcontent.com/pod-product-compliance
Lightning Source LLC
Chambersburg PA
CBHW060325260626
47160CB00007B/2678